Burning Desires

Burning Desires

L.J. DIVA

★ Royal Star Publishing ★

Chances is an imprint of Royal Star Publishing
www.royalstarpublishing.com.au

First edition paperback published in 2024
All Rights Reserved, Copyright ©L.J. Diva 2024

Trade Paperback ISBN: 978-1-922307-75-0
Large Print Paperback ISBN: 978-1-922307-76-7
Dust Jacket Hardcover ISBN: 978-1-922307-77-4
E-Book ISBN: 978-1-922307-74-3
Audio Book ISBN: 978-1-922307-78-1
A catalogue record for this book is available from the National
Library of Australia.

Cover design: Royal Star Publishing and ©Designed with Grace
Typesetting in Minion Pro by Royal Star Publishing
All photos from Depositphotos

Dedications

Dear lovers,

*I'm tasting you…*Aussie band, 5 Seconds of Summer, you inspired the "interviews" that got the whole idea started. For future reference, I prefer drummers…

*I'm craving you…*wildly hirsute and hot as hell Brett Goldstein, you inspired my shy and retiring detective, who, when the suit came off and the cuffs went on, unleashed his wild inner animal.

*I'm burning for you…*sexy as fuck, Roy Kent, you inspired my sexy as fuck band manager, whose gruff interior is always outdone by his very hairy sexy man beast exterior.

The sex was always wild!

Love, L.J.

PS. To Angela Bishop, thanks for inspiring my entertainment reporter.

Prologue

He crescendoed on the base drum and the orgasm hit her hard. Her breath groaned from between her lips as his leg slowed to a stop. Hers slid down until her feet landed on the floor.

"You really know how to fuck a woman."

He exuded the scent of sex, drugs, and rock 'n roll as her fingers danced over his bare chest and up to his lips.

Her lips hovered in front of them. "You *really* know how to fuck."

His lips slowly curled into a grin. "And you know how to make fucking adventurous." His hands grasped her waist and lifted her as he stood, sliding her off his cock and placing her on her feet. He tucked himself away and zipped up. "Never banged a woman while I banged out a beat on the drums before."

"First time for everything," she murmured, smoothing her short denim skirt. "They say drummers bang it harder. You certainly proved just that." Licking her full, cherry gloss covered lips, she trailed her fingers over his muscular arms. "And now I know the rest of you matches that, muscle for muscle."

"I have been doing this for years," he muttered into her ear. "But even that's running low on the enthusiasm scale." He grabbed a towel from the table behind the drum kit and wiped himself down.

Her brows furrowed. "What do you mean? Isn't drumming doing it for you anymore? Had enough of the travelling band life? The rich and the famous. Girls throwing themselves at you. Millions of dollars rolling in. Number one singles and albums."

"Just made me money to waste on drugs and alcohol." He threw the towel down and opened a bottle of ice-cold water, taking a long swig before pouring the rest over his head.

"Yeah." She moved over to the table and took a bottle for herself. "I did notice the line of coke you snorted off your hand before starting the rehearsal." Eyeing him as she opened her water, she noticed his physical unease, and carefully added, "Planning on doing that the rest of your life? Or are you sick of that, too?"

He slumped down on the corner of the table and swiped the back of his hand across his mouth to catch a few drops of liquid. "Yeah, getting sick of that, too."

"You can do things about that, you know." She stood in front of him. "Rehab or leave the band altogether. What is it you're actually feeling?" She reached out and lightly shifted his auburn curls out of his eyes, her fingers sliding over his rounded cheek that was lightly freckled. "What is it that you actually want? Right now. Don't worry about what the band will say or do, or what your manager will say or do, or the record company will say or do. Just think about you. What do you want right here, right now?"

"To disappear and never come back."

She was surprised. "Blunt and to the point. Are you done with the band? Done with music? You've been together what…fifteen, twenty years, now?"

He heaved a deep sigh and shook his head. "I feel so done sometimes. Other times, I'm still riding high on tours and number ones."

"And on other things, clearly." She stepped closer and lowered her voice. "How much do you want this to stop? How much are you done? How much do you want to *be* done? How long have you been doing drugs?"

He gazed into her vibrant green eyes and felt the highs of the cocaine drift down to the depths of normality. "Very done. And too many years." He thrust upward, his face inches from hers. "Drug addicts normally don't want to stop. They constantly want that high. But I've come to hate it." He stalked away. Around the table. The drum kit. Back and forth across the room.

She watched, waiting for him to speak.

He ran both hands through his tangled mess of curls and stopped. "I want it done. I want it gone. *I* want to be gone. But I was hanging on for tonight."

Confusion settled over her. "Tonight? Why tonight?"

He gave her a wry grin and huffed a little. "You asked how long we'd been together. Well, it's our twentieth anniversary today. We got together twenty years ago and tonight will be our anniversary party. Our anniversary show."

"Wow." Her brows rose and she nodded slightly. "You've held on how long? Wanted to stop how long?

Would you leave after tonight?"

With his hands on his hips, he glanced around at nothing in particular. Tonight, they'd be playing in the hottest club in the country, run by the hottest woman he knew. He weighed up his thoughts. "Yeah. I would. I might. I'm done. I'm drained physically. I'm exhausted mentally. The record company wants us to head into the studio and start writing and recording, but fuck it, I'm done. I can't keep doing this." He rubbed his eyes and fell to the floor, rolling onto his back, legs bent at the knees, staring up at the ceiling. "I'm sick and tired of touring, not sleeping properly, not eating properly, not having any downtime in between tours. They want us to record, and then we have to release and promote, and then tour again. It's exhausting and *I* am fucking exhausted."

She knelt beside him. "Do you want all of it to stop after tonight's show?"

"If it could, that'd be great," he mumbled. "But even I don't know if they'd let me take time off for rehab, or a holiday. They don't have any problem with us doing drugs. We're more productive, and they're the ones who pushed it onto us in the first place, so we'd get more done. All for them. All to make *them* more money."

"Seems to be the way," she murmured, and settled on the floor next to him. "Do you want someone to help you leave?" She glanced around to see if anyone was lurking in the shadows. "I know people who can help."

He looked at her, thinking she was joking. "Wait… you're serious?"

She nodded. "Yes. I am."

He pushed himself up on his elbows and stared at her. "Are you actually serious? If I want to leave tonight, you'd help. And take me where? Do what with me? What would happen? How would it happen? When would it happen?"

She looked furtively for his people. "After the concert," she murmured close to him, still on the lookout. "There are rooms for people to enjoy pleasures in. No one will notice you're gone unless you tell them."

He sat up, his heart hammering at the prospect of sneaking away. "But how?"

"Can't tell you." Her gaze darted around. "Best kept secret. But if you want to leave after the show, I'll help you. Problems will only arise if you shoot your mouth off." Studying his face, she could see the wear and tear of years of drugs, late nights, partying hard, and no time off. "It's worn you out. That's obvious. You look older than thirty-seven. And if you're deadly serious about changing your life, then I can help you tonight. But..." She inhaled deeply and thought some things through, on the lookout for his people. "Because of your anniversary you'll have a reporter and camera crew there all night. And I take it you'll be doing interviews before and after the concert, so it's going to be a long night and you'll need to keep your mouth shut about leaving or taking time off." She glanced at him sharply. "Can you try and not take anything so that you don't blurt any information out by mistake?"

"Can't promise that," he said with a shake of his head. "The record company supplies munchies for our, *and their*, enjoyment before a show. And it expects us to take them." He sighed. "You know. We started off healthy as teenagers. But we very quickly fell into the nature of fast food and sugary drinks. When our health got bad and our performances suffered for it, they brought in a nutritionist and cook. Things got better, but it wasn't fast enough, or good enough for management, and that's when the extra *supplements* came into the diet. We didn't know at first. Thought they were normal vitamins. That's what we were told. But it was too late when we found out. We were hooked, and they kept them in moderation, so we didn't OD." Wiping his nose, he thought about the line of coke he'd done earlier. "Unfortunately, it made us want the hard stuff and you saw that before."

"Do you want to stop that? Seriously? Twenty years together, however many years on drugs, now the hard stuff. Do you *seriously* want to stop and walk away? For how long? Forever? For a year? For months? What? I need to know so I can make the plan for later."

He bit his lip while thinking about it. "Not forever. But a good year or two, maybe three or four. The whole band needs to detox and get rid of management. We're due to sign a new deal with them tonight. The others have been questioning it, wanting a break as well. But they just want time off. I want to disappear."

"I can help with that. Where would you like to go? The desert or the seaside?"

"Can't stand the desert, but love the water. Seaside. Why?"

"I can arrange that. Is there anyone you'll be leaving behind? Partner, children, family?"

A wry grin slid over his face. "My family's on my back about rehab, and there's no partner or children. Where would I have found the time?"

"From the schedule I've seen of tonight, you'll be doing interview, concert, fan chats, interview. After that you'll be partying. It'll happen then, towards the end of the night. You need to be ready. You need to want this. You need to be willing."

Breathing deeply, he nodded. "I'm ready. I'm willing. I want to do this."

"Then keep it to yourself and I'll make the plan. I'll see you tonight." She got to her feet and adjusted her skirt.

"Will we fuck before I go?" He grabbed the waist of her skirt and pulled her close. "That was quite something."

"Oh, don't worry; we'll make them think that's what's happening. Until tonight." She pried loose his hands and left him to his rehearsal.

PART ONE

TASTE

Chapter 1

"Hello, ladies and gentlemen. Welcome to the country's hottest *and* coolest club to be for the best music and live performances in town, *The Cavern Club*."

From her spot on the stage, Remi Steele glanced around her club and the adoring two-thousand-strong crowd there to see Jagger who was celebrating their twenty years together with an intimate performance for their rabid fans. They had run a competition to give away those tickets, and within minutes their website had crashed. But the fans had still scored their tickets.

Remi put her hand up to quieten the crowd. "Now, as you know, you are all competition winners and have received your packs with information on how tonight will go. The boys will be doing an interview upstairs before the performance, and one after. They'll sign your merch and take photos with you. No pushing or shoving—you'll get to see them. We have free drinks at the bar, and will be playing their music for you to dance to while you wait for them to come on stage. And until they do, enjoy yourselves. Free merch, free drinks, free performance. What's not to like?" She scored screams in return and walked off the stage.

Sisco Reynard, the club's manager, appeared by her side. "Rem, the reporter wants to interview you as well."

"Me? Why me?" Remi walked past the bar, turned right into the private hallway behind it, and into her office. "Why me?"

"Because you're famous in your own right." Sisco shut the door behind them and watched Remi slump on her couch. "Want a drink?"

"God, yes please," she groaned and put her boot-clad feet on her coffee table. "I'm worn out already. Don't know how many more years I can put up with this." She accepted a cold soda and Sisco sat beside her.

"Bullshit! You love it, and besides, that's what you have me for. To manage the place while you're not here."

After several mouthfuls of icy soda, she blew out a breath. "True. But I think I'm just as exhausted as the bands that play here. Are the plans for tonight done?"

"All set. Interview, performance, meet and greet, interview. Which brings me back to the reporter who wants to do an interview with you."

"About?"

"Your life, your career, your everything. You're just as famous as the bands and singers that come through those front doors."

"And go out the back ones." Remi smirked. "Is it in the before or after interview?"

"Before the before. She'll talk to you and then the band."

An idea came to Remi's mind. "What about if we do it together?"

Sisco cocked his head. "You're up to something."

"Am I?" Remi's eyes rounded innocently. "Why would I be up to something?"

"Because you usually are—" He was interrupted by a knock on the door. "I'll get it." He quickly got up and opened the door, finding the reporter on the other side.

"Hello." Donatella Prince was a thirty-year veteran with one of the TV networks. "Are we on for that interview, yet?"

Remi sighed, lifted her feet from the table, and stood wearily. "Sure. I'll just freshen up and be up in a few minutes."

"Fantastic. See you then." Donatella walked away and Sisco closed the door.

Remi groaned and bowed her head. "I'll be out in a minute." She took her time freshening up and then strode upstairs to where the camera crew was set up for that night's performance and interviews.

The club had multiple levels, laid out similarly to a theatre; you had the floor in front of the stage, a mezzanine level above it at the back where they were, and multiple levels of private booths around the sides.

"Donatella."

"Remi Steele, look at you. Still hot-to-trot at forty-two," Donatella said, microphone in hand and legs on display in a short, sequinned dress and stiletto heels.

Remi's brows rose. "Yeah, thanks for reminding me how old I am. Let's get this done, shall we?" She turned on an angle so she could look at Donatella and the camera easily, without cracking her neck or getting whiplash.

"Well, there's nothing wrong with age," Donatella replied. "And you've done a hell of a lot in your lifetime, including set up this incredible club. But what people may not know is that you had your very own music career as a singer songwriter. Number one hit songs, hit albums, tours; year after year you did something new, released something new, were massive around the world in dozens of countries, and then you gave it all away to set up this club."

"Ah, that's not accurate, Donatella," Remi corrected. "I started at eighteen and recorded and produced and toured for twenty years, until just four years go. I started this club ten years ago as an extra outlet for my craft. I stopped working for my record company once the club became more profitable than my singing career."

"Are you saying your record company ripped you off?"

Remi gritted her teeth and let out a slow breath. "Don't put words in my mouth, Donatella. Making product and touring became less fun and less profitable. There are a lot of artists out there making money, and I decided to go a different path and exit stage right into my club. I believe it's my twenty-year career that helps make this club what it is. Famous."

"And speaking of famous, you've had some pretty famous bands, singers, and musicians come through the doors to perform on your stage. Are they people you've known throughout your career, or ones you've forged new friendships and working relationships with?"

"Mmm, good question," Remi said. "Many I have known throughout my career love coming to do intimate shows for their fans, and many start here with their careers. Every now and then we'll do a talent show and have managers, press, and record execs here to see what talent is out there now, and so I forge relationships with up and comers as well."

"Jagger have performed here a few times over the years, and they chose *The Cavern Club* for their intimate twentieth anniversary performance. They've reached the same milestones you have; some of you are stayers in the music community."

Remi nodded. "We have to be sometimes, but it can get very boring hanging around so long. I had absolutely no problem hosting the boys tonight. And their people went all out for it, even down to the food. They have jelly confectionery in the shape of the boys' tattoos, so I am off to suck on Jace's snake." Remi took that moment to wave goodbye and dash off, passing Jagger, who were coming for their first interview, as she went. Jace smiled and reached for her hand. She squeezed it as he passed and kept on going until she was downstairs. Glancing up, she saw the boys meet up with Donatella for their first interview.

Letting out a sigh, she headed for the merch tables to sample some of the confectionery the record company had laid out and picked up a red treble clef and a chocolate snake. A wicked thought sprang into her mind. Trying the snake, she sucked on its head for a few moments before ripping it off. She swallowed, and quickly devoured the rest as she walked up the stairs to the mezzanine. She hurried along, making sure her timing was just right and Donatella was looking the other way. Pretending to just be walking past, she heard, "The last thing she told me was she was off to suck on Jace's snake." Remi stopped next to the reporter and said, "Oh, I did."

Startled, Donatella turned to her. "Did you try it? How was it?"

"I sucked its head off and then I swallowed." Remi wiggled her brows at the camera while Jace burst into a fit of giggles. She pretended to walk off, but then stepped back. "No. I need to make a correction. It's not a snake, it's a python, and I sucked that head off and swallowed it down, down, down, down. For the record"— she pointed at the camera— "it tastes like chocolate, and also for the record, I've never deep-throated a python before. Weird experience, especially when that sucker slid deep."

"Oh, my God, you can't say that!" Donatella cried, looking from Remi to the boys, to the camera.

"Can't say what?" Remi asked her. "Deep? Weird experience? Python? Throat? And how do you think Linda Lovelace made a name for herself?"

Donatella turned bright red and glanced at the camera.

Once more, Remi pretended to leave, but as she was having too much fun, and the boys were egging her on, she added, "By the way, boys, I have a recording studio in my basement. You're free to use it anytime. Especially Jace."

"Oh, that sounds like a euphemism," Reece said from beside Jace.

"I'd love to work in your basement," Jace told Remi. "And bang those drums real hard." He stepped closer and laid a hand on her hip.

"Good." Remi rocked against him and grabbed his crotch. "I'd love to have you in my studio. I need a python in my basement."

Jace doubled over in laughter, wrapped his arms around his waist, and fell to his knees.

"Oh no, you broke Jace." Reece stared down at his fellow bandmate.

"Oh, no, sweetie," Remi cooed. "He won't know what broke is until I'm done with him." She glanced at the camera and waved her fingers. "Toodles." Walking off, she heard laughter behind her, and grinning, went downstairs. Walking behind the bar to check on things, she saw a few record executives, managers, and publicists in the crowd, or in the private upper booths, and spied Rex Titus, band manager extraordinaire. One of his bands was 10x4, a hot new teen band on the rise. They'd had one of their first gigs at the club and Rex had seen them and signed them to his label.

Remi was sipping an ice-cold cola when he walked up to the bar.

"Remi."

"Rexy."

He eyed her shapely legs in her boots and denim skirt, and as his gaze moved up, her well-proportioned breasts in their low cut slashed up Jagger top. She'd worn it for the band.

"Good to know you still want to eye me off." The corners of her lips curled. "You're not looking too bad yourself." She drank in the skin-tight dark blue ripped jeans held up by a leather belt with a large silver buckle featuring two naked women. A few chains hung from the buckle to a side jean loop. He wore a white tank top and black leather jacket, and the curls on his chest matched the curls on his face and head; dark, thick, and luscious.

Remi had always wanted to run her hands through his hair. All of it. Every last curl on his tanned, muscular body. The way they moved, the way they taunted her with their sexuality, made her want to rip his clothes off and fuck every last curl on his body.

"Remi. Good to know your eyes still want to rip my clothes off and fuck me." He nodded at the bartender and received a beer. "We could actually do that, you know."

She walked around the bar and hitched a leg onto a stool to slide onto it. "Do what? What are you inviting me to do, Sexy Rexy?"

He set down his beer, wiped the foam from his beard, and leaned in.

His sexy, manly scent wafted around her, and she willingly breathed it in, getting high on the pheromones. "Rexy," she breathed seductively, her eyes hooded with lust.

He spoke in her ear, his curls tickling her, his lips tormenting her. "I'm inviting you to fuck, Remi. You know what that is, don't you? You've tried it a few times, or more, with the boys in the bands that play here."

She breathed in sharply and blinked a few times to clear her thoughts. "You calling me a whore, Rex Titus?" Pulling away, her fury burned. "Are you? Because in that case, you'll never get to sample, let alone try out, what I have." She noticed the surprised look on his face, but she didn't care. She spun around on her stool, and stomped off to her office, leaving him shaking his head.

"What the fuck!" Rex muttered, bewildered by her sudden change of mood. He stared at the door until he realised she wasn't coming back out, picked up his beer and took another swig, and then with a frown, turned his back to watch the club scene. "Fucking hell."

Remi stewed for twenty minutes, and then heard the band start playing. Gathering herself, she took a deep breath and walked back into the club.

After watching the boys on stage for a few moments, she slowly walked around the room, weaving through the screaming crowd watching the band on stage. Her love of music was deep-seated and she loved watching each member of each band as they performed. It was always the drummers that caught her eye. Up the back of the stage, they weren't always obvious or noticeable, not in or under the main spotlights like the showman of the bands, who was usually the lead singer. Drummers were solid, sturdy, muscular and meatier. Their flesh was juicy and succulent, always engorged and ripe for the picking. And this drummer, Jace, was an animal; a driving beast who knew exactly which skin to pound and when, using all of his energy and masculine power to beat them. He knew exactly what to do with those drumsticks and it sent a thrill of electricity down her spine.

He noticed her, nodded, and kept on pounding. His dark wet curls bounced over his amber-green eyes that flared brightly at the attention. A smile crossed his lips and showed off dimples that were almost buried by the voluptuous round cheeks of his face. His shirt had come off when he'd come on stage, as it always did, and she made note to explore all of his tattoos before he left. She'd booked a bed in the sex room, a sectioned off part of the club for party goers to get sexual, and she had what he needed waiting for him. A blush raced across her face, and she moved on, hearing the lead singer get the crowd going.

"Come on everyone, scream my name," Reece crooned, leaning toward the fans, reaching out his hand for them to touch. "Scream my name, baby. I love the way you scream my name." He stood and cupped his ear to listen to the crowd chant his name, a huge grin on his face. "Louder now. Scream my name for me."

Jett, the bassist, and Linc, the guitarist, played a low tune, while Jace played a soft beat, all so they could hear the crowd.

"Come on, baby," Reece groaned to one girl as he held her hand. "Groan my name for me." He held the microphone in front of her and she groaned his name before fainting. "Can we get the medics over here?" he asked, pointing to the girl.

The medic team rushed in and carried her to the side of the club to revive her.

"That's what I like to see." Reece stalked back and forth across the stage, reaching out to fans. "I love to see how you react to me. To the band. I love the way you scream my name in those sexy tones. Can you scream for Jett?" He motioned at the bassist and heard the crowd scream his name.

"Can you scream for Linc?" He pointed to their guitarist and the crowd screamed for him.

"Can you scream for Jace?" He waved his hand around in a theatrical manner and bowed in front of the drum kit.

The crowd screamed the loudest for Jace and he waved his sticks in the air before throwing them both into the audience. The crowd surged forth and lunged for them, with two very excited girls getting one each.

"Wait…" Reece told the crowd, strutting around the stage in his tight white jeans and half-open shirt. "Did you just scream the loudest for Jace?"

The fans screamed back and a wave of whoos went through the crowd.

"Oh, no, that's just not fair," he said, undoing another button on his shirt. "Who did you scream the loudest for?" He flipped open another button and pulled one side of his shirt out of his low-slung jeans, gyrating in front of the crowd until five more fans fainted, and staff had to run around handing bottles of cold water to the rest of them. "I love the way you're screaming my name, and the way you do it with no shame. Let's get on with our song, boys, let's hit it," he called, and they launched into their hit, *Scream My Name.*

Standing up the back of the club watching the band, hands in his jeans pockets, Rex watched Remi as she wandered. He'd seen the exchange of looks with the drummer, saw her blush, and wondered if Jace was another on her list. Not that he knew if she had a list; it was just a rumour that the owner of *The Cavern Club* loved to indulge in sexual activity with band members, particularly drummers, when they played at the club. For all he knew, it was nothing but a rumour. For all he knew, after seeing the exchange, it was completely true.

So what! he thought with a shrug of a shoulder. *She's a grown woman; she can be with who she wants. But why isn't that me?* He'd desperately wanted to bed Remi since he'd met her four years ago, but she wasn't interested in getting intimate even though she flirted outrageously with him. He was just a manager, not a drummer, and clearly didn't have what she was after. He watched her pass by the bar and chat with Sisco in the hallway to her office. She nodded and walked behind the bar, picked up her drink, and downed half. He wanted to be that cola. Going down, down, down her throat. His gaze lowered to her throat, her breasts. *Damn, I want to drink from those breasts. Fuck it, Remi, why won't you fuck me?* His gaze moved up and caught her watching him with raised brows. His brows descended to almost meet at the bridge of his nose and he spun on his heel and stormed off. He needed to relieve himself right now.

Perplexed, Remi turned her attention back to the band as they wrapped up their performance. She didn't have the time or the energy to worry about Rex or what he thought of her, but how dare he think she was a whore because of rumours? She had the rest of the night to deal with.

The band took a fifteen-minute break while things were set up for the meet and greet, and then they came out and spent another hour taking photos, signing merchandise, and doing videos with their fans. It was heading for eleven when they finally made it upstairs for the after-show interview.

Donatella welcomed them to the couches and offered drinks, making sure everyone was comfortable before starting the interview.

They were ten minutes in when Jace said he wanted Remi to join them.

"You want to share your interview with the club owner?" Donatella asked and glanced at the others. "You boys have a problem with that?"

They replied no and Jace leaned over the back of the couch and yelled out to Remi. "Come up here and do our interview with us."

She glanced up wearily from behind the bar.

"Come on," he encouraged and gave her a big wink. "Let's have some fun."

She snickered and grabbed her drink before making her way upstairs. "Where am I sitting?"

"Right here." Jace pointed to his left and moved over, pushing Reece out of the way. "Right next to me, babe."

"Babe," Remi huffed. "Am I your babe now?" She settled in and managed to get her cup into her left hand as Jace swung his leg over her right one. "You right?" She looked at him. "Sure you don't want to sit on my lap?"

"Ooh, can I?" he asked and gazed at her expectantly.

"No," was all she said.

He leaned closer. "Do you want me to get off?"

"Didn't you already?" She eyed him up and down and watched him laugh nervously.

"Whoo. We've got a live one here," he called.

"It's fairly obvious that isn't a drumstick in your pocket." She gave him a saucy wink and casually glanced at the other members who were bright red and giggling.

Jace's eyes grew wide, and he fanned himself with his left hand while picking up his water bottle from the coffee table with his right. He took a swig and then poured some on his head and patted his neck and half bare chest. "Is it hot in here or what? Whoo."

The band laughed, and Donatella reached across Remi to shove the microphone into Jace's face. "It looks like you've got the hots for a certain club owner."

"Who wouldn't?" he replied and waved a hand up and down her body. "Look at her. Look. At. Her."

Remi blushed and took a sip of her drink before placing it back between her legs so it didn't fall over.

Jace picked it up and drank from it while watching her nonchalantly. "Who wouldn't have the hots for a woman like this? Look at her." He took another sip. "What is this?"

"Tropical juice and lemonade." She watched him, knew the band was watching him, and the reporter was watching him.

"Mmm," he murmured, raising both brows. He sucked and swallowed, and then seductively placed the cup back between her legs, pushing it up a little further his gaze never leaving hers.

Unable to say a thing, Remi just breathed and shook her head.

"You know what they say about drummers?" Donatella said to Jace.

"What?" Jace replied, watching the scene before him.

"Drummers bang it harder," Donatella said.

"Then bang me like a fucking bass drum," Remi muttered, her eyes hooded and her blood pulsating through her veins.

"Should we be talking about this on camera?" Donatella asked, looking at her producer who gave her the signal to keep going. This was TV gold and she wanted more.

"Oh, don't worry, he's just telling me he wants to put other things between my legs," Remi said, her gaze never leaving Jace's.

"Didn't I already do that this afternoon?" Jace murmured, staring at Remi's thick red lips. "Let's go again."

"Okay, let's rein this in a bit, shall we," Donatella said and asked Linc and Jett a couple of questions.

Remi and Jace eyed each other, sly smiles lifting the corners of their mouths. Remi had planned a little going away present for him and had hoped to get him alone before he left.

"So, Remi, you're obviously a fan of Jagger," Donatella said and pointed at Remi's t-shirt that had been artistically cut up. "You came dressed for the occasion."

"Why are you pointing at my breasts?" Remi asked cheekily.

"Yeah, Donatella." Jace spread his hands across both of Remi's breasts. "Stop pointing at her breasts."

Remi stared from his hands to his face, to Donatella's, speechless.

Donatella kept it cool. "You know, she could #metoo you for that move."

Remi raised a brow at him, trying not to laugh. But all he did was raise one back.

"Aren't you going to say something, Remi?" Donatella asked.

Remi slowly glanced at her. "What *does* one say at a time like this?" She glanced at his hand, picked it up with two fingers, and dropped it in his lap.

"Don't you feel sexually harassed? Manhandled?" Donatella asked, seeing the heat rise from both of them. The attraction was blaringly obvious.

"I do." Remi nodded and looked at her. "I feel *very* manhandled, and I have absolutely no problem with it whatsoever."

"Whoo." The boys in the band catcalled and whistled, applauding her.

"But aren't you in love? Aren't you in a relationship?" Donatella asked. "Rumours have it you are, so why flirt with someone else when your partner's where? At home?"

Remi had always been private about her personal relationships, and the current one hadn't lasted long enough, or made it into the press, so how Donatella had found out, she didn't know. "Actually, I'm just coming out the arse end of it."

"Oh, that doesn't sound good." Donatella shoved the microphone into Remi's face. "What happened? Who broke up with whom? Who did it first?"

"Well, to begin with, it didn't last all that long, and was great while it did. But in the end, he got what he wanted, and I've been left alone and feeling very used."

"That's not good." Jace turned to the camera. "To the arsehole out there who got what he wanted out of this woman and then left her like a piece of rubbish"— he thrust his finger at the camera— "you are an arsehole and you suck." He leaned back and put a protective arm around Remi's shoulder.

"I'm just glad I didn't." Remi glanced from the camera to Jace, staring him in the eye and waiting for him to get the joke.

He stared back and finally got it, then laughed his head off. "Oh, my God, I love it."

"Are you in love, Jace?" Donatella reached across Remi.

"Absolutely," he replied. "I'm in love with this woman right here." He held his hand above her head and pointed his finger down. "She's incredible, talented, amazing, sexy and intelligent, and some arsehole dumped her. Your loss, my gain, and she didn't suck!"

"Okay, so we'll wrap this up with a few more questions." Donatella tried to control their laughter. "Now that you've celebrated twenty years together, and have had your anniversary, and come off your most successful tour of your most successful album, what's next for Jagger?"

Remi held her breath and glanced down. Sipping from her cup, she avoided looking at everyone else.

"Oh, I don't know. I think it's time for a holiday," Jace said, keeping things casual. "We've been touring non-stop, recording non-stop, performing non-stop for twenty years. It's time for a holiday."

"And how long would that be for before you're back in the studio writing for the next album?" Donatella asked.

"I don't know. We've done this for twenty years, so how long should a holiday be? Twenty seconds? Twenty minutes?" he joked and looked at Reece.

"Twenty hours," Reece added.

"Twenty days," Jett said.

"Twenty weeks," Linc went on as the boys laughed.

"Twenty months, twenty years. Who knows, but we bloody well deserve it." Jace ran his hand through his hair and glanced at their manager and record execs standing behind the cameras with confused expressions. He'd spoken to the boys about taking a break, but no one else, and they'd agreed they wanted one too. "Twenty years sounds good. Same amount of time we've been working."

"Regardless of how long the holiday is, you bloody deserve it," Donatella replied. "Any idea where you'll go?"

"I might hang out under a palm tree on the beach," Linc said.

"I've always wanted to hang out in Paris for a few months," Jett replied. "Get arty, find some Parisian influence."

"Paris sounds good," Reece said, nodding. "I want to hang out in the Greek islands on a yacht."

"It's not as if you can't afford it after twenty years," Donatella said. "Jace?"

Jace picked up Remi's cup and took a sip. "Desert, seaside, wherever my whims take me. I'll see the world while the world can't see me."

"Sounds poetic. Any idea when you'll come back and start writing and recording a new album?" Donatella thrust the microphone at Jace.

"No idea. As of tonight, we're no longer with our record company, so we get to take all the time in the world off and do what we want when we want. No one has any say except for the four of us."

Remi glanced up sharply, her brows furrowed, but Jace gave nothing away. She breathed in and glanced away.

"Did you know about this?" Donatella asked Remi.

Remi shook her head. "Why would I? It's just as much a surprise to me as it is for their manager and the record execs."

They all looked over at the men behind the cameras. All were on their phones, trying to figure out what to do.

"We didn't resign because we're done," Jace said. "Not forever, but for now, while we have a well-earned break." He looked at the camera and put his hands together in prayer. "Thank you so much to all of our fans for your love and support over the last twenty years, but we need a break and we're going to have one. Thank you very much. Let's go boys. Thanks, Donatella." Jace grabbed Remi's hand and pulled her to her feet as he left. The boys followed, as he'd always been their unofficial leader as the eldest, and their manager and record people trailed behind. They'd already talked and made the decision, all had been overworked, all were over drugged, and all were alcoholic. And all wanted a break and time to detox. They also all had other plans.

Jace pulled Remi down the stairs and headed for the red curtained cordoned off entrance to the sex rooms. He waved goodbye to the boys, and they slipped between the curtains. "Let's fuck before I go, because I take it you're shipping me off somewhere."

Remi opened a door off the hallway. "Why didn't you tell me you had that organised?" She locked the door behind them. "If you've all decided to take a year or two off, why do I need to help you escape?"

With his dick already hanging free, Jace pulled Remi against him and kissed her. "They only decided this afternoon. We all had the same plan but hadn't said anything in case someone at the record company found out and stopped us." He pulled her skirt up and slammed her against the wall. "Let's get this over with before I leave."

One minute of grunting, thrusting, and coming later, they took a moment to get their breath.

"Okay. So, you all had the same plan. Do they need help getting away?"

"Not from what they said this afternoon." Jace tucked himself away. "They've got their plans sorted. The only problem was the contract."

"And that ended this week? Today? What was it?" Remi slid her skirt down and adjusted her top.

"It ended at midnight last night. Or this morning. And we refused to sign the whole time they've pressured us into signing it. We kept telling them we'd have that chat after this show. But it all came out when we spoke this afternoon."

"Okay, so I guess I'd better get you out of here before anyone asks questions." Remi opened the door and glanced out, but all she saw were her men. "Come on." She led him down the hall and out the back door.

In the band room, their manager was trying to convince them to stay. "We're only one day past the contract. You can still sign it."

"We're done," Reece told him as he packed his bag. "Mentally, physically. We all need a break. A long one."

"And you can have that," a big bruiser of a record exec said. "After you sign your new contract."

"You do realise we don't actually have to sign with

you again, right?" Jett asked as he hoisted his bag over his shoulder. "We're not signing with you because we no longer want to be with your company." He picked up his guitar case. "Sayonara, suckers. I'm off to Paris."

"And I'm off to my tropical island." Linc followed him.

Reece brought up the rear. "Where's Jace? Has he left already? His stuff is gone."

The record execs rushed upstairs to the entrance off the sex rooms, but bouncers stopped them.

"No one's allowed back here."

"We need Jace."

"He's already left with Remi. They were giggling like kids when they left via the back door, so I suggest you go too."

With a grunt, the execs stormed off to formulate a plan.

Chapter 2

"Freddy, make sure we're stocked up on the hard stuff. I noticed we'd gone through a fair bit of it last month." Remi's finger slid down the list of alcohol they regularly ordered, and she noticed they were missing a few. "I have a feeling some of our guests might be absconding with bottles out the back door after being privately entertained."

"Sure, boss." Freddy stopped polishing the glass in his hand. "Ah, boss, you've got a visitor." He watched the man walking across the club floor.

From her spot at the bar, Remi glanced up to the mirrors on the bar wall and saw him coming.

Black suit, grey shirt, his hair black and neatly trimmed. A close shaved beard expertly highlighted his cheekbones, and thick brows and dark lashes framed his dark brown eyes.

"Ah, excuse me. I was told the club owner was in. Are you Remi Steele?"

"I am." Remi finally glanced over her shoulder. "And you are?"

"Detective Drew Reilly." He flashed his badge and

glanced from the woman to the man behind the bar. "Can we talk in private?"

"What's it about?" Remi turned around and crossed her arms. Leaning against the bar, she had a close-up view of the man in front of her. Five ten to eleven at most. Trim, but fit build that his suit hung slightly loose on. He was quite attractive in a dark and hairy Mediterranean way. Just the way she liked some of them. Dark and hairy. Like Rex. Like Detective Drew Reilly.

"It's about a missing musician." Drew slid his badge into his pocket and pulled out his notebook, flipping through a few pages. "Trent Sexton. Goes by the name T-Sex from the band, Sexton. Apparently, they played here a few weeks back." He looked at Remi. "He hasn't been seen since and his family asked me to look into it."

Remi's left brow rose. "Asked you personally, did they? Special favours for friends."

Drew blushed. "Ah, no. I meant they came to the police to file a report and it was passed on to my division. I got the case and spoke to the family, band members, management, etc. They asked me when I spoke to them."

"Ah." Remi nodded thoughtfully. "Do you know that he's actually missing? I mean, he could have just walked away." She turned back to the bar and her paperwork. "Some people do, you know."

"Do what?" Drew asked, taking in her shapely figure from behind.

"Walk away." Remi tidied her notes. "Sorry, detective, can't help you. As you said, they played a few weeks ago. What Trent did, or what happened to him after that, I don't know."

"Except it wasn't after that." Drew moved to her side. "It was that night that he disappeared."

"What night?" Remi cast a glance his way. "The night they played here?"

"Yes. Which is why I'm here. To find answers." Drew's gaze moved around the club. "I take it you have rooms for the band to prepare." He tapped his pen against his notebook and slowly walked past the bar, seeing the red curtains. He pointed his pen at them. "And what's behind there? Some special area for celebrities? Did Trent go in there? What's back there?"

Remi walked up behind him. "Private rooms for celebrities, wealthy business men and women. People who want to enjoy the music while having a private party. Anything else?" She placed her right hand on his back and turned him towards the entrance to move him along, her left hand motioning the way to the door.

He grabbed her left arm and they stopped as the electricity crackled between them.

Her breath came out in a gasp, and she gazed from his hooded eyes to his dimples hidden just under the precision cut top of his beard. His lips were well proportioned, and the hair neatly trimmed around them.

"Sorry." He let her arm go. "I didn't mean to… Did I hurt you?"

"Um…" Remi breathed out and glanced away, aroused by the softness of his voice. She rubbed her arm. "No, I oh…" Breathing in, she rubbed her lips together. "I don't think I can help you. I'm sorry. I have no idea what happened to… What was his name? Trent from whatever band. They come, they play, they stay to play in the club, and then they leave. What happens after that…" Her voice trailed off and she shrugged a shoulder.

"I understand," Drew said. "I'd still like your footage from that night if you don't mind." He looked up at the ceiling for the cameras. "A place like this would have a lot of protection against lawsuits and whatnot. You'd surely keep the footage for longer than seventy-two hours or a week." He dared not look at Remi. His heart was still pounding and his dick had aroused from its slumber.

Remi sighed and thought through a few things. "We do, in case of legal action. I guess my manager could find the night in question and send it through to you. Or hand deliver." Her stomach clenched and released in quick time, adjusting itself to the beating of her heart. Not many men attracted her. But Drew Reilly was one of them. Just like Rex Titus. And just like Jace. She cleared her throat. "Do you have a card, or contact details? My manager will get it to you by the end of the day." Her gaze darted to him and then away.

"Sure." He pulled a card from his pocket. "He can get it to me here."

Remi took it and read the plain black font on the matte white card. *Detective Drew Reilly. Metropolitan Police Force.* She committed his number to memory. "I'll make sure you get it."

"Thank you." Drew's gaze moved from her to the stage before he did a slow 180. "What's that back there?" Pointing to the back of the club, he took a few steps forward. "Special booth?"

"Yes." Remi slid the card through her fingers. "Guests

can book it out and have up to twenty people. Champagne, caviar, whatever. We call it The Golden Ring. Freddy," she called out. "Flick on the lights for the ring."

Freddy nodded and ducked down behind the bar. Seconds later, the seating area lit up in gold.

"Whoa." Blinded by the light, Drew flung his hand up to shade his eyes as he walked over to it. "The best seat in the place, huh."

A circular velvet couch sat in the ring, with a ring of gold lighting around the outside atop a circular wall that rose as it curled around the back. A metre wide gap was in the front to walk through. A round gold coffee table sat in the middle, and sparkling party lights dripped down from the ceiling above it.

"No wonder you call it The Golden Ring." Drew walked up the five steps to the platform it sat on and turned around. "You can see the whole floor, the stage, everything but the level above us. A perfect position. How often is it booked out?"

"Mainly Friday and Saturday nights when bands are in, but if it's free and you come in another night, you can have it."

"So, you only have bands playing on those two nights?" Drew descended the stairs and stopped in front of Remi. "What about other nights?"

Her pulse did the tango. "Sometimes, depends on their schedules. But we are still a club. We still have music and are open six nights a week. We have Sundays off. But I really do need to get back to work, detective. The club doesn't run itself. So come this way." She made a hand gesture to Freddy who turned off the lights in the ring, and she waved her other hand to usher the detective to the door.

"Once I get the footage, I'll probably have more questions, Ms Steele." Drew stopped just before they reached the door and faced her. "If you remember anything or have any idea where Trent Sexton might have gone to, or are covering up for something that happened here, then I will definitely be back."

"Nothing happened here, detective," she said a bit too quickly and sighed. "He played, he left, end of story." Finally looking him in the eye, she added, "If that's it, detective, there's the door. I need to get back to work."

He gave her the once over and mumbled under his breath, "I'll be seeing you, Ms Steele." He pulled his sunglasses out of his blazer pocket, slid them on, and walked out into the daylight.

"Sisco," she yelled, and headed for her office. "Fuck, fuck, fuck. I can't have him find out what happened. Sisco!"

He appeared from the hallway. "What's wrong? And who was that delectable man you were talking to?"

"A detective." Remi grabbed his hand and pulled him into her office, locking the door behind them. "He knows Trent Sexton is missing. His family contacted the police and now they're looking into it. He wants the footage from the night the band was here." She paced and bounced her fingers together. "Go through that footage before taking it to him or emailing it, or whatever. We need to make sure nothing's on it."

"Except for him going into the back room and not emerging." Sisco crossed his arms and leaned his weight on his left leg. "Is that going to be a problem?"

Remi stopped and faced him. "It hasn't been until now, so let's hope it won't get worse. Here's his card. Get it there today."

Sisco took the card and read the name. "Might I say you and Detective Drew Reilly had some sparks?"

Remi directed a stern look his way. "No, you may not. Now go and do it."

Chapter 3

That night, Remi did a circuit of her club, walking through the mezzanine, popping into the private booths on either side, making sure her patrons had what they wanted. She reached the ground floor and gazed around. The curtains were drawn on the stage until the band came on, and the disco balls hanging from the ceiling sent shards of coloured light in a million directions. The ring was lit up for that night's patron.

Her gaze landed on the man and the people who'd come with him. He was standing in the centre like Jesus, straight and tall, arms bent at the elbows, hands out, palm side up, preaching to his choir who were fawning at his feet. The light directly above him highlighted his ridiculous costume. Black top hat, long black overcoat, black pants and top, and black fingerless gloves.

He had long hair, a pale face, and what looked to be vampire teeth. She hadn't got close enough to see the details, but Sisco had escorted the party to the ring and told her about it. Now she wanted to find out for herself. Taking a deep breath, she walked over and up the stairs to the ring. "Good evening, I'm Remi Steele, your host and owner of the club. Do you have everything you need?" Her gaze flitted from person to person and landed on the showman.

He stared down at her, taking in her appearance, scorn upon his deathly white face. "And you have interrupted my sermon."

Remi's brows rose in distaste. "There's no preaching in here. You come for the entertainment, or you leave." She had no time for jerks and had no problems having them thrown out of her club.

He stepped toward her until they were toe to toe. He was a decent head taller and thought that gave him the advantage.

Her nose screwed up and she pulled her head back. "You stink. That had better be body odour and not some type of drug on you because I won't tolerate it. Clean yourself up." Out of the corner of her eye she saw two of her bodyguards come up to stand either side of her, arms crossed, looking as wide as they were tall. "Oh and meet my security." She waved a hand at the one on her left. "Try any shit and you're out."

The Jesus look-alike glanced from guard to guard then zoomed in on Remi. "Ms Steele." A sly, smarmy, shit-eating grin curled up his lips, showing off gold teeth. "I was not preaching religion. I was preaching about the benefits of music and letting it fill every fibre of one's being in order to fully be free." He leaned closer. "*Especially* the mind."

Remi noticed that what she thought was just two fangs on the top, were actually a full attachment of gold teeth from incisor to incisor. Disturbed by his smile and freaky vampire teeth and get-up, she stepped back. "Fine. But make sure religion doesn't come into it or you're out."

"*Of course*, Ms Steele, you have my word." He narrowed his heavily lined eyes at her. "And may I say what a wonderful club this is. Owned and run by the very famous Remi Steele. Will we be getting a performance from you tonight?"

Remi took another step back, a deep frown on her face. "Possibly. But remember what I said. No religion, no drugs." She turned and trotted down the stairs, unable to get away from him fast enough, her guards on her tail.

"*Of course*, Ms Steele," Jesus-look-alike murmured, watching her go. "*Of course.*"

Remi headed for her office and found Sisco behind her desk. "Who's the dickhead in the ring? We need to keep an eye on him. I'm getting bad juju vibes."

Sisco handed her the paperwork. "Don't know, but he looked weird when I saw him."

Remi ran her hand down the appointment and admittance booking sheet. "What?"

"What?" Sisco repeated, now intrigued. "Who is it?"

Remi looked up; her face screwed up in distaste. "Dr Teeth."

Sisco got up and moved to her side to look for himself. "Dr Teeth? Who the hell is that? Is he a celebrity?"

"I don't think so. I've never seen him before and he's dressed like a freak. Have you seen his teeth up close?"

"Gold vampire fangs." Sisco chuckled and sat back

down. "What a show-off."

"Half insert actually, from incisor to incisor. Show-off all right," Remi said. "He probably wears them because of the name. It can't be his real one."

"Or he changed his name to suit his teeth. Sure they're an insert and not real?"

"As sure as his name's not Dr Teeth. I mean, what, are *The Electric Mayhem* going to come next and want to do a show?" She saw Sisco's frown. "As in *Dr Teeth and The Electric Mayhem*."

Sisco gave her a blank stare. "Who?"

Remi groaned and rolled her eyes. "From *The Muppets*! So, let's hope this dude is just an influencer or performer and not some Muppet himself."

*****

An hour later, and after a bite to eat, Remi ventured back into the club and listened to the band, Night Highway, playing their set. She kept an eye on the crowd, looking for signs of smoke or delirious patrons who might have drunk too much or taken something they shouldn't have. Keeping her club drug free, smoke free, and shithead free was top priority and a full-time job in itself. The crowd was always jumping, filling the club every night it was open, and a lot of the same people came night after night. It was the place to be seen after all. Seen entering that was, as many influencers, reality show contestants and bloggers, vloggers or Instagrammers always competed with the TikTok stars for who could get the drunkest, or stupidest, and many tried out the private rooms and left by the back door. And many didn't, stumbling out the way they'd come in, still looking like the shit-faced fuckwits they'd walked in as. God, she hated them, but they brought in more people because of their stupid videos.

"Always fucking wannabes," Remi muttered, watching a couple of girls in their early twenties taking selfies in front of the band, although they seemed more interested in keeping themselves fully in the frame. "Bunch of fucking pissants." She saw multiple phones in the air recording, which annoyed her no end, because God only knew how much else they recorded. Phones were only allowed in the main club, nowhere else. They were confiscated by every guard, at every door, to every room in the rest of the club as a way of keeping privacy and publicity to a maximum. They would get their phones back when they exited the room they'd entered.

Having been in the industry for twenty years, Remi knew about having her privacy splashed all over the covers of tabloids, magazines, and gossip websites that could never get their facts straight and preferred to print lies day after day rather than the truth. "Truth does not pay," Remi muttered. "They fail epically every single day." Her gaze landed on a young couple she remembered from the ring. They were biting each other's necks, throwing their heads back in wild abandon, and flinging their arms skywards.

"Oh, no." She grabbed a small walkie-talkie from behind the bar. "Whoever is on the floor, keep an eye on the delirious hippie couple. I think they're biting each other's necks and I see what looks to be blood.

Keep an eye out in case of collapse." A few voices let her know they'd received the message and she went back to watching the band.

A few minutes later, she saw another couple biting each other's necks. "God, what is this? A new mating ritual?" She chuckled. "Love bites are making a comeback." She walked behind the bar and poured herself a drink. Taking a sip, she acknowledged the couple making their way between the red curtains. Those rooms were pre-booked, just like the private upstairs booths, and the ring, and you needed to show the special code in the email you'd received to prove you had it booked. Sniggering, she wondered which room they were going to as all three were booked for the night.

Giggling, and calling out for drinks, a young couple came up to the bar, falling all over it, and each other.

Remi noticed their mouths as they threw their heads back in laughter. Teeth. Vampire teeth. Just like Dr Teeth's. Her gaze travelled to their necks. Tiny trails of blood slithered down their flesh from two little dots. She moaned under her breath. *I hope this isn't the start of some new fetish, or drug haze.* She watched them trying to drink with the teeth in, but when they sputtered and slopped it over themselves; they removed the piece from their mouths and tried again. "This had better not be a problem," Remi muttered.

"Thank you so much for coming tonight, ladies and gentlemen," Jackson from the band called out. "We see you've been enjoying yourselves, so before we go, we'd like to invite our good friend, an incredibly famous singer in her own right, up on stage to sing with us.

Owner and creator of this incredible club, *The Cavern Club*, Ms Remi Steele."

"No, no, no, no, no." Remi waved her hands back and forth in front of her. "No!"

"Come on, Rem," Jackson encouraged, waving her up. "Come and sing with us."

Her head fell back in resignation, a combination of a sigh and a groan left her, and she made her way to the side of stage, where she walked up the stairs and accepted Jackson's hand.

He escorted her to his microphone at the front of the stage. "Ms Remi Steele, ladies and gentlemen."

The crowd enthusiastically applauded and Remi gazed over all in the club. Her focus landed on Detective Reilly who'd just walked in the door. *Shit! What's he doing here?*

"So, Rem, which song would you like to sing? You can do one of ours, we can do one of yours, or we can do something else by someone else."

Remi breathed in and tore her attention from Drew to look at Jackson. "How about a sexy Latin version of *Smooth*."

"Ooh, nice. I love that song of yours." Jackson turned to the boys. "Ricki, take it away with the beat."

Ricki started pounding the base drum and followed it with a rat a tat tat on the snare. The band launched into the song with a sexy Latin beat and Remi started singing.

"*Your eyes follow me everywhere, your hands long to touch my skin. Your lips kiss a trail to heaven, your tongue longs to teach me sin.*"

While singing, Jackson stood behind her and she melded to him. They rocked sideways in a sexy dance beat, with him singing over her shoulder, his hand on her abdomen, with hers over his. But while her mouth may have been churning out the words, her eyes followed Drew around the room. He headed for the bar but stopped to check out Dr Teeth in the ring, then continued, ordering a drink and sitting to watch the performance.

Remi and Jackson rocked out to the last beats of the song and the crowd burst into applause. "Thank you, thank you." She waved at them. "That song was number one all around the world in its pop version, and now you've heard the Latin version. Thanks so much for loving it. I'm out." She made the peace sign and walked off stage and over to the bar. "Detective, you can't have finished watching the footage so soon." She went behind the bar and took a sip of her drink.

Drew eyed her, appreciating the skin-tight leather pants and cropped t-shirt. "Actually, we have, and I'd like to ask you about it."

She watched him take a sip of what looked to be rum or whiskey. "Should you be drinking on duty?"

His gaze never moved from hers. "It's cola, so I'm not. Now, where can we talk?"

His deep brown eyes burned through her, and she found his hirsute exterior incredibly attractive. "My office," she managed, and led the way. Closing the door behind them, she offered him a seat. "So, what questions do you have?" She walked behind her desk and took her official posture of business woman. "You didn't find anything untoward, did you?"

"Not on the first run through, no." Drew placed his drink in her desk, noticed her gaze flicker to it, and sat back in his chair, getting comfortable. "But I have a few questions."

"Such as?"

"Such as where did Trent go once he walked through those red curtains, and what *is* behind those red curtains?"

Remi placed her elbows on her desk and steepled her fingers in front of her face. "Where Trent went once he left the club, I have no idea."

"Not what I asked." Drew stared pointedly. "Where did he go once he walked through those red curtains?"

"And, as I told you today, they are private rooms. He clearly went to one—"

"But he never came out or re-entered the club. Where'd he go after the room?"

Remi debated how much to tell him and decided on the basics. "There is a private entrance out the back. Celebrities can come and go through it or come through the club and leave via the back door."

"And Trent exited via the back door?" Drew leaned forward.

Remi gave a slight shrug. "I guess he did."

His gaze searched hers. "You don't know? I find it hard to believe as owner of the club."

"You can believe what you like, detective. But once customers go into those rooms, many of them leave via the back entrance. I have no idea where or what happens after they do. Trent could've walked out of here and gone somewhere without telling his family."

"Or; he could've been dragged out of the club, murdered, and dumped somewhere." Drew thrust up into a standing position and placed both hands flat on the desk, leaning towards her. "Tell me, Ms Steele. Where is Trent Sexton?"

Remi shoved her chair back and slammed her hands on her desk, her body language mimicking Drew's. "I don't fucking know, detective. And it's time for you to leave." She stomped around her desk and pulled open her door, motioning for her two guards standing off to the side. "Please escort Detective Reilly to the front door. He needs to leave." She waved Drew past her. "Detective, it's been nice chatting to you."

He slowly stepped past, his gaze zeroing in on hers. "I'll be back, Ms Steele. Once we look into this further."

"I have no doubt you will be." She slammed the door behind him and collapsed onto her couch. "Fucking hell. What am I gonna do?"

Chapter 4

Luckily, she didn't see Drew for the rest of the week, and slept in on Sunday, her only day off from the club. Even though Remi could sleep in any day of the week and roll into work when she felt like it, she had chosen a daily schedule of business hours to work to keep her life regular, just as she spent some nights at home instead of at the club. Outside of work, she had a small circle of friends, and she was meeting them at a local restaurant bar for lunch.

Stretching, her jaw cracked with her yawn, and she lazily reached over and checked the clock on her bedside table. It read ten. She just as lazily rolled out and sat on the side of the bed, taking a moment to wake up and grab a small remote from the table. One click of a button and the curtains glided back to frame the floor-to-ceiling window of her eleventh storey penthouse to showcase views of the city to the left, and the beach to the right.

"What a way to start the day," she muttered, and padded into her luxurious ensuite consisting of a walk-in shower for two, two sinks, private toilet, and a spa bath in front of another floor-to-ceiling window.

An hour later, she was dressed in a simple blue dress and taking her chauffeur driven car to the restaurant, thinking about the lobster drowning in champagne she was going to have for her meal.

Rex saw Remi leave the apartment building and followed. He'd been waiting outside trying to convince himself to go up and press the buzzer so he could talk to her but had chickened out. Three times he'd tried to get out of his car to do it. Three times he'd backed out. He'd been busy all week and unable to go to the club to see her, and he had decided he just needed to be upfront with her and demand his needs be met. There were sparks between them that ignited into smouldering heat when they moved closer; a heat and a throbbing he could no longer deny. He wanted Remi, wanted to kiss her naked body all over. Wanted to ride her all night and into the morning. No other woman had made him feel that way. Even though he'd felt that way once, about a girl, a hell of a long time ago. But she was gone, and Remi was here. And he wanted to do something about it. What he was going to say, he had no idea. What he was going to do, he had no clue about either. He just knew he needed to tell her straight.

He followed her into the carpark of a well-known restaurant bar and grill and managed to find a free car space, to watch her alight and walk inside.

His breath sighed out of him. "What am I gonna do, what am I gonna do?" He contemplated the situation for a good half an hour before working up the courage to get out of his car and walk inside. He stopped in the entrance and glared left and right. The restaurant was to the right of him, the bar to the left. He saw her in the bar talking to a group of women and holding a glass of wine.

He blew out a long breath. "It's now or never Rex Titus. Get your shit together." He brought out his inner animal, the rough and gruff personality he constantly had on display, wore constantly as a suit of armour, when really, he was pretty much a pussy cat in private. With another deep breath, he set his shoulders back, and walked into the bar.

"Oh, my God, is that the band manager you've told us about?" Melanie, Remi's long-time friend since school, was watching him walk towards them.

"Who?" Remi frowned and glanced over her left shoulder to see Rex right behind her. "What are you doing here?"

"Remi, a word," he muttered in her ear.

Titillated, she took a step back. "How did you know I was here?" Fully aware of her friends' eyes firmly on her, she tried to keep calm.

"I came for a drink and saw you, so let's have that word." He motioned to a private area off to the side of the bar.

"I suppose." Remi let him lead her away from her friends and into a small alcove. "What did you want? And did you really just happen in for a drink, or have you been following me?" She caught his surprised look. "I've seen you out and about, watching me. You're a stalker." When he said nothing, just stared at her like a lovesick drug-fuelled idiot, she said, "Rex, what's going on?"

Rex stepped closer, leaning into her ear. His right hand slid over her abdomen towards her pelvis. His left hand slid across her lower back. His hands made the same motion on either side of her body, arousing the deep desire within her. The activity made her insides quiver, her pulse quicken, and her breath come in palpitations.

His lips pressed to her right ear. "I have a message to pass on. My penis wants to meet your vagina to say hello. And he wants to do very wicked things with her. *Very* wicked." He leaned back and watched the blush flame across her face. "Make sure she gets it."

Remi shivered with sexual excitement and couldn't think of anything to say.

With a deep throaty grunt, Rex walked away, leaving her aroused and unable to breathe, until her breath came out in a whoosh, and she leaned against the wall with one hand. "Holy mother fucking bloody," came out stunted. "What in the fucking…?"

"Oh, my God, Rem, what did he say?" Melanie laid a hand on her arm. "You okay? It looked like the two of you were going to explode from the sexual heat. We could feel it across the room. *Was* that Rex Titus?"

Remi leaned against the wall and looked at her friends in a daze. "Yeah, that's Rex."

"Fucking hell he's hot. No wonder the two of you keep lighting fires every time you see each other." Lacy Mackenzie had known Remi for over twenty years, starting with her in the music business, and she was currently single and in the mood for a hot fuck from a hot man. "Is he single? If you don't want him, I'll have him."

"Ah, yeah." Remi turned her gaze to Lacy. "That's Rex. And I never said I didn't want him, I do, believe me, I'd love to be fucked by him, but he keeps saying stupid shit that annoys me, so then I'm alone until the next time." She pushed off the wall. "He's a hot mother fucker, but he keeps insulting me, so I storm off. If he stops insulting me, maybe it'll happen. Until then, we play these stupid games."

After a long lunch in the restaurant, Remi bade her friends goodbye and went back to the bar for a drink and a listen to the band on stage. She had no idea who they were, and she didn't really care. She longed for silence so she could figure out what Rex was up to. They'd talked about him almost the whole way through lunch, with each one suggesting a way they'd like to fuck him. But it hadn't given Remi any answers. She and Rex always played these games. He'd flirt outrageously, she'd comply and flirt in return, but then he'd always say something stupid that insulted her on some level, and she'd go cold and walk away. They'd known each other four years, and it had always been the same. The sexual attraction was palpable, explosive, but she'd never gone there even though she'd wanted to. She didn't want another fiasco like when she'd dated another band manager and it had ended badly. She just didn't want to go back there.

Sighing, she faced the bar, crossed her legs, and took a sip of her favourite cocktail, and that's when she felt a presence beside her. Turning her head, she looked up to see Rex leaning over her left shoulder. His unruly curls, and even unrulier beard made him sexy as hell and she breathed in the pheromones he was dropping left, right and centre. He could arouse her in an instant.

He pressed his lips to her ear. "Did you pass the message along to your friend? Because my friend wants to get this meeting happening. He's very eager and can't wait to say hello." He placed his hands on her hips and slid his lips over her ear and into her hair.

The throbbing between her legs matched the pounding of her heart. Her mouth was dry and the inability to swallow was all too much. Her eyes closed against the onslaught of emotion belting around her body and the bar slid away into oblivion. All that existed was her and the furry as fuck man beast breathing in her ear.

"My friend can't wait to say hello," Rex breathed, kissing her neck.

Remembering she was out in public; Remi opened her eyes and gathered her wits. She picked up her bag, swung around on her stool, and swayed to her feet. She side-stepped and flung her arms outward to catch her balance. Rex reached for her.

"I'm fine," she said, shaking her head to clear the dizziness. "Just got up a little too fast. I'm fine, I'm fine. I don't need help." She brushed him off and headed for the entrance.

He caught up, grabbing her arm, spinning her around to trap her in his embrace. "Remi, stop running away from me," he growled in her ear. "You're attracted to me; I'm attracted to you. You know full well you want to fuck me, and I fucking want to fuck you. So stop running."

"I don't want to get involved with a band manager," she managed to say against his chest. His arms were so tight she was being crushed against him and breathing was hard. "I'm a free agent. I see who I want. When I want."

"Then why don't you fuck me? We're attracted to each other. My dick gets hard when I see you and I bet your vagina just waters at the sight of me." Every fibre of his body, trapped against hers, was straining to get to her. "Why won't you fuck me, Remi? You fuck everyone but me."

An icy wash flowed through her, and she froze. "What?" Pulling her head back, she looked him in the eye. "What! You think I'm a whore and fuck everyone but you?" Her strength broke free from his grasp, and with both hands on his chest, she shoved him backwards. "You think I'm a whore," she spat. "How fucking dare you!"

Shocked, he was momentarily speechless. "What? No." He watched her climb into the back seat of her car and leave. "Fucking hell!" he growled, swiping a hand over his face and through his hair. "What the fuck! How the fuck does this happen?"

Furious, Remi stewed all the way home, all the way through a simple quick dinner, and all the way through a steaming hot shower and slow languid spa bath.

She needed to relax her overwrought muscles, and not just the ones in her shoulders and neck, but in her jaw as well from all of the stress clenching.

She watched the sun set and the city lights come on, watched the last pinks and reds of the sky turn to black, watched the suburban streetlights and living room lights brighten her neighbourhood before getting out of the spa and towelling herself down. She wrapped a silken robe around her and wandered into the expansive living room which boasted more floor-to-ceiling windows which ran the length of the room. Remi was finally relaxing when there was a knock at the door.

A frown crossed her face, and she wondered which neighbour it would be at that time of night. She checked the surveillance screen before answering.

Flinging open the door, she spat, "How the fuck did you get in? I didn't buzz you in."

Rex had been nervously waiting for her to answer. "I sneaked in when someone came out. I figured if I buzzed you wouldn't let me in."

"Damn right, I wouldn't. What do you want?" She placed her right foot behind the door so he couldn't push his way in and crossed her arms defiantly over her hardening breasts.

"I want to talk, Remi. I want to apologise for what I said today." He knew he had to stay calm if he was going to get what he wanted.

"Apologise for calling me a whore. Great, go ahead." Remi waited, watching his eyes grow wide.

"I didn't call you a whore, Remi. I said you seem to fuck everyone but me, which is true." He rested a hand on the door frame and thrust the other onto his hip. "Why is it you love to fuck musicians, but don't care for a band manager? Why is it you love to fuck boys, but don't want to fuck a man?"

"Excuse me! I hardly fuck boys. Anyone I have sex

with is over twenty-five, and they're not all in their twenties." She thrust her finger in his face and stepped closer. "But who I fuck is none of your business. You're just pissed that I won't fuck you. Don't you have enough notches on your belt and bedposts? Why do you want to add me?"

"I don't have notches," he fumed, standing straight and pushing against her finger so her hand ended up on his chest. "But if I did, I wouldn't want to be another notch on *your* bedpost, regardless of how much I want you to be one on mine."

"And why the hell would I want to be another notch on the bedpost of a porn addicted male in his early forties who's been having a mid-life crisis since puberty? No thanks." Remi grabbed the door and tried to close it, but Rex stopped it with a hand flat against it.

"Fuck this shit," he growled. "I want to fuck you. You want to fuck me. Why isn't this happening? I want to fuck you like a wild animal and then make love to you, then fuck you like a wild animal again." He pushed through the doorway and slammed it shut behind him. He took her by the arms, crushing her to him. "I want you, Remi." He breathed heavily, his forehead against hers. His lips brushed hers. "I desperately want to kiss you. My tongue wants to invade your mouth and shove itself inside like a love-sick lunatic. I want to shove my tongue in your mouth, down your throat, inside of you all the way down. I want to shove it in places no other man has been."

Feeling herself give in, Remi melted into his arms, her fingers sliding through his beard to his lips. "And my tongue awaits your arrival and welcomes it with open mouth." She clamped her mouth over his and their tongues danced a wild tribal beat.

His arms wound around her, his body bent to hers, his tongue didn't leave her mouth as he lifted her and carried her into the bedroom. They fell onto the bed in a tangle of arms, legs, and tongues, and in moments, his clothes were on the floor, along with her robe, and they were igniting between the sheets. Heat sizzled, and his full body of hair made her cry out as the friction rubbed her raw. The orgasm was explosive.

He rolled off her and her body followed, half leaning on his. Her leg draped over his hips, her face and hand buried in the wild forest as they leaned on a pile of pillows, panting, heaving and sweating.

"Fucking hell," she murmured into his chest before throwing her head back for air. "Fucking hell."

"And that was definitely worth the wait." Rex pushed the hair off his forehead, slick with hot sweat from their wild mating. He'd waited all his life for sex like that and Remi had been worth it.

She rested her head on his shoulder, and gazed into his sultry eyes, her fingers on his lips. "I'll second that. Even though I *had* sworn off managers. But I will say this. You are far more of a man than any of the musicians I've fucked."

A grin slid across his lips, revealing big man-eating teeth. "Good to know, Rem."

"Is it, Rex? What about all the notches you've had?"

A chuckle escaped through his lips before they closed and he thought a moment. "You're the only notch I want on my belt or bedpost." Gazing into her eyes, he added, "The only one."

"Naw, aren't you sweet." Her lips curled into a small smile and her fingers made their way through his beard, down his neck, into the wild forest on his chest, down to the jungles on his lower abdomen and pelvis. "Jesus, Rex. I knew you were hairy, but this is just…"

"Wild," he murmured. "Yep. I was born this way, so it's all real."

"Do any manscaping?" Remi's fingers walked themselves back up before sliding into the nest over his sternum. "Where's all this from, anyway? The Mediterranean? The Middle East? Where's your ancestry from for you to have all of those glorious, luscious curls all over your hot naked body?"

"The Middle East? What? You think I'm a terrorist?" he joked, and his hand grabbed hers and brought it to his lips.

"Well, you've certainly been terrorising me these last few years with your hot curly self." She pulled her fingers away and kissed his lips. "So yeah, you're a terrorist."

He laughed. "Nice one. But no. My father's of Egyptian descent."

"Ah." Her eyes flickered with interest. "Exotic."

"What's so exotic about Egypt?"

She took a breath and her eyes widened in surprise. "You're kidding, aren't you? Pharaohs, sphinx, pyramids, Gods." Her eyes didn't leave his. "Exotic."

He breathed deeply; his fingers traced along her arm. "I can see how you'd think that."

"I more than think it." She slid over him, her body

igniting with the thick hair over all of him. "I definitely know it's exotic," she murmured, kissing him until he rose between her legs. Sitting on him, she went to work, holding his hands on her breasts. He squeezed with every thrust and bounce, kneading her nipples with his thumbs. He bent his legs up and held her to him until she climaxed with a scream and collapsed backward over his knees.

While she rested, his thumbs moved down, finding their way to where the base of his penis met the opening of her vagina. They played with her clitoris, making her squirm, cry out, and grab his hands. In moments, she jerked and came again.

"You bastard." She collapsed against him and rolled to her side, pulling him with her, their legs entwined. Her fingers went to his beard. "You're quite something, Rex Titus. And pretty fucking crazy."

"Am I?" he murmured. His fingers found their way into her hair, pushing it back from her forehead, before cupping her cheek. He took a breath. "I'm fucking crazy about you, Remi. I haven't been this crazy about a girl in decades. No one has come anywhere near you and the way I feel. I'm fucking crazy about you."

Gazing into his eyes, in the soft shades of the city lights beaming into the room, she could see he was serious.

"I'm crazy about you too, Rex. But it's just attraction. We're just incredibly sexually attracted to each other. We both lead single lives, doing what we want, going where we want, working the hours we want. We're not into relationships. It's just fun and fucking." Her fingers stroked his face. "And you really are good at fucking."

A small grin lit up his lips. "Yeah. Lots of practice. But so are you. It doesn't stop me being crazy about you."

She pressed her lips to his. "Show me how crazy you are about me."

"Challenge accepted." He rolled her onto her back, still inside, and thrust up, grasping her hips.

She gasped and wrapped her legs around his waist.

He knelt, lifting her with him, thrust until she screamed out, and pushed her hard into the pillows. Her eyes clenched tight.

A gasping laugh came from her. "You're still a bastard." Through hooded eyes, she watched him slide out and lie on top of her. They were nose to nose and he gently pushed her hair back.

"Do you want me to show you how crazy I am? Crazy about you. Crazy in general," he said softly.

She reached up and stroked his cheek. "Yes. Show me how crazy you are about me, Rex Titus."

"Don't say you didn't ask for it, and that I didn't warn you." His lips move from hers and the curls of his thick beard teased her as his tongue did the tango across her cheek to the soft flesh behind her ear.

An appreciative groan escaped deep from her abdomen. Her breasts surged up against the forest of fur on his torso, hers full against his, and the breath whooshed out of her.

His tongue danced down her neck to her collarbone, to her shoulder and back. It danced its way down her chest and sambaed its way across her breasts, his beard leaving a blazing trail of wreckage behind.

The curls on his head brushed against her lips, leaving

a woody scent. There was a hint of mint on the tips as her fingers wound their way through each curl, clenching around them as she directed him where to go, and she curled into him as he moved down her body.

His lips and tongue sizzled down between her breasts and across her stomach, making their way into her own grouping of curls. Touching, tasting, teasing. Her lower lips opened as her legs pulled up and her breasts hardened still. Her hands stayed locked on his curls as his lips and tongue stayed locked on her. Dipping in and out of her, sucking and blowing like an arctic breeze.

His tongue teased and tortured, bringing pleasures that blew her mind. She was rarely on the receiving end of oral sex and preferred to never have a dick in her mouth, so she never performed it. But Rex was showing just how crazy he was and she was enjoying it. She gazed at the curly head between her legs. His beard created friction that was insanely turning her on and she knew an orgasm was near. Her pelvis pulsated, throbbed, and opened for him and the explosion to come, but all she saw were the curls in her hands caressing her own with their endurable strength. She gasped in, opened her legs, and thrust up. The guy was fucking Samson and his hair was his strength. But they were between her legs and hypnotic and so incredibly arousing.

She arched in spasm as his tongue flicked her clit. A cry escaped her. His tongue and mouth had done their job. They had brought her to her knees and the brink of ecstasy while on her back, while the rest of him had taken over.

But he wasn't done. And neither was she.

She thrust her pelvis upward and her curls mixed with his. Her clitoris tingled and her hands held him to her as she ground into his hair. They were fuckable curls. He was a fuckable man. And she'd never met such sexually arousing hair on a man before. Or a man with such incredibly arousing curls. She guided his head left and right, up and down, grinding herself, her mound, into his curls. Curls that were so fucking hot. She thrust up and pushed his head down. Rode him, rode his head, rode the curls that were so fucking attractive. She'd had the perverse desire to fuck them. His head moved down, she clenched them tighter, thrusting as if being thrust into. Small grunts came in time with the thrusts, and he wrapped his arms under and around her legs to keep them there. This was new for him, and since he had kinks leftover from his porn addiction, he went with it.

They were so fucking hot.

She cried out and got off.

Chapter 5

Monday night, the club was rocking out to the sound of Ecstasy, a band that Rex managed. Fans filled the room to capacity with frenetic screams every time one of the band members pulled off a piece of clothing or leant down so the audience could touch their idols.

Remi covered her ears at one particular scream, shook her head, and turned towards the bar. She'd never got used to the screams of her own fans, or others, and the high decibels always pierced her eardrums. And those were also piercing her brain, so she escaped towards her office, stopping in the hallway long enough to take a last look at the crowd which included Rex, and he was coming in her direction. She grinned and turned her back.

Rex strode across the floor, hands by his sides, his gaze laser beamed on her, focussed until he was behind her. "Remi," he grunted.

She casually turned and raised a brow. "Rexy."

"Let's fuck."

Her other brow rose, and she stepped closer until the toes of her boots touched his. "No."

His brows furrowed deeper than they usually did. "What do you mean no?"

"No," she repeated. "I don't want to fuck. I want to be underneath your hands to the point I'm writhing, grasping at the sheets, moaning and groaning and toe curling until I explode."

A sly grin slid across his lips. "I could do that, and then my dick will make you explode."

Remi smiled wickedly. "If we get that far." With one hand she grasped his t-shirt, with the other she opened her office door and pulled him in, locking the door behind him. A quick flick of the light told her no one else was there before she planted her lips on his and they groped and kissed their way over to the Murphy bed she managed to pull down before they tumbled to the floor.

He did as promised and made her writhe and groan under his hands, screaming his name and thrusting her head into the mattress before he took what he wanted and made her scream louder than the fans out in the club. When he was done wreaking havoc, he rolled onto his back and lay gasping, his hot sweaty body glistening in the light.

"Fuck, Rex." Remi gasped, parched from heaving in air. "Where the fuck did you learn to do those things? That's not natural. *You're* not natural."

"As I said, lots of practice," he grunted, and placed his arm under his head.

"Clearly." Remi reached over to the fridge beside the bed and removed a bottle of water. "But what do all of your victims think?" Sitting up, she swigged a couple of mouthfuls and handed the bottle to him.

He leaned up on his elbow to face her and swallowed a mouthful. "Victims? Believe me, they're very willing participants."

Remi chuckled. "I'm sure they are. Especially after seeing this hot naked body." Her fingers trailed up his body and splayed across his chest. "And what *is* it that you do with your penis? It's rather magical."

"Nah, it's nothing. Just a hip thing I do. Makes my penis seem like it's got a bend in it and drives the girls wild." Rex handed back the bottle. "We going again, or do you need to get back on the floor?" His fingers slid up her arm to her shoulder and down her chest to her breast. He flicked her nipple. "Think we could go round two before we're needed?"

She pondered the thought a moment. "We could. Do you need to get out there?" Pushing him back until she was leaning over him, she added, "Does your bandy wandy need their widdle manager to watch over them while they're here?"

"Bandy wandy?" he said, and rolled over till he was on top. "They may behave like juvenile delinquents, even though they're in their late twenties, but I wouldn't call them a bandy wandy. And no, they don't need me to watch over them while they're here. But I can watch over you." He kissed her. "Do you know how to behave like a juvenile delinquent? I can spank you for it."

She grinned, reached down between them and smacked his left butt cheek. He flinched and grunted. "I think I just got in first."

An hour later, they were back on the club floor, both going about their business.

Rex checked in with the band, and Remi did another round, checking on patrons, the staff, and making sure all was running smoothly.

She saw that more than a few were wearing fake vampire teeth and knew that Dr Teeth was back in the ring. She also knew he'd booked it out for the week.

She made her way along the mezzanine, then stood above the ring and watched him. He exuded something. Arrogance, narcissism, a confidence of something she couldn't put her finger on…and that god awful stench that was wafting up.

His followers crowded around him or were on the floor dancing with wild abandon. All were wearing teeth just like him. Was it a new trend she didn't know about, or was there something else to it? Maybe it was something that had come from another club.

Her hands rested lightly on the railing, and she glanced around the rest of the room. Guards were paying close attention from their positions in corners, and she knew her bouncers didn't let just anyone in. That was the rule. But something was annoying her about the man beneath her and the disciples he'd brought with him. She looked down and saw that he now stood in the centre of the ring facing her and looking up, watching her as she watched her club.

She shivered as a cold slithering tendril made its way up her spine. It was creepy, and so was he. Pale skin and red lips, no doubt make-up. The same long black overcoat, fingerless gloves, and top hat. The same long greasy hair, snake-ish smile, and disease-filled eyes that captivated hers so she couldn't break their gaze. She saw Rex walk across the room in her peripheral vision, stop at the steps of the ring, look up at her and yell, "Oi."

Dr Teeth spun around, giving Remi a chance to breathe and escape to her office. "Is something wrong?" he asked Rex, his grin slithering from ear to ear. "Is there something I can do for you?"

"Yeah, stop freaking people out with your stupid fucking shitty outfit." Rex looked him over. "It's fucking ridiculous and you fucking stink. Have a shower next time or get out and go have one now." He growled and stalked off.

Not going to happen, Teeth thought. *Not while there's so much work to do.*

Rex barged into Remi's office. "You okay?"

She cried out and spun around. "Fuck! Don't scare me like that." Grasping her chest, she gasped for air. "Yeah. But fuck that guy's creepy."

"Seems to be." Rex nodded and left the room.

Remi picked up her walkie-talkie. "Keep an eye on the creepy freak in the ring. He gives me weird vibes."

"Will do."

After having a drink and calming herself, Remi went back into the club and sat in her seat to the side of the bar. The band was on a break, and everyone was still dancing to the music being played until they came back on.

Remi carefully watched those on the floor. Her gaze flicked to Dr Teeth every twenty seconds, trying to keep up with all going on. She saw his disciples dancing like manic windmills, arms and legs flinging into the air, heads spinning around, long hair flying on the wind it all created.

A bad vibe sprang up in Remi's gut. They were *too* manic. She watched a young woman in a flowing purple floral '60s style muumuu arch backwards, glazed eyes staring at the ceiling, her body slowing to a halt just moments before she hit the floor.

"First aid teams to the dance floor, first aid teams to the dance floor," Remi yelled into her walkie-talkie and took off through the crowd, as did some of the guards, towards the girl.

The music died, the disco ball stopped, and the teams swarmed onto the floor and around the prone victim.

"Stand back, make room," one of the guards instructed, and they herded the crowd back and formed a barrier around the girl.

Remi pulled her phone from her pocket, ready to dial for an ambulance, but Sisco appeared at her side already on the phone to the call centre.

She watched the girl fit, and her eyes roll back into her head. There was no control over her actions. "What's going on? Is it a diabetic fit? Epileptic?"

"I'd say it's drugs," the club's doctor said, his fingers touching her neck. "And it looks like she's been bitten. There are two puncture wounds." He lifted her top lip. "She's also wearing plastic teeth."

Remi's head spun to her right. Dr Teeth had disappeared and so had the rest of his followers. The ring was empty. Damn it!

"They said there's an ambulance nearby and it's on its way," Sisco told her.

"It also means the cops will be on their way." Remi groaned. "That's all I need."

"Anything I can do?"

Remi glanced over her shoulder and saw Rex. "Tell your band they may be late getting back on tonight. If at all."

"Will do." Rex nodded and walked off.

Paramedics came through the door with a stretcher and were waved over. They were there only a minute before Drew Reilly walked in.

Remi frowned at the sight of him. "Detective. What are you doing here?"

He glanced from the scene to Remi. "I was in the neighbourhood when the call came through. I heard the address and came over. Seems you might have a bit of a problem, Ms Steele. I'm afraid we'll have to do a check and end the party now."

Remi growled in her throat, pissed off that some cretin had ruined the night. Looking past Drew, she saw Rex walk into the club from side of stage. He saw her, then Drew, his eyes widened for a moment in shock, then his brows sank low, a scowl crossed his face, and he turned on his heel and disappeared back the way he'd come.

Interesting, she thought, and her eyes narrowed. *Why would Rex react like that?*

"We'll get everyone aside and start asking questions," Drew was saying as the paramedics lifted the stretcher and rolled the girl out.

Absentmindedly, Remi asked, "How long will that take?"

He noticed her staring off into the distance behind him and turned around to look. Seeing no one in particular, he turned back. "It could take all night, Ms Steele. We'll start with you, shall we?"

Sighing, Remi finally looked at him and nodded. "We'll go into the hall off my office for some privacy."

He followed her, pulling out his notebook and preparing his questions. When she stopped and turned around, he barely managed to pull himself up in time.

"I'm hoping it's diabetes or epilepsy," Remi told him. "Or some other brain or health issue. Drugs would literally kill my business." She crossed her arms and gazed past him at the scene they'd left behind.

"It usually does," he said. "So, tell me. What happened?"

She recalled what she knew. "And then you walked in, and she was rolled out."

"Did you see anyone take drugs? Snort, inject, swallow? Did you see her do any of that?" Drew took in her sexy attire, and full breasts nestled above her crossed arms.

"I can't say that because I wouldn't know if any of my customers have brought anything in or took something before they got here. We don't search them at the door, just their bags, but if we do see anything we shut it down immediately and permanently ban the customer. I don't do that shit and refuse to have it in my club." Remi walked a few steps to the left and then walked back. It set her off pacing. "I mean, Jesus. I've worked hard to keep this club clean, but even I have no problem saying stuff gets past me and my people. We do what we can, so if this *is* drugs"— she swept a hand through her hair and faced him— "that's going to really piss me off, detective. *Really* piss me off."

He found himself attracted to the firebrand before

him; to the demeanour, stance, sexy curves and fiery red-brown hair. There was movement in his pants, and he cleared his throat. "We may need to go through your surveillance—"

Remi sighed and closed her eyes. "Again?"

He shrugged lightly. "We still haven't found our missing drummer, Ms Steele, and now you've had a patron collapse from a potential overdose."

Remi grumbled under her breath. "Yeah. Whatever. We'll get them to you."

"I'll be back later to pick them up, after I see the vic at the hospital."

Remi glanced sharply at him. "You're going now?"

"Yes, why?" His Spidey senses perked up.

"Well, it would probably be a good thing for the owner of the club to go and see the patient. Right?" she asked him. "Take some flowers, pay for the bills, etc."

His eyes narrowed. "What are you up to, Ms Steele?"

"Detective." She stepped in front of him. "Someone collapsed in my club, so it's only fair that I, said owner of the club, pay them a visit. Are you going now?"

"Yes," he murmured. "And I'll take you." He put a finger up to stop her protest. "That way, I can keep an eye on you. To make sure you don't do anything."

"Detective." Remi's eyes grew wide. "Why would *I* do anything? Hand on heart, that's not what I'm going for." She placed her right hand on her chest.

Drew couldn't help looking at that chest. He swallowed the lump in his throat and raised his eyes, seeing her watching him with a raised brow. "I'll be keeping an eye on you, Ms Steele."

She leaned towards him and seductively said, "Please do, detective. Although it looks like you already are." Brushing past him into the club, she told Sisco where they were going and to prepare the footage for later.

He nodded and watched them leave, the sparks flying between them.

*****

Remi and Drew walked into the emergency room fifteen minutes later.

"I'm after the OD victim who just came in." Drew flashed his badge at the nurse behind the desk.

"Still in with the doctor. They're doing tests." The mid-thirties nurse glanced from him to Remi and her eyes grew wide. "Oh, my God," she breathed. "Remi Steele."

Surprised, Remi smiled lightly. "Apparently."

"The patient," Drew urged.

"Oh." The nurse blushed. "Cubicle behind you."

"Thank you." Drew was already turning away when she stopped him.

"But as I said, the doctor's in there."

In three steps, Drew was at the cubicle and flinging back the curtain. "Doc, is it drugs?"

"*Seriously*, detective. You could have waited." The harried doctor was still checking the patient over. "We've done a tox screen, checked her sugar levels, and looked through her bag. Until we know more, it's a suspected overdose."

"Bag." Remi frowned. "She didn't have a bag." All eyes turned to her, and she faltered. "Um, I remember watching her dancing. She had no bag on her and the people she was with disappeared before the cops came."

"Where's her bag?" Drew's head spun back to the doctor.

"Here." A nurse handed it to him, and he walked back to the nurse's desk, spilling the contents all over it. He pulled gloves from his jacket pocket and snapped them on before going through the contents. "Not much here. The normal stuff women carry, but I don't see any drugs." He unfolded the black leather wallet. "A bit of money, notes and coins, and here's her ID."

Remi had been staring at the bag trying to remember if she'd seen it or not, or how it made its way to the hospital, but now she looked over his shoulder. "Merriam Webster. Never heard of her and I don't recall seeing her before tonight."

"But she could have been there before tonight." Drew folded the wallet and looked at Remi. "Could she have been there before, and you not know? Do you know who comes in? Do you keep records? Have a client list?"

"Only when it comes to reserving certain areas, like the ring…" Her gaze travelled up the wall as her brain thought back. "She came with Dr Teeth."

"Who?" Drew finished packing the bag and turned to her. "Who's Dr Teeth?"

"Some creepy weirdo who booked the ring out for four nights last week, and again this week. All week." She bit her lip in thought. "Don't know his real name, and guests' names aren't put down. He just booked it each night for a party of thirteen."

"Does that include himself?"

"Yeah, it does. Why?"

He sighed and lifted the bag. "We may have her name, and this could be her bag or not, but if she didn't have it on her, how did it come here with her?"

"That's what I was thinking before." Remi stared at the bag. "It's not the type you sling over cross body style. It's too big." She pointed at the tan suede bag with fringing. "It's what— '60s boho, hippie style. Too big to dance with, and I was looking straight at her when she collapsed, and she did *not* have it on her body."

"So how did it come here with her?" Drew repeated.

Giving a shrug, Remi said, "I guess we'll find out when you watch the surveillance footage."

"Yes, we will, and I'll be back for that later. Meantime…" Drew started leading her to the entrance. "I'll get a car to take you back. I need to get to the station first."

"Don't need a car, I have mine." Remi waved at her driver, and he rolled up in front of them.

"How did he know to come here?" Drew reached for the back door and opened it.

"Sisco told him. I'll see you back at the club." She slid into the back seat.

He closed the door and watched her drive away before walking back into emergency for another chat with the doctor.

*****

Remi walked into her club to find most of the guests

gone and the police wrapping up the final interviews. Her staff had hovered around, staying out of the way, but upon news of her return, swarmed her as she strode towards her office. She stopped in the hallway and faced her people. "So far, she's okay, but she was here with that creepy dickhead, Dr Teeth, in the ring. When the cops are gone, I want it searched. Even under black light. Got it." Her guards nodded and left. "Everyone else, start packing up like any other night. We won't be starting up again. Sisco, is Rex and his band still here?"

"Don't know." Sisco looked at his watch. "I told them to go home half an hour ago. I can see if they're still here."

"No, I'll go. I need to talk to Rex if he's still here. You wrap things up. Make sure the rooms are clean and the back doors are locked."

He nodded. "On it."

Sighing, Remi grabbed a quick drink from the bar before heading backstage and then downstairs to the band rooms. They had a private entrance for the musical guests to come and go unbothered by fans. With rich coloured carpeting, soothing colours on the walls, Hollywood style lighted mirrors and vanities, private bathrooms, and multiple leather couches and chairs with dozens of cushions, each room was stocked with a fully loaded drinks fridge, and each guest always had their special foods and flowers brought in, so they felt at home.

"Rex," she called, walking from room to room. "Rex."

"Yeah." He poked his head into the hallway. "You're back."

"Yeah. You haven't left yet." She leaned against the

door frame and heaved another sigh. "The band gone?"

"Just sent them off and I'll be done in a minute." He packed something into his black leather overnight bag. "Is everything okay? That girl alive?"

"For now. But as for the other thing, you tell me."

"Tell you what?" He gave her a quick look and packed his diary into his bag.

"Is everything okay?" She watched him place a small folio into his bag and zip it up.

"Why wouldn't it be?" He faced her and leaned back against the vanity table.

"Because…" She stepped into the room, closer to him, and crossed her arms. "When you saw the detective, you went into shock. I saw your eyes widen, and then that furry monobrow of yours plummeted into its usual place," she joked, waving her finger at his full and heavy brows. "Just like now. So, what's going on?"

He crossed his arms, and one foot over the other. "Nothing. Just surprised to see cops here so quick."

"Mmm," she murmured. "I don't believe you." Moving closer, she leaned against him. "Do you wanna try again, or do I have to make you tell me?" She rested her breasts on his arms and wiggled her hips into his. "You coming tonight?"

Unable to help himself, he grinned. "I wish, Rem. But I'm leaving with the band tonight. They're going home to get their stuff. I need to do the same."

"What?" She leaned back. "For how long? How long is my vagina supposed to go without mating with your penis?" She pulled at his t-shirt. "Huh? How long?"

A chuckle left him. "The only time I've got is right

here, right now. So, unless you want to get your gear off, it won't happen for a month or two."

"What! You're gone for a month," she complained. "I won't get your dick for a month?"

He walked over to the door and locked it. "No, but if you want it now, get your kit off and let's fuck."

Aroused with the excitement, Remi quickly dropped her knickers and mounted Rex's hardened penis. They fucked their way from the centre of the room to the door, to the couch, and coffee table, ending with Remi's legs in the air and the top half of her body hanging over the edge of the couch and her breasts in Rex's mouth.

"Ah, fucking hell," she said through a dry mouth. "How do you fuck me like this?"

"Lots and lots of practice." He moved her right leg forward and shifted away, stumbling to his feet and pulling his pants up. "Fuck, Rem. I'm gonna miss my flight."

"Oh, boo hoo." Remi rolled onto her knees and climbed off the couch. She pulled on her clothes while Rex grabbed his things. "What time is your flight?"

He looked at his watch. "Midnight. Just over an hour and a half. Private jet, no less. But I still have to get to my place for my luggage."

"Surprised you didn't bring it all with you so you could go from here." Remi followed him out the door and over to the private entrance.

"We thought of it, but then forgot, so I need to go and get it. I'll see you in a month or so, Rem. Try not to kill anyone while I'm gone."

"Ha-ha." She gave him a smacking kiss on the mouth.

"Bye, Rexy. My coochie is going to miss your poochie."

A deep rolling laugh came out of him. "Love it. Bye, Rem."

"Bye, Rex." She waited until he was in his car and gunning the engine before nodding to the guard and locking the door. Taking a moment, she breathed and walked upstairs, finding Drew watching her people searching the ring. "Detective, back so soon?" She stood beside him. "Do you have the surveillance footage yet?"

"I do. Your assistant gave it to me." He waved the disc back and forth. "What are they doing? Shouldn't we be doing this?"

"Since your people left without doing it, I'd say no." Her people wrapped things up and packed away their gear. "And Sisco's the manager, not my assistant."

"Sorry. Didn't know that. So, what do you plan to find?" He tilted his head in her direction. "Are you CSIs in your private lives?"

That got a smile out of her. "No. But if Merriam was here with Teeth, then who knows what he left behind. And I really want to find out who dumped her bag into the mix, especially if it was there." She pointed to the ring. "But it ended up with her there"— her finger moved to the spot she'd collapsed— "without anyone seeing. Someone must have dumped it near her and taken off."

"I asked my people if they'd interviewed someone of Dr Teeth's description, they said no. They must've been gone before we got here."

"You'll soon see on the footage. Want to watch it now? I'm curious. We could watch it in my office. I'll fast forward to her collapsing."

Drew considered the offer. "Sure. As long as I can get a drink on the house."

Remi cocked her head. "You're on duty."

"Who said anything about duty? I need a cola with ice, stat," Drew said, and headed for the bar. When he had his drink, he followed Remi into her office and watched while she booted up the computer and moved through the footage until the collapse. He eyed the rumpled Murphy bed.

"Here." She pointed to the screen, and he hurried around her desk and leaned over her shoulder. "She collapses here." Remi briefly glanced at Drew's chocolate eyes. "And then you what?" She continued the footage. They watched her fall and a moment after someone threw her bag at her and disappeared. "That's interesting," Remi murmured and decided on another angle. Slowing the footage down, they saw Merriam fall, Dr Teeth point to her, and another follower rush past with her bag as Teeth and the others ran for the door.

"Just before my people got to her," Remi said, backing up the footage and pausing it. "My team moved fast, but they moved faster, almost as if he knew it was going to happen."

"He gave the order to dump her bag as she was falling. He knew." Drew paced the room, sipping from his glass, thinking it all through. "Who the fuck is Dr Teeth? Real name. We'll just have to find that out. Who are his guests? We'll have to find that out, too. Did he give her the drugs, or did she take them before getting here? Or maybe someone else gave them to her." He stopped in front of the bed and his top lip twitched. "Been taking a nap, have we?"

Remi walked up behind him. "Sometimes. The nights can be long, and I have a cat nap sometimes before the club opens."

"Had one tonight?" He swigged back the last of his drink. "Use it often?"

"I did. And I do."

"Alone?"

"As if that's any of your business."

"So, if I turned off the overhead light and turned on a black one, I'd find specimens of sexual activity?"

Shocked, Remi leaned back. "I don't think that's any of your business, detective."

"Maybe I should make it my business." He turned around and handed her the glass. "I should make it my business very much, Ms Steele. Call me if Teeth turns up." He looked over his shoulder as he reached the door. "Or even if he doesn't. Sweet dreams." He left, leaving her perplexed, but strangely aroused.

Chapter 6

Remi received a call from Drew two days later that Merriam had passed away from an overdose. Her death was being labelled suspicious as they couldn't claim it as suicide *or* homicide. They knew she had drugs in her system and they were the cause of her death, but couldn't say if it was self-administered, or from a secondary party.

Drew asked her again to keep an eye out for Teeth which she did for the rest of the week. Even though he'd booked out the ring, he and his disciples didn't turn up. Finding this highly suspicious, Remi let Drew know there was no sign of him. But she also had other things to worry about, including the three bands playing the club that week. Each night was packed to capacity with fans, so Remi had more than enough to deal with, especially when Demon's Run played on Thursday night.

All were in their 60s and had decided this was their final year on the road.

"Remi, my love, how's it goin', babe?" Gerry Millsap, the lead singer, kissed her on both cheeks. Wrinkled from drugs, alcohol, and age, he still wore the cut-up jeans, white holey tank top, and battered leather jacket that he'd worn since the '80s for each performance. Remi had told him every time they played the club that he needed new jeans because he was flashing the audience.

"Fine, Gerry." She smiled at the rest of the band. "I see you've changed your pants."

He thrust his crotch forward and looked down at it. "Changed them? Nah, love, just had me old lady put a patch on them coz my left ball fell out. Still the same old jeans, coz you know they're my lucky ones." He looked at her through his pale blue watery eyes. "She didn't want all the girlies getting an eyeful of the lads. Ay, ay." He goaded his fellow bandmates. "Wants them all for herself, she does."

Remi kept her lips pursed as she nodded. She was all too aware of Gerry's humour. Very British, very stale, very archaic. And one might also say very misogynistic and sexist. But the band was still huge and still brought in fans, which meant more money and more popularity for the club, especially from the older patrons. "Good for her," she finally said. "You know where your rooms are, and they're ready and waiting. You'll do a rehearsal this afternoon before tonight's performance."

"Of course, Remi. Care to escort us?" He held his elbow out for her. "Or would you let an old geezer like me escort you?"

Remi's brows rose. She was unamused by sexual innuendos, unless they were from Rex. So, coming from an old geezer, she wasn't interested. "Sisco will escort you down, even though you know the way, and make sure you've got all you need." She waved her manager over. "Have fun, boys."

She watched them grumble their displeasure and follow Sisco before escaping back to her office. It was going to be a long night with Demon's Run in the club.

The club opened at eight, and the band came on at ten.

"No point starting early," they had told her every time they played. "No one would be in the mood for a fuck or a good time."

It was a coarse way of looking at performing, and not one Remi adhered to, but they were old, and they were British— at least that was their constant excuse.

She watched a few minutes of their set before taking refuge once more in her office, and spot on midnight, the band finished up.

"Thank you, thank you." Gerry held his arms in the air. "We hope you've enjoyed yourselves. We're going to take a break for a while and will come out with something new next year. Meanwhile, if anyone wants a fuck, you know where to find me."

The crowd went berserk, and Remi groaned and dropped her head into her hands. "Jesus Christ! I can't wait for this night to be over."

*****

Remi was surprised to see Dr Teeth back in the ring Friday night, and her brows slid into a frown. What the fuck! After Merriam's death, she'd been sure he'd never show his face again. She contemplated calling Drew but chose not to. Instead, she quietly warned her team to keep an eye on him and his disciples, who looked like different people from last time. He still gave her the creeps, but she was also angry that whatever had caused Merriam's death, it was because of him. And she knew it in her bones.

In her office, she monitored him on the surveillance cameras, so she didn't have to look at him in person. He was definitely one creepy mother fucker, and luckily, there was no repeat performance of his last time in the club. He left spot on midnight, his disciples following like the sheep they were.

*****

Remi was going over paperwork the next day when Drew slammed open her door and strode into the office. The door hit the wall and bounced back.

"Where the fuck is he?" He slammed both hands on her desk and leant in. "You tell me where the fuck Trent Sexton is or I'm going to arrest you."

"Remi? Everything all right?" Sisco asked from the doorway. He'd noticed the detective storming through the club and had been admiring his posterior before speaking.

"So far, Sisco. Stay for the entertainment. I may need you." Remi leaned back in her chair, trying to keep her insides from quivering. She hated any man forcing himself into her space and playing the role of dictator. She was not one to be dictated to. "What do you want, detective?"

"I want to know where Trent Sexton is," Drew muttered through gritted teeth. "He was last seen at this club on the night he played. He hasn't been seen since and his family haven't heard from him. What do you know? I know you know something."

"And what do you know about Merriam's death and that creepy dickhead Dr Teeth, because he was here last night with a bunch of new suckers following along." She knew changing the subject would get his mind moving in another direction, so with luck he'd forget why he was there.

Drew straightened. "He was here? Why didn't you call me? Why didn't you tell me? We haven't been able to find him to talk to him, not that we can pinpoint him to the crime, just have him in the same vicinity. Why didn't you call me?"

"Did I need to?" Remi asked in return. "It's not *my* job to do *your* job and find *your* suspects. Besides"— she noted his expression but couldn't quite put a finger on what his emotion was— "we kept an eye on him because he hadn't been in since the night of the overdose. I was surprised he turned up, but again, not my job to inform you, detective." She watched the brows slowly move down, the head tilt forward, the lips separate to show clenched teeth and she could see the displeasure all over his face, oozing from every pore.

"It may not be your job, Ms Steele, but you said you'd call if he turned up and you didn't. So, to me, you can no longer be trusted to do what you say you will." His fingertips pushed into the top of the desk and he leaned across it. "Just as I can't trust you about my missing musicians. Now, where are they?"

She sucked in a shaky breath but held it together. "I don't know, detective."

"Then I guess I'll have to find out for myself then." He pushed himself off the desk. "I'll just check out those private rooms and have a look at that back door and where it leads, shall I?" He turned on his heel and strode out the door.

"No!" Remi dived out of her chair and raced after him. "Stop right there, detective."

He halted in front of the bar and turned around. "Why, Ms Steele? What are you hiding back there? Really?" He stepped up to her, his face only inches from hers. "What are you hiding, Ms Steele?"

His sexy spicy man scent wafted around her, and inhaling became difficult. She was light headed and couldn't speak.

Sisco, seeing his boss's reaction to the delectable detective, spoke up. "They're private rooms, detective. We cater private parties and keep our customers' private happenings private. We cannot disclose any of it. That's part of the contract."

"Contract?" Drew managed to draw his gaze from Remi's dilated green eyes. "What contract?"

"All parties that enter into those rooms sign a contract as do we. That all will be kept private. Whatever happens in those rooms stays in those rooms. We don't break our contracts, detective. We'd be sued and the participants would be outed."

"Participants? Like who?" Drew glanced between Sisco and Remi. "The musicians that've gone missing? Actors, politicians? Who? Who goes in there?"

Sisco spread his hands and shrugged. "Anyone. Everyone. Famous, not famous. Anyone who can afford to go in. There is a fee."

"And that's what?" Drew pulled out his wallet and rifled through his notes. "Ten, twenty, fifty, a hundred?" He leered at Remi. "You told me they can book it out. For how much? Do *I* have to pay to get back there?"

"You're not going back there, detective." Remi pulled herself up, her wits back in charge, and she faced Drew. "Those rooms are off limits, and you can leave. I've had enough of your harassment."

"My harassment?" he scoffed and thrust his finger at her. "I'm nowhere near harassing you, Ms Steele. You're hiding information from me, and I am sick and tired of it. Three men have been reported missing from this club and I want to know why, when, and how."

Remi flared. She pushed against his finger and let her finger fire away. "First off, *detective*, they did not go missing from here. So were not reported missing *from here*. Second, what they did after they left is *their* business. As for why and how, no freaking clue, but the when was *after* they were here. Stop blaming me." Her breath came hard and fast, and her face was mere inches from his. She tried not to melt into his chocolate eyes, but found it incredibly difficult, so she let her anger stay in control. "I'm done, detective. Time for you to leave."

"Not yet, Ms Steele. If you won't talk to me here, then you'll have to do it down at the station. Ms Steele, I'm arresting you on suspicion of kidnapping, you may not wish to say or do anything that will affect your day in court."

"What!" Remi stepped back in shock.

The crowd around them mumbled in waves of murmurs.

Drew pulled cuffs from his belt. "Ms Steele."

"Wait!" she yelled, putting her hands up in front of her. "Wait." She gazed around at her employees. "I'm fine. I'll be fine. Keep working. Sisco, keep on schedule." Breathing in, she slowly let it out. "You don't need to arrest me, detective. I'll come willingly to the station on one condition."

Drew glanced at the animated crowd of bouncers, all twice the size of himself. "And what would that be, Ms Steele? You don't get to call the shots. *I'm* arresting *you.*"

"And *I'm* telling *you* there's no need for that," she said. "My condition is that you get your top bosses into the room so we can end this today."

"End what, Ms Steele?" Drew took two steps closer. "And why do you need my bosses in the room?" He swung the cuffs on his finger and saw her eyes dart to them. Her lips parted. He stopped and wrapped his fingers around them. Her gaze moved back to his. *That's interesting,* he thought, and his gut stirred with desire.

"I don't mean *your* bosses. I mean the higher-ups. The ones who can close this case today and we never have to speak of this again."

Drew exhaled a huff and shook his head in disbelief. "Ah…Ms Steele." He rubbed his weary eyes. "You're telling me that after weeks of misdirecting me, and possibly lying to me, you're finally going to tell me what happened? Why should I believe that?"

"Because you're threatening to arrest me," she said.

"That's a bad move on your part and bad press for me. But that's why I want your higher-ups, not you. Take it or leave it, detective. I'll go of my own volition."

"This has to be a joke," he muttered, and put the cuffs back on his belt. "Okay, let's go."

"I need to get something from my office first. Won't take a moment." She turned around, but he reached out and grabbed her arm.

"Not so fast, Ms Steele. I don't trust you."

"And I don't trust you, but I need my handbag and something from the safe." Her left brow arched, and her eyes narrowed. "You're welcome to follow and watch."

Exasperated and over the entire encounter, Drew nodded her on and followed. He watched her collect her bag from the desk drawer, and watched as she pulled a wall panel aside and unlocked a huge wall safe. He saw her reach in, but he didn't see what she extracted or where she put it.

"Right." She locked the safe and slid the panel back into place. She grabbed a bottle of water from the drinks cabinet and walked out of the room, Drew on her heels. "Don't worry everyone, I'll be back soon. Sisco, keep getting ready for tonight. We need to see if Dr Teeth turns up. Detective Reilly has a murder case to solve, after all." She cast a dark glare at him and continued walking all the way to his car where he placed her in the back seat.

"Well, this is embarrassing," she muttered, and shrank down to hide.

"You should have been honest with me then." His eyes reflected back at her in the rearview mirror.

Her eyes burned with fury back at him. "Easy for you to say."

After arriving at the station, Drew placed Remi in an interrogation room and went to call his superiors. At the mention of her name, they immediately said they were on their way and Drew waited for them in the adjoining room.

"Did you call them?" she asked the mirror, knowing full well it was double-sided. She uncrossed her legs and sat straighter. "I know full well if they knew I was here I wouldn't be waiting, Detective Reilly."

"So, what's this about?" Chief Superintendent Richards sighed. He knew Remi Steele and didn't want his connections to her known or made public.

"I've been on her for weeks about the musicians that are missing. They were last seen at her club. She won't tell me, so I brought her in." Drew flipped through his notes and started to speak again but was cut off.

"Enough, detective. You said she'd only talk in front of us so this could be over," Superintendent Passover said. "Well, we're here, so let's get this over with and solve this case, shall we. I hear you have an overdose in her club to solve."

"Which resulted in death, yes." Drew nodded and gestured for the three senior officers to leave the room before leading them into the interrogation room. "Ms Steele, Superintendents Richards, Passover, and Macky are here to listen to your story. I read you your rights at the club."

Remi watched Drew move to her right, and the three senior officers lean against the wall in front of her.

"Gentlemen, I will say on record, I'm here against my will. But this whole saga needs to be over and dealt with quietly so I can get on with it." She'd never expected to ever be arrested, but was glad she had the confidences of the three men who visited her private rooms so frequently they had gold passes. "The details need to be kept private, for everyone's sake. And I don't need to tell any of *you* about privacy."

"Ms Steele, you don't get to run the interrogation," Drew snapped and leant on the table.

"Neither do *you*, detective." Her eyes flared and she nodded in the officers' direction. "They do. Now listen carefully, detective, while I give you just enough information that this case will be closed." Drew opened his mouth, but she shushed him. After a breath, she looked at each man and began. "Behind the red curtains at the club are three private rooms. Each is for different things." Her gaze directed to Richards. "Guests can book those rooms for the fun they can have in them, but some people who enter through those curtains turn right and walk down the hall and out the back door. They step into a waiting van and get driven to a private hangar at the airport, where they will walk onto a private jet and fly to a private island, where they will walk into a private *rehabilitation clinic*." She stared at Drew whose frowning eyebrows slowly relaxed.

Richards groaned and hung his head. "So not missing at all."

"No," Remi told them. "To the families, yes, but technically no."

"How long has this been going on?" Drew crossed

his arms and felt his case circling down the drain.

"About eight years." Remi cracked open her bottle of water and took a sip. "A year after I opened, an old friend talked about the rehab clinic he'd been in. He wanted to help other musos into it. I suggested using the club and set up a plan for it. He started mentioning it to his friends, and they came to me. The plan is set in motion and away they go."

"So, Trent Sexton, Romeo Valera, and Kirk Knight?" Drew asked.

"They are three, yes." Remi nodded and took another sip of water. "But, if they haven't contacted their families to let them know, then something's wrong and you need to contact the clinic."

Drew scratched his head and sighed. "I can go there tomorrow."

"By flying a hundred k off the coast? No." Remi shook her head. "They won't let you in. You need to call there and let them know the families have filed reports." She dug around in her bag and pulled out her phone. "I'll get you the number." Scrolling through her contacts, she stopped at one. "Here." She held her phone up and Drew dialled the number. "Put it on speaker." Remi motioned at the phone and after a second, he did.

"*Holiday Inn Meditation Centre*, how may I direct your call?"

"Ah…" Drew looked at Remi in confusion. "This is Detective Drew Reilly calling from Australia. I need to speak to the person in charge."

The silence lasted a few seconds before the woman spoke. "Do you want to book in?"

"Rachael, it's Remi Steele. Please put us through to Doug; it's important."

"Ah, of course, Ms Steele." The phone went silent.

Doug came on the phone a few moments later. "Remi? What are you calling for? You have a detective with you?"

"I'm at the police station *almost* under arrest. I've told them the basics only. You need to speak to the detective."

"My name is Detective Reilly, and I have three missing person reports concerning three musicians that are apparently in your care."

"Ah…" Doug sighed. "Yes. Trent Sexton, Romeo Valera, and Kirk Knight, right? They don't want to contact their families. The initial email was sent upon their arrival, saying they were taking a break, but the first month's phone call has not happened in Trent's case. Sorry detective, we can't make them call, and part of the contract is they don't talk about rehab to anyone until they've left. It helps to keep everything private while they're here. Imagine if we had boats and choppers on our doorstep? We couldn't do our job."

Drew sighed and rubbed his eyes. "So, they are there."

"Yes. Still here and doing well."

"What do I tell the families?"

"That they are alive and fine. Thriving on their holiday and will contact them soon. I can't say anything else, detective."

Drew looked at his superiors. All three waved at him to end the call. "Thank you for that information. I'll let the families know."

"Thank you, bye Remi."

"Bye Doug."

Drew ended the call. "I guess I wrap this case up and close it, then?"

"You do." Richards straightened his jacket before buttoning it. "But considering how delicate the matter is, keep it private and don't mention rehab in the paperwork."

"And since you have an actual death to solve," Passover added, "when the paperwork is done, get into that."

"Yes, sir." Drew nodded at each one as they exited the room and waited for the door to close before exhaling. "Jesus, Remi, why didn't you just tell me that? It would have saved so much fucking trouble. *And* embarrassment in front of my superiors." He turned around and sat on the edge of the desk.

"It's *Ms Steele* to you, detective." Remi fired up. "And where would the fun be in that?" She stood and stretched her back. "I take it I can go? I have a club to run."

"And I have a death to solve." He swiftly spun around to stand in front of her. "Is Dr Teeth booked in at the club tonight?"

Remi stepped back and cleared her throat. "I don't know. Why?"

"Because if he is, I can do my job." Drew leaned towards her. "Find out."

"Ah." Remi took another step back. "I'll look it up when I get to the club."

"Now. Call your assistant." Drew pointed at her bag. "I need to know now."

"He's not my assistant."

"Yeah, yeah, he's your manager," Drew grumbled with a wave of a hand.

Unnerved, Remi fumbled for her phone and called Sisco.

"Remi! You okay? You need help? The cavalry? Superman?"

Relief washed over her and she chuckled. "No. I'm fine. On my way out. Can you look up the bookings for tonight and see if that dickhead has booked out the ring?"

Sisco shuddered. "Ugh, you mean that hideous Dr Teeth? Yes, he has. I was just going over the paperwork. He has twelve guests again."

"Thanks, Sisco. Is my driver outside?"

"Of course. See you soon."

"Bye." Remi disconnected and threw her phone into her bag. "Anything else, detective, now that you've harassed me around for a few hours. Lorded it over me. Fake arrested me—"

"I *did* arrest you." He picked up his notebook. "I just didn't cuff you."

"Cuff a lot of women?" slipped out from between her lips.

"No." His eyes bored into hers and he took a long pause. "But there's one I'd like to cuff."

Her lips opened and she sucked in a shaky breath. Electricity shot through the air.

"Ah…" He broke the spell and blinked rapidly. "I shouldn't have said that." Awkwardly, he looked around and gathered his things. "You're free to go, but

I'll escort you to the front desk to let you out." After double checking his files, which he nervously dropped and then fumbled to pick up, he finally opened the door and escorted her downstairs, unlocking the door so she could enter the lobby. "Ms Steele. Thank you for finally clearing things up."

Remi stepped through the doorway and glanced over her shoulder. "Keep it private, detective. Their physical and mental well-being depends on it."

He thought for a moment and nodded before closing the door.

She sighed and left the building.

*****

After a refreshing shower, a bite to eat, and a power nap at home, Remi was back at the club at eight. Her afternoon trip to the police station had been quite an event and one she didn't want to repeat.

She also didn't want to see Drew again. Although she found him attractive, he was too clean cut, too stiff upper lip, too staid. But…he had handcuffs. A tingle fluttered through her pelvis and her sex organs convulsed. They only did that when thinking about a man. Or sex.

"Maybe I should call Rex," she murmured, and grabbed her phone. She shot off a quick text before taking her seat at the bar.

The club was jumping as usual. The crowd ranged from eighteens to what looked to be sixty-eights. Or they could have been older considering there looked to be people whose faces said 40s while their bodies said 80s.

Her phone beeped and she read the reply from Rex.

I'd be sucking your vagina if I were there.

So why aren't you?

Busy with the band. Miss me?

Fuck yes!

Or is it my dick you miss?

That too!

I'll be back in a few. We'll hook up then.

Can't wait.

Neither can my dick. He can't wait to fuck your hoochie again.

You're disgusting, Rex.

So are you, Rem. You fucked my hair.

It's hot hair. Let it know I miss it.

Will do. But my dick is jealous now.

Tell it I'll fuck it too, as well as the thick luscious curls around it.

You just want me for my hair.

You have a lot of it.

I have a lot of dick too.

So you do, and I can't wait to feast on it.

And I can't wait for you to do that. Gotta go, Rem. Love you.

Love your dick. Bye Rex.

Fuck you!

I will. You too.

She giggled and finally looked up from her phone. It wasn't the first text exchange they'd had, and they were always dirty. The dirtier the better. They'd even had phone sex a few times. But it was nowhere near the real thing. Her head nodded along to the song, and she crossed her legs, her foot tapping to the beat. She scanned the crowd slowly and saw Dr Teeth lead his procession of rats to the ring. "Just like the pied piper," muttered from between her lips, and her eyes rolled hard in their sockets. "Here we go."

They entered the ring, Teeth in the lead, and he stood in the middle, arms out to the sides, while his guests took their seats. He slowly turned to the club floor, head back, staring at the ceiling. A sly grin was on his lips. His outfit was the same. His pallor was sickly white as always, his lips blood red, but cracked and dry. His fangs glinted gold in the lights.

"Fucking hell," Sisco murmured, standing right behind Remi. "That dude has a serious God complex."

"He does, so keep an eye on him and tell the guards to as well. He's responsible for that young girl's collapse and he left without a care for her health or safety," Remi said over her shoulder. "And call Detective Reilly. It's really not my job, and after today, I don't want to talk to him."

"He is a rather tasty morsel of Mediterranean flesh, isn't he?" Sisco leaned his arms on the bar. "And in fine shape as well. Although not as fine as Rex Titus."

Frowning, Remi glanced at him. "Mediterranean? Is he? I wouldn't've thought it. And yes, Rex is very fine."

"And all yours, I take it." Sisco grinned. "Is that hands off for the rest of us? Because I certainly wouldn't mind dipping my pen into that pen's ink."

Remi screwed her face up at the terminology. "Ew, gross. Your pen, oh, you mean penis. Jesus, Sisco. Rex doesn't swing that way, but I know nothing about

Detective Reilly." She thought about his looks. "I don't think he's Mediterranean."

Sisco shrugged. "Middle Eastern, Egyptian, Greek, whatever. I do like the dark, silent type."

"After today, I'd hardly call him silent." Remi directed her gaze at Teeth. "You'd better make the call, though. Even though he knows Teeth has booked the ring."

Sisco pulled his phone from his blazer pocket along with Drew's card. It went through to voicemail, and he left a message. "Not there, but you know I left a message, so he can't say we didn't call him."

"Nope." Remi nodded and went back to watching the crowd.

After a break and a bite to eat, Remi wandered through the club chatting to her patrons, making sure they had what they needed. She was on the mezzanine overlooking the dance floor when she spied Drew. Or a man who *looked* like the detective. *No*, she thought and peered closer. *That can't be.*

On the dance floor, Drew was dancing up a storm. He hadn't cut loose like this since his late teens when he and his best friend had hit up every club in their hometown. Every Friday and Saturday night was spent trolling the clubs, hooking up with girls, and drinking to their heart's content. They'd even won a couple of dance competitions. But that was a hell of a long time ago, another era, another life. Another Drew.

Remi leaned on the railing, staring at the man on the floor. He sort of looked like Drew, but the hair was wild and free, he wore ripped jeans and black boots, and a tight black t-shirt with a deep v, and a black vest over it.

"Fucking hell," she muttered, shaking her head, the beat driving through her brain. "Fucking hell." With one last look, she continued on her way and made it back downstairs. She pulled Sisco into the hallway outside her office. "Guess what. The reason you couldn't get through to Detective Reilly is because he's on the dance floor."

"What!" Sisco's eyes widened. "Where?" He spun around and craned his neck, eager to see for himself. "Where?"

"Black t-shirt, vest, jeans and boots," Remi said over her shoulder. "In the centre, but don't point. Teeth is here."

Sisco glanced at Teeth and noticed him staring. "Teeth is interested," he told Remi and gazed across the club to not draw attention. "Ah…wow, you sure that's him? Definitely not the strait-laced cop I thought he was." Sisco glanced at the bar. "Wonder if he drinks. You know…" He spun around to Remi and moved her back into the corridor. "Teeth was watching. Do we want to let Detective Reilly know he's here?"

Remi's attention had been flitting back and forth between Drew and Teeth. "I have a feeling Detective Reilly might be doing some surveillance. Why else would he be in plain clothes? He's clearly not on duty, so I'm not sure if he'll drink. But don't draw attention to him. Do we need to tell the guards?"

Sisco peered out into the club. "Tell them what? That Teeth's here?"

"No, they already know that, and are keeping an eye on him. I mean tell them we have an undercover detective in our midst."

"We sure he's undercover?" Sisco crossed his arms

and pursed his lips. "The delicious detective could just be cutting a rug for the evening, and he's very good. Almost *too* good for a straight man."

"Your gaydar is showing," Remi remarked. "And I don't think he's gay. I also know that many straight men are very good dancers."

Sisco smirked. "Oh, they are darling, but who said they're straight?"

Remi wasn't shocked by most things, but every now and then Sisco came out with something that startled her. "That's gross, Sisco."

The smirk still in place, he said, "For you maybe. I'm back to work. Maybe I should go and dance myself." He sashayed away, heading for the pounding beats of the music and the syncopation of the light-up dance floor.

"Fucking hell." Remi shook her head and let her gaze move back to Drew. "Why are you here? Is it for Teeth? Why else would you be here?" She let out a sigh and took her place beside the bar.

The sweat was dripping off Drew. Down the side of his face, his neck, his back and chest. He was soaked, but he didn't care. He only cared about finding Teeth and any evidence he could get against him. He didn't care about the girls who'd thrown themselves at him. He would dance with them and move on. He'd even ended up dancing with a dude who was clearly gay and about to score something somewhere. Drew had known he'd have to immerse himself into the role of an undercover. Not that he minded. He loved music and had managed to remember his moves from over twenty years ago. He swayed to the beat and did a few fancy steps, clapping and moving. He spun around to find a woman with a sexy figure in a skin-tight cat suit that left nothing to the imagination.

"Hey." She nodded and swayed closer to him. "You're hot."

A rare grin lit up his face. "I've been told. So are you." His hands went to her hips and his legs moved inside hers.

She rested her arms on his shoulders and they moved together in circles around the floor, their bodies melding together. His left hand slid down across her buttocks to rest in the crook of her leg, and his right hand slid down to her lower back, pulling her even closer.

"Keep touching me like that and I'll have to fuck you," she said in his ear.

He stared into her light eyes as the music beat wildly around them. "You could anyway." His hands slid around her waist and lifted her up.

She wrapped her legs around him, locking them together, locking her to him. Her pelvis throbbed and she kissed him passionately.

He kissed her the same way in return.

Remi watched from the hallway to her office, pain searing through her. Pain of jealousy. Her sex organs throbbed in anger and frustration and needed relief. But Rex wasn't there, and it wasn't as though she was interested in Drew. Of course she wasn't, and he wasn't interested in her. He was all over the blonde like a rash, so no, he wasn't interested in her. She growled and leaned against the wall behind her. She hadn't been this turned on in weeks, and maybe she should just pull

Drew aside, and no, why was she thinking about Drew when he wasn't thinking about her, and if he was on duty and undercover, then why was he playing tonsil hockey with some random in the club?

Remi tried to remember who was currently in the private rooms and if she could find relief in one of those. If not, she'd have to resort to her handy dandy vibrator, or Drew. "Nope," she muttered. "*Not* Detective Reilly." She marched off down the hall, unlocked the door separating her from the private rooms and opened it. She hesitated, considered her next move, and closed the door behind her. She knew rooms two and three were the ones she needed and knocked on the door to room two. Peering inside, she saw Jericho, the guitarist from Sex Bandits, a rock band who'd had a stellar ten-year career touring America. He was draped in two women, his jeans and jocks around his boot-clad ankles and he was leaning against a pile of pillows.

"Remi! Come and join us."

Remi eyed the two girls. "Girls, how about you wait out in the hallway. We won't be long."

The girls started protesting but Jericho slapped each one on the bum. "Don't start, Remi's the owner and the one letting you be here. Play nice and go wait in the hall."

The girls climbed to their feet, slipped robes over their underwear, and slid out the door.

Remi locked it behind them. "This won't take long." Walking over to him, she grabbed a condom from the bowl on the coffee table and threw it at him. "Put this on and I'll get these off." She pulled up her skirt and shimmied out of her lace knickers.

"Only one," he complained. "We could have some fun, Rem."

She climbed on top, said, "This won't take long," and proceeded to pound out to her own beat.

*****

The song came to an end and blended into the next, but Drew knew it was time to stop. He set the woman on her feet. "Let's get a drink. I need to rehydrate."

"I know what I can drink." She pulled at his belt.

He caught her hands. "Cute. Let's get a drink." He led the way to the bar, collapsed against it and they ordered drinks. When Drew's arrived, he swallowed it in four gulps and ordered a refill.

The blonde piled her hair into a knot on the top of her head. "You clearly needed that." She picked up her champagne and sipped it. "Care for some of this? It will get you high."

"I'm already high." Drew took another mouthful of cola. "The music gets me high; dancing gets me high; life gets me high."

"Does love get you high?" She slid her left arm around him and snuggled close. "What about other things?"

He knew where that was going and nuzzled her neck. "What about other things?"

She giggled and rubbed her crotch on his leg. "Oh, I don't know. Other things."

"Such as?"

"Oh…" She glanced away coyly. "Sex, drugs, rock 'n roll."

"Into rock 'n roll, are you?" He finished off his second cola. "Anything else?"

"Kink."

He raised a brow. "Ah. You into that stuff?"

"Could be. Wanna try?" She let the last drop of champagne slide down her throat and placed her glass on the bar. "I happen to have a few things on me."

His interest piqued, he asked, "Like what?"

She opened the small bag around her waist and pulled out two small Ziploc bags. "These."

Puzzled, he took one and held it up. "What are these?"

"Teeth," she said. "You put them in and get a thrill."

"From what? Being bitten." Drew handed it back. "I don't get it."

"Then let me show you," she said, her voice sultry and close to his ear. She pulled one set out and pushed the fake teeth over her own. "See, you wear them like this and then bite each other. It's some new craze kink. You bite each other on the neck and pretend to be vampires or something. It's all the rage these days."

"Really." He wondered if they had to do with Dr Teeth. Nodding towards the dance floor, he moved her in front of him so he could get a look at Teeth who was still in the ring, but not looking their way.

The blonde pulled Drew into her arms and nuzzled his neck. She made sure the teeth were in place and then latched onto Drew's flesh.

"Ah." He jerked, but she held on. "What the fuck! That hurts." He pulled away and slapped at his neck, seeing swipes of blood on his hand. Flaring at her, he said, "Did you fucking bite me? Did you seriously fucking bite me?"

"Calm down, it's just a tiny sting." She pulled him back against her. "That's the point of the teeth. To bite each other like vampires. It's a kink. It'll stop hurting in a moment."

Drew's brow was deeply furrowed, and a million thoughts a minute swam past his eyes. What was in those teeth? What were they made from? What was in there? Were the ends just sharp or was there something else in them? Could it be syringes? What was in them? Merriam had two holes in her neck, as if she'd been bitten. Was this how they did it…?

The thoughts trailed off and the lights and sounds around him took over. He was floating in a multi-coloured flashing cloud, pinks to reds to orange, yellow, greens, blues to purples back to pink. The music washed over him like God anointing him, and his soul felt freer than it ever had. No more hatred, anger, resentment. No more sorrow, sadness or fear. No more pain of love unrequited and loss unresolved. There was no more. Nothing but light and music. His soul was free of his body. His body was free of all restraints.

He closed his eyes and let the musical cloud take him away…

PART TWO

CRAVE

Chapter 7

Drew breathed in, deep into his gut, filling it until he couldn't expand it any more. He held his breath for a few seconds, and then slowly exhaled. His senses became aware of his surroundings and his eyes slowly opened to take in his room. Except it wasn't his room. He also realised, he wasn't alone. Blinking a few times and wiping his eyes, he carefully leaned up on one elbow to study the woman beside him and recognised her from the club.

"Fuck," he muttered and looked around the room. It definitely wasn't his with its feminine bedding, curtains, and decorations. "Fuck." Trying not to disturb her, he rolled out of bed and quickly stood. "Ah." He clutched his head. "Too fast. Dizzy." He sat back on the bed and breathed in. What the fuck! His vision cleared and the pounding resided. "What the fuck?"

"What the fuck indeed." The woman clicked a button on a small square remote and the curtains silently slid back to the wall either side of the wall-to-wall window.

"Ah… I was trying not to wake you." Drew avoided her gaze, breathed in, and stood slowly. "Just trying to find my clothes and then I'll be on my way."

Completely naked, he tried not to be self-conscious. His genitals were free for viewing pleasure, and he considered covering them, but also considered just letting them flap around as she'd clearly seen them during their exploits the night before. Whatever those exploits may have been. He wandered around the bed, one hand casually in front of him, and saw the scattered clothing. "I'll just get dressed and be on my way."

"Take your time." The blonde slithered out from under the pearl grey satin sheet. "I'm having a shower. If you're gone before I get out, make sure the door locks behind you." She eyed him up and down. "I had fun. Maybe we could do it again. I love men with wild jungles on their body. Adds to the friction."

Startled, he stopped with his pants in mid-air, and his gaze flew to her, seeing her perfectly sculpted body, the colour of cream, and everything in proportion. He glanced away. "Maybe," he said and reached down and grabbed his t-shirt. "If I see you there." Heat swept over him. "I don't normally go clubbing. I'm always busy and it's not something I've done for a good couple of years," he rambled, willing himself to shut up. He was still naked but holding his clothes to his body.

"Maybe I can convince you to do it more," the blonde said, and sidled over to the bathroom, a hand casually leaning on the frame as she paused and glanced over her shoulder. "Let's do it again." She closed the door behind her.

Drew heard the shower start and moved. Pulling his clothes on as fast as he could, he scavenged under her clothes and the bedding for his keys, wallet, and phone. He found his ID still in his jeans pocket, and the rest on the floor.

Shoving his socks into his pockets, and his feet into his boots, he took one last look around to make sure he had everything. As his gaze searched across the bed, he noticed several packets of plastic teeth, like the ones she'd shown him the night before, on her bedside table. Hearing the shower still going, he hurried over and picked one up. Noticing there were more in the partially opened drawer, he replaced the one he had so she wouldn't see it missing and took a couple from the drawer. Holding them up for a closer look, all he saw was two sets of plastic teeth. He shoved them into his pocket, and with one last glance around, quickly left.

*****

Drew arrived at work two hours later, to the jokes and jibes of his fellow detectives, and the angry expression and tone of his superintendent.

"I'm sorry I'm late. I ended up staying at someone's house and had to call a taxi." He paused and grew red. "After I found out where I was."

Laughter spread around the room.

"He didn't know where he was," one detective said. "Must have been a hot broad for you to stay the night and not know where."

The blush deepened Drew's face to a tomato shade and his right leg pulsed nervously. Embarrassment and shame flitted over him. "I had to find out where I was to tell the taxi where to pick me up." He straightened and rushed on. "Needless to say, it was a very long taxi ride home, and then I had to take the taxi to where I'd left my car, but I got there and now here I am. Ready to work." He tried to block his ears from the comments and wished the ground would open up and swallow him.

He received a nod from his boss and scurried to his desk, leaning on it as dizziness overtook him. "Ah…" He rubbed his eyes and breathed in. "Why's the room spinning?"

"Too much to drink?" Detective John Burrows grinned and threw a small soft football toy across the desks at him. "You better sober up, Reilly."

The ball hit Drew in the chest, and he fumbled for it before slumping down in his chair. "I don't drink, so I'm not drunk *to* sober up."

"But something's clearly wrong." Richard Wong rolled himself over in his chair. "You snort, swallow, or inject?"

"None of the above," Drew snapped and threw the ball back at John. "I don't drink, I don't do drugs, I live clean."

"But, again, something's clearly wrong," Richard repeated and rolled back to his desk. "Maybe you should do a test in case. Who did you go home with?"

Drew sighed and pulled a pile of manila folders towards him. "That's none of your business." He closed his eyes and leaned his elbows on the desk, putting his face in his hands.

"Well, if she used something…" John cast a sly glance at his fellow officers. "Or *he* did something, you'd better find out."

Drew sent a scathing glare his way. "I'm not gay."

John shrugged while the others sniggered. "Either way, if you've been drinking—"

"I haven't," Drew snapped. "Because I don't drink."

"Reilly." Their boss strode up behind them. "Breathe into this." He shoved a Breathalyzer unit at him. "You know we don't tolerate drunken tardiness in this unit and if you're drunk—"

"I'm not," Drew insisted. "I just don't feel well." He eyeballed his boss and the machine. "Give it here." Snatching it, he breathed into the tube and handed it back. "I said I don't drink, so I'm not drunk."

The other detectives gathered round until the machine beeped 00.00 and flashed green.

"Told you!" Drew grumbled and pulled out his desk drawer. "Anyone got any Panadol? I took some at home, but they're not working." Looking through his drawer, he found none. But he did find his boss still standing behind him. "Well?"

"Well." Waylon Winthrop the Third waved the breathalyser in Drew's face. "You're in the clear. This time. But if you're sick, you should go home. Something's wrong."

"Probably picked up a bug." Drew shrugged and glanced around. "Maybe there's a flu carrier in this room. We need to be able to open the windows."

Waylon grumbled something under his breath. "Okay, everyone. Back to work."

Drew rubbed his eyes and leaned on the desk. *What the fuck happened last night?* he thought. He'd been trying to connect the dots since he'd walked out of her house. And except for remembering the woman in the club and dancing with her, he had no clue how they got to her house but figured they'd had sex. How many times, he didn't know. But since they'd woken up naked, it was a safe bet it had happened.

"I'm going to the bathroom," he muttered to no one in particular and pushed back his chair. After quickly making his way down the hall and into the gents, he was relieved to see it empty and turned to the sink. He splashed his face multiple times before turning off the tap and looking at himself in the mirror. His eyes were still a little red. He'd noticed that at home. His pallor was a little more pale than normal. He turned his head left and right and noticed a red dot on his neck just above his collarbone. He leaned in for a closer look, rubbing at it. Pulling his collar down, he saw a second red dot and frowned. Flashes of the woman biting his neck came back to him and he leaned back. "Fucking hell!"

*****

Drew rolled up to the club and strode inside, waving aside the guards at the front door. After making his way to Remi's office, he found her talking to Sisco. "I thought you said you didn't allow drugs in this club."

They looked at him, and then each other.

"I'll just…" Sisco pointed at the door and made a move towards it.

"No, stay," Remi told him. "If the detective's going to accuse me of something else, I may as well have a witness."

Sisco sidled back to his previous spot and watched them both intently.

"I believe I told you, detective, that I do what I can. But I can't stop anyone from pre-loading on drugs or bringing it in some orifice we don't search."

Sisco sniggered and quickly covered his mouth.

"Then what the hell happened last night?" Drew slammed his hands on her desk. "I'm dancing with some woman and woke up in her bed this morning—"

"Lucky her," Sisco murmured.

Drew sent a scathing glance his way. "I don't remember going back to her place, or what we did, but I woke up there this morning."

Remi frowned and glanced at Sisco.

"Now, Merriam Webster dies from an overdose that more than likely happened in this club, and that case is still open. So…" Drew thrust his forefinger towards Remi. "What the fuck is going on and what the fuck happened to me last night?"

"You got laid, detective," Sisco said. "Why do you need to know anything else?"

"And," Remi butted in. "You can't prove she got the drugs in the club. She could have pre-loaded before she got here."

"But Merriam collapsed *in this club*," Drew retorted. "*You're* responsible for that."

"The fuck I am." Remi stormed to her feet. "No one can prove where she got her drugs, or where she took them. The only thing we know for certain is she collapsed here and died in the hospital. *That's it.* If drugs got past our staff, then that's a problem, and we've been looking into it." She'd walked around her desk while talking and now stood face to face with Drew. "As for your other problem, you couldn't keep your hands off that blonde, nor she you. You danced, you drank, her champagne, you cola, she bit your neck and the two of you stumbled out of here. *Happy*?"

Drew's brows furrowed and his fingers went to his neck. "She bit me?"

Remi's gaze moved to his hand, and she nodded at it. "Right there. You must have seen the marks."

His head shook slowly. "No, not until before. I… Little plastic teeth. She said they were a kink."

"Apparently," Remi muttered and crossed her arms. "I've seen a few people with those stupid teeth in. They seem to get off on biting people."

"So, you're not the one selling them?" Drew's thoughts flew through his mind.

"Nope. Not giving them away, either. They either get them before they come, or from someone else, like that stupid Dr Teeth. What was the point of you being here last night, anyway? Undercover?"

"Yeah," Drew said, distracted by the case. "Thought I'd see what the crowd was doing."

"And?" Remi studied his face. Brows deep, eyes thoughtful, lips pursed together.

"Huh? Uh, didn't find out anything. I ah…" Drew's gaze shifted to her and then around blankly. "I gotta go."

Remi watched him leave and her brows slid down in thought. "Something's very wrong. He was distracted—"

"Away with the fairies, but still so delectably hot and hirsute," Sisco supplied and took his place on the couch. "If only he were into men."

If only he were into me, Remi thought and her

brows slid lower. With Rex still away, her nights had become incredibly lonely, and even though she had the occasional fuck with a drummer when bands came to the club, it still wasn't the same. Drew wasn't the same as Rex, but he still titillated her and the glimpse of chest hair she'd seen last night told her he had a good body of it. Heaving a sigh, she got back to work.

*****

Drew walked into the club just after nine with no intentions of replaying the night before. He was there to find out who was supplying drugs and was determined to get to the bottom of Merriam's overdose and subsequent death.

He danced his way through the crowd to the bar and ordered a cola on the rocks, sipping it while scanning the club goers. He recognised a few from the night before, including Dr Teeth with new disciples in the ring. He still hadn't found any information on him. There was no social media unless you accounted for Dr Teeth from *The Muppets*. No one by that name had a license, Medicare card, nothing, so it was clearly a stage name, and unless they got fingerprints, DNA, or an actual name, it was going to be a lot harder to find out who he was and what he was up to.

He saw Remi schmoozing with her patrons on the mezzanine and admired her taut behind in her skin-tight leather pants. *God how I'd love to yank them off* floated through his head. He snapped out of it. *Nope, can't be thinking that way. I have a murder to solve.* He finished off his drink and made his way into the throng.

Remi was pulled over by Sisco when she got back to the bar. "I see our studly detective is here again. Wonder what he'll get up to this time?"

Remi barely heard him above the music but glanced at Drew who was thrusting his pelvis at a hot brunette with dark features. "Looks like he's having fun," she replied dryly and escaped to her office.

Close to midnight, Drew found himself in the toilets taking a leak. Washing his hands, he saw the two dots on his neck, redder than before, and rubbed them.

"You too, huh?"

Drew looked towards the voice and found it belonged to a twenty something, tall, skinny redhead. "What?"

"You too. You got bit, too." The redhead nodded at Drew's neck. "A lot of us are into it. I prefer biting to being bitten. It's very sexual and erotic."

"Ah…" Drew thought fast. "Yeah, it is. I just can't remember much after it."

"That's the point." The redhead fixed his hair and gave himself the once over in the mirror and nodded. "That's the whole point. Get high, don't remember." He clucked his tongue twice, said, "Cheers," and walked out.

Get high, don't remember. Drew thought about his words. *Get high on the kink? How do you get high from being bitten?* The thought stayed in his mind as he walked out and found the brunette waiting for him.

"Well, hello again," she murmured, sliding her arms around his neck. "Ready to get kinky?"

"Get kinky how?" His hand slid to her waist, and he escorted her to the dance floor.

"By going into one of the private rooms?" Her mouth was at his ear. "And by using these." She held up a packet of teeth just like the ones he'd taken from the blonde's bedside table that morning.

"And how do we get kinky with plastic teeth?" He played along. "You bite me, and I feign subservience because you're secretly Dracula?"

Her left brow rose. "You feign subservience? Oh, no, my hot stud. You won't be feigning it; you'll actually be doing it." She ripped open the packet and pushed the teeth over hers. "Ready?"

"And we're going to a private room?" he asked as she led him by the hand. "Where?"

She looked over her shoulder. "You'll see. Have you not been before?"

"No. Not here," he said as they stopped at the red curtains.

The brunette flashed her pass at the attendant, and he scanned the code and nodded. Pulling aside the red velvet curtains, she led Drew between them into the darkened hallway and shoved him against the wall. "Let's get this party started now so it kicks in." She laid the fangs in before he could stop her.

His eyes widened at the sharp pain. "Hey! What are you doing?" His hands grasped her arms and his head bent. "What the fuck!"

She pulled away and removed the teeth. "Don't worry; it'll kick in in a few minutes. Have you never done this before?"

"I've never done it, no." He breathed deeply to clear his now fuzzy head. "But it's been done to me, twice now. Ugh, what is that?" He doubled over and leant on his knees. "What the fuck is that?"

"That…is fun kicking in," she said. "And I've booked into room three for some fun. Let's go." She led him down the hall.

"Room three?" He blinked under the lights. There were dimmed but seemed like bright shining spotlights to him. "What the fuck is happening to me?"

"Fun." She knocked on the door and opened it to find the other guests already there. "Ready?" she called, seeing eager eyes turn to her.

"Ready for what?" Drew was lightheaded, dizzy, but strangely euphoric.

"For this." She pulled him into the room and closed the door.

He saw naked women on top of or under naked men. Others were doing it standing. "Wait…"

She whipped open his black shirt to reveal his full torso of hair and pushed the shirt off his shoulders.

"I love a hairy beast." A woman being pumped from behind eyed Drew. "Me next."

"You next what?" Puzzled, Drew frowned and saw the brunette in front of him go to her knees. "What are you…whoa!" His head fell back as the warmth of her mouth enveloped him.

"Holy fuck that's a big dick," a woman yelped as the man inside her pumped his final thrust. "Can I try?"

Dazed, Drew looked from the woman who'd spoken, to every other woman in the room who were advancing on him, to the woman sucking on his dick.

The room spun, and he was gone.

Chapter 8

Drew woke to another bleary bedroom. He tried remembering what had happened the night before, but his mind was a blank. His stomach rumbled and he rolled over, wiping his eyes clear. Flicking on the bedside light, he saw he was in his own room.

Thank fucking Christ for that, he thought, falling back on the bed. *Thank fucking Christ.* Breathing slowly, he unpeeled his tongue from his palate and tried swallowing, but his mouth resisted. Turning his fogged head, he saw the bedside clock blinking 9 a.m. "Fuck," he croaked. He was going to be late for work again.

He rolled out of bed, and stumbled into the bathroom for a cold shower, followed by a quick shave, and a drink of tap water and a couple of paracetamol tablets. He dressed quickly, grabbed his phone, ID and keys, and raced off to work.

His boss was none too happy. "Reilly. My office, now," he called from his office doorway. He'd been drinking his coffee when he'd seen Drew run to his desk.

Drew paused at his desk, eyes sliding closed. "Fuck!" he muttered.

"Guess who's in trouble." Richard sniggered.

Drew gave him a dirty look and turned tail, heading for his boss's office.

Waylon stepped aside and closed the door once Drew had entered. He paused and walked behind his desk. "What the hell is going on, Reilly? This is the second day in a row you're late and hungover—"

'I'm not hungover," Drew butted in. "I proved that yesterday with the breathalyser. I don't drink. I'm not drunk. I'll do another one to prove it."

Waylon leaned back in his chair and waved for him to sit. "Then you tell me what the hell is going on."

Drew relaxed back in his seat. "I don't actually know. I don't remember much. I've been going to the club where the young girl overdosed. *The Cavern Club*, owned by that pop star, Remi Steele. I've been going undercover—"

"Off or on the books?" Waylon crossed his legs and picked up his cup.

"On the books. I logged in and wrote up what happened," Drew replied. He tried to swallow. "You don't happen to have a bottle of water, sir? My mouth feels like a desert."

"On the cupboard." Waylon indicated to the drinks bar he had set up with coffees, teas, and other refreshments.

Drew walked over and grabbed a bottle, cranking it open and downing half before speaking again. "It's in the report from yesterday."

"In your own words."

Sighing, Drew began at the beginning. "Because the young woman, Merriam Webster, collapsed at the club,

I've been trying to find out if she took the drugs before or after she got there. The medical report couldn't specify a time for ingestion, so I've been going undercover at the club to see what I could find out, who I could see, if anyone was selling."

"And are they?" Waylon placed his cup on his desk and leaned both elbows on it, arms crossed. "Are they being sold or given out in the club?"

Drew sighed again and slumped in his chair. "That's just it. I don't know. Remi runs a tight ship, but even she knows things slip past her guards and bouncers. She does what she can. And I haven't seen any money or drugs being passed between hands. So, I don't have any evidence yet."

"Remi?" Waylon asked. "You're more familiar than you should be, detective."

A blush crept across Drew's cheeks. "Well, that is her name."

"Maybe so, but it's Ms Steele to you for this case."

Drew gave a small nod and fiddled with the bottle lid. "Sir." His head dropped in embarrassment.

"If you're not drunk, are you high?"

Drew's head shot up. "I don't do drugs just as much as I don't drink."

Waylon pointed as he spoke. "Your eyes are bloodshot and dull; your skin is a little pale. You're dry, so have a need to drink, and you have spots on your neck as well as a headache, I'm sure."

Frowning, Drew reached up and rubbed his neck, feeling the tiny bumps under his fingers. "I said I don't…" A flashback of the woman popped into his head. What had they done? Had they slipped him something? No… they'd both…

"Detective. Any ideas?"

Drew snapped out of his reverie as the idea popped into his head. "I think it's maybe the teeth, but I can't be sure."

Waylon's brow furrowed. "Teeth? What teeth?"

"The teeth. The plastic teeth, the vampire teeth." Drew stumbled over his words. "Everyone said it was just a new kink. That you put them in and bite people on the neck." He rubbed the spots again. "But what if it's not just a kink? What if it's a way of delivering drugs and people wouldn't know?"

Waylon nodded at the spots. "And you've been bitten."

"Twice…" The light dawned for Drew and his head bowed. "Ah, Jesus. I didn't even realise, but it would account for my memory loss. I don't remember what happened afterwards except for waking up late and feeling like shit."

"Okay, you've been compromised on this case, with or without your knowledge, so I'm taking you off it for a few days and handing it over." He picked up his phone and tapped a button.

Drew leaned forward in his seat. "You can't do that. I'm clearly getting somewhere. If the teeth are another way they're getting drugs to people, then we're halfway there."

John and Richard came through the door. "Sir."

"Close the door and listen," Waylon told them, and once they had, he said, "Reilly's taking a few days off so you're helping out on the overdose case at the club." He pointed at Drew. "Reilly here thinks the drugs are being administered in fake plastic teeth, and we believe he's been compromised because of it. I need you to go down to the club and check the ground outside for any evidence. I'll get the CSIs to meet you down there."

Perplexed, John shook his head. "What are we looking for? I don't get it."

"Fake plastic teeth. Like vampire teeth. But you don't need to go to the club, I've got some at home…" Drew's voice trailed off because he realised what that meant.

"You have what at home?" Waylon demanded. "Where did you get them from and how do you have them?"

Blushing, Drew found his voice was croaky. "I… may have…taken them from the woman I woke up next to yesterday." The redness spread across his face and neck as John and Richard teased him.

"Enough." Waylon put his hand up. "Take Reilly back to his house to collect the evidence and then get down to the club to see if you can find more. At least we'll have a clean set for the lab to examine, and we might get some DNA off the used lot. Meanwhile, Reilly, you've got the rest of the week off, so once that's done, go home and rest, and I hope I don't have to send you to rehab."

Drew rushed to his feet. "But I'm getting somewhere. We have means, now we need motive and a perp."

Waylon stood up. "Enough, detective. You've been compromised. Go home after the club. You can fill in the others on the way." He stopped Drew's protests and waved them out the door. "Go home. I'll call the CSIs."

He watched as they closed the door behind them and headed for their desks to collect their coats. That was all he needed, another drug-addled detective on his team.

*****

Burrows and Wong followed Drew back to his house, and waited while he went to collect the packets of teeth, before following him to the club.

They discussed what had just happened on the way, as they didn't know much about the case overall, and hadn't read the files yet, wrapping up their conversation as they pulled up behind Drew. The CSI van was already there, and they alighted and walked over.

"I hear you've got some evidence for me, detective." Wednesday Mitchell held out a bag. "Drop them right in here." A twelve-year vet, she'd worked with the boys before. She saw the teeth in the packets. "Nice. Some good fresh evidence could be on there." After sealing the bag shut, she handed it off to one of her co-workers. "So, we're after used teeth. Any place in particular?"

"Probably the back alley, but there may be some out front, in gutters or bins," Drew said, and quickly filled all three in on what was happening with the case.

"Interesting new way of delivering a hit of anything." Wednesday nodded. "Let's go."

The team spread out, searching under rubbish, behind crates, whatever was left in the alley. Out the front, the gutters were searched, and after an hour, they'd found several specimens to provide them with DNA evidence.

"Detective Reilly. What the fuck are you doing to my club?"

Drew turned around and saw Remi standing outside the police tape, arms crossed, right foot tapping, and a scowl on her face.

"Oh, my God, is that Remi Steele?" Wednesday gawped. "I love her so much."

"She's hot." John nudged Richard in the ribs and grinned. "Hey, Drew, she single?" He received a scowl in return.

Drew hurried over to Remi. "Ms Steele, this isn't about the club, it's about collecting evidence."

"In front of, and behind, *my* club," she spat. "Of course, it has to do with it. What the hell are you after?"

"Teeth."

"What?" Puzzled, Remi shook her head. "That dickhead that comes to the club?"

Drew shook his head. "No, the plastic teeth your patrons wear to bite each other."

"The…what? Why would you be after fake teeth? That's just a kink."

"Apparently not," Drew told her. "We think that's how the drugs are administered, so we need some to do tests on."

"The plastic teeth are for drugs…" Remi's brows knotted. "But that means…"

"Biting each other wasn't a kink. It was doping each other."

The realisation crashed over her. "Fucking hell! That means I've been letting drugs into my club and didn't know. I thought they were harmless plastic push-ins. It didn't even occur to me it had to do with drugs."

"Ah…Reilly, maybe you shouldn't be talking to our main suspect," Burrows said from behind them. "It is her club."

Remi leaned past Drew to see the two detectives. "I'm not a drug dealer, or your main suspect," she retorted in anger. "So, you can fuck right off. If you've found them outside then people are obviously getting them outside the club. It's nothing to do with me."

"Okay, stop." Drew put his hands up to hold them at bay. "All we're here for is evidence, nothing else, and since we have what we came for, we can go." He looked at his fellow detectives. "Burrows, Wong, go back to the station." He turned to Remi. "Ms Steele, we just needed to find some teeth. We've done that; we'll be on our way. Boys." He waved them on and followed them back to their cars.

"Um, Ms Steele."

Remi turned to see Wednesday standing nearby. "Yes?"

"Could I get a picture with you?" Wednesday nervously pointed at her phone. "I'm such a huge fan and still have all your cds."

Remi regarded the woman before her. "Ah…sure." She posed for a few snaps then stood in the club's doorway, watching the remaining police vehicles pack up and leave. "I fucking knew Teeth was trouble," she muttered under her breath. "But how the fuck do we prove it?"

*****

As much as he wanted to be at work dealing with the case, Drew knew his boss would just order him back home, so home he went. He went straight into his ground floor office where he had wall mounted whiteboards he could lay the case out on. Someone was supplying drugs, potentially in the teeth, to club goers before they entered the club, or while they were in the club. That meant someone was taking them in and handing them out.

Merriam arrived with the suspect named Dr Teeth. Or at least was there with him. After she collapsed, he and the others took off, and didn't come back to the club for a few days. She died from her overdose and had two small red dots on her neck.

He stopped writing and touched the small red lumps on his neck. He vaguely remembered the blonde from the first night; she'd pulled out teeth and bitten him. What happened after that, he had no clue except for waking up in her bed in her home. And she had a supply of teeth on her bedside table.

He made the bullet points on the board.

Last night, he didn't remember either, but at least he'd woken up in his own bed. "Not that I know how the hell I got here," he muttered, and rubbed his neck. It ached as if it *had been* freshly bitten, and he wondered if the teeth had been laced with drugs, and what kind. *Didn't think plastic fucking teeth could hurt so much.*

He made some more notes; added Remi's name and stood back to survey his handiwork. While there was a suspect, he might not be the only suspect, and until forensics on the teeth came though, they wouldn't be any closer unless they could get Teeth's DNA or fingerprints.

Ah, that's an idea. He called the club. "Can I speak to Ms Steele?"

"Who's calling?"

"Detective Drew Reilly."

"Ah, detective." Sisco's tone became smooth. "So nice to hear from you. Anything I can do?"

"You can put me through to Ms Steele."

Sisco bristled. "Fine, fine, don't talk to me then." He handed the phone to Remi. "It's the hot detective."

Remi chuckled and took the phone. "Now what do you want, detective?"

"Does Teeth eat or drink or touch anything in the club?"

"Not that I've seen. Why?"

"I'm just hoping he's touched a glass or bottle that we could get fingerprints from. Are you sure he doesn't eat or drink while he's there?"

"Ah." Remi bit her lip in thought. "I don't think I've actually seen him do that. Hang on a minute." She held the phone away and looked at Sisco. "Have you seen Teeth eat or drink, or do you know if we serve them drinks? I guess his minions would, but has he?"

Sisco's gaze rose to the ceiling, a place he often looked at when in thought. "You know, I can't say I've actually seen him do that. Why?"

Remi went back to the phone. "Neither Sisco nor I have seen him eat or drink. That's not to say he hasn't. We'll keep an eye out the next time he comes in."

"Which will be?" Drew asked.

"Tonight. He has the club booked all week. He's been here the last two nights that you've been here."

Flashes of last night came back to Drew. "Yeah, ah, I

think I remember."

"You think?" Remi's brows knitted together. "At one point you stopped dancing and looked straight at him."

Drew's brows slowly furrowed. "I did what?"

"You stopped dancing and stared straight at him," Remi repeated. "It wasn't for long. Maybe ten, fifteen seconds."

"Huh," Drew muttered. "Don't remember. Okay, if he drinks or eats tonight, keep the evidence in a bag and I'll pick it up. No…" He sighed and rubbed his eyes. "I'll get the boys to pick it up tomorrow."

"The boys from today?"

"Yeah."

"Why?"

"Because they're now on the case and I'm not."

"Why not?"

"Because I've been bitten, and if the teeth do have drugs in them, then I've been compromised and can't be on the case."

"Oh," slowly came out of Remi's mouth. "Fuck. Sorry. I didn't know."

"Didn't know there were drugs in the teeth, or that I've been bitten?"

"Both. Was it the woman, the blonde from night before last?"

"Ah…" Drew hesitated. He wasn't sure how much to say, but he wasn't on the case anymore and she would have seen them. "She was one."

Remi's brows rose in surprise. "Was *one?* There were more?"

"Last night. A brunette."

"Ah, well I didn't see much last night. Busy with clients." She clicked her fingers at Sisco to get his attention then waved at the surveillance system. "So, you had a brunette bite you last night and a blonde the night before. You do work fast."

"Ha-ha," he replied dryly and paused. *Should I ask her? Should I not? Well, I don't remember so why not.* "Um, you don't know what happened after the blonde bit me, do you?"

Remi thought back. "I don't know when she bit you, but you left not long after getting a drink."

"Ah, okay." Drew figured that was when they'd headed back to her place. But had she driven, or did they take a taxi or Uber? "And last night?"

"As I said, I didn't see you. We could check the surveillance for you. Do you really not remember what happened?"

"Not after I was bitten, no. But at least I woke up in my bed this morning."

Remi choked and her fingers flew to her mouth. "And you didn't with the blonde?"

"Ah, I have to go. I'll drop by later to find out what happened. I might need it for my report. My super wants it on his desk tomorrow."

"Okay. What time?"

"After dinner, maybe. I'll have a poke around outside to see if I can spot anything or anyone."

"Okay, we'll keep an eye out. Bye detective." Remi ended the call and looked at Sisco. "Well?"

Sisco stood aside, eyes wide. "We've got trouble."

Remi walked around her desk and stood in front of

the monitoring system. She saw Drew with the brunette who was leading him through the red curtains to the private hallway, pushing him against the wall and biting him. "Fuckity, fuck, fuck, fuck," burst out of Remi. She watched the woman lead him into room number three and her eyes widened. "Fuuuuck."

"Do we have a problem?" Sisco asked. "Because…" He sped through the footage to the point they emerged from the room. Drew was rumpled, his shirt barely buttoned, his fly undone, his hair mussed. He'd been in the room for three hours.

"Fuck," Remi said again. "If he finds out what happens in room three, he might just be pissed. But at this stage, he doesn't seem to remember."

"How are we going to stop him finding out?" Sisco hit pause and a rumpled Drew froze on the screen.

A deep sigh from Remi's gut left her. "I'm not sure we can."

Chapter 9

It was 9:30 p.m. before Drew arrived in the lane out the back of *The Cavern Club*. He'd been so involved in the case and writing his report, that time had flown, but he'd managed to drop it off on his super's desk and grab a quick bite to eat before parking on the side street.

With a torch in hand, he scoured the alley from the ground to the first floor of the buildings either side, stopping to take pictures if he found anything out of the ordinary, or pulling out Ziploc bags from his pocket if he found anything interesting. Such as more teeth.

He collected a couple of bags of samples before turning to the industrial bins against the wall of the club. There were three in total, about five metres from the club's back door. That was the actual back door and not the secret back entrance celebrities used to sneak out of. "Might have to check those too," he muttered, and flipped the lid of the first bin back. The putrid stench hit him full on and he jerked back to breathe. "Fucking hell." He whipped a handkerchief out of his pocket and covered his nose. "What the fuck is in this shit?" Aiming his flashlight into the bin, he saw garbage bags piled to the stinking brim. "Ugh." He slammed the lid down, took a breath, and said, "Fucking hell," before opening the middle bin. He was peering inside when he heard a sound behind him and turned, his instincts on high alert.

A person, all in black, and wearing a mask, with a stench to rival the garbage in the bins, lurched at Drew, right arm raised as if to strike.

Drew dashed out of the way, getting in a kick to the man's leg, bringing the assailant to his knees for a moment, but before Drew could draw his weapon, the man threw something at him, blinding him for a second, giving him enough time to spring to his feet and jam the syringe into Drew's neck.

Remi barged through the back door and saw the two men struggling. "Hey!" she shouted as the lights came on. "Get off him."

The man let go of Drew, who stumbled to the ground, and advanced on Remi.

She gave him a couple of swift karate kicks and he fell to his knees. She scrambled over to Drew who was grasping his neck and trying to get up.

Drew dazedly stared past her. "Look out," he managed.

Without thinking, she grabbed his gun from its holster, turned around, and fired three bullets into the man's torso. He staggered a few steps before falling face down. Once she was sure he wasn't moving, she turned to Drew. "Fuck, you okay?"

Her guards belted out of the back door. "Get him inside; find the spent cartridges I just shot off and get the doc. Help me get him in." She holstered Drew's gun and helped him to his feet. "What happened?"

"He stabbed me with something. A syringe, I think," Drew managed before collapsing.

"Get him inside," Remi yelled and handed him to two guards. "We need to look for a syringe." It didn't take them long, with Remi snatching it off the ground and racing inside to the private doctor's room where Drew had been taken. "I got the syringe. What is it?"

The doctor looked up from Drew sharply. "I can't tell unless there's a vial."

"Fuck." Remi glanced over at the dead man and sprang into action. She searched him, almost vomited at the stench, and found a vial in his pocket. Holding it up, she thrust it towards the doctor.

"A party drug that's harmless in small batches," the doctor said and turned his back to raid his cabinet. "But lethal in large doses. How much did he get?"

Remi picked up the syringe. "It's half full. Maybe not much."

The doctor plunged a clean syringe with clear fluid into Drew's body. "This should counteract it. But if it wasn't even a half a syringe, he should be lucky."

Drew groaned and squinted under the light of the medical room. "Where am I?"

"In the club." Remi rested her hand on his shoulder. "Doc's taking care of you. You'll be okay." She watched his eyes drift shut.

"He'll need rest and a proper bed." Doc checked his vitals. "The bed in your office would be fine for the night."

"Yeah," Remi mumbled and glanced at the assailant. "He's dead. We'll need to dispose of the body."

"Got somewhere in mind?" Doc asked and pulled off his gloves.

Remi ripped off the man's mask and frowned. "I think I've seen him before."

"Oh, where?"

She thought back and realised he'd been at the club with Teeth. "Fuck him!" She pulled out her phone and took pictures. "I suppose Drew would want to call the coroner and call it in, but"— she glanced over her shoulder at him resting— "I shot the dude three times. I'm not getting into trouble for that." She called in her guards. "Get Drew to my office on the bed, and get this dude"— she pointed at the dead body— "ready for transportation."

"To where?" one guard asked.

"The island." Remi hurried to her office and pulled down the Murphy bed. Once the guards safely deposited Drew on it, and she shooed Sisco away, she put in a call.

"*Holiday Inn Meditation Centre*, how may I direct your call?"

"Rachael, Remi Steele. Is Doug in? It's important."

"It always is," the voice on the other end snapped. "I'll put you through." Musac played and Remi's brows rose. "What the fuck!"

"Remi, good to hear from you. Another patient?"

"Not quite. Do you still have that pool of sharks that swim around the island?"

"We do. Why?"

"They hungry?"

"Probably. Why?"

"I'm sending them some food and I hope they eat it all, otherwise you'll need to dispose of the remains."

There was a long pause. "Jesus, Remi. What have you done?"

"Saved someone's life by any means necessary and it *was* necessary."

A sigh came down the line. "Could we use it for experiments first?"

"Knock your socks off; just make sure you dispose of everything, one way or another."

"Will do. When's the arrival?"

"It's on its way to the airport."

"A couple of hours, then. Anything else?"

"Ah, no. Thanks Doug," she replied, not sure what else he'd been expecting.

"Bye Rem."

"Ah, hang on. I got a snide remark from Rachael just now. Anything I need to know?"

"Just a couple of holidayers got out of hand and she copped a drink to the face."

"Water, I hope."

"Red cordial. It left a rather large splotch on her white top."

"Yikes. You give your junkies red cordial? They need to come down not get high all over again."

"Very funny. Bye Rem."

"Bye Doug. And thanks." She replaced the phone in its cradle and looked at a sleepy Drew, replaying everything from the last half hour. She'd seen him in the alley on the monitors, then seen the assailant lurking in the shadows, and bolted out the door not thinking of her own safety. "Thank God for self-defence and kick boxing classes," she murmured.

While Drew rested, Remi roamed her club. The staff were on high alert for Dr Teeth and his disciples, and they were front and centre in the ring. The bar staff had been put on alert about food and drink delivered to the ring and to bag and tag anything left.

Remi kept her eye on them as she moved through the throng. Teeth was sitting in the middle of the circular couch, arms spread either side along the back of it. His legs were crossed, and his foot tapped along to the beat of the song.

Bad vibes radiated off him, and she felt them on her side of the room. She shivered, knowing bad things were happening because of him. He was doing something, and if the teeth were his, then there'd be hell to pay.

She kept on moving, watching to see if he ate or drank, or if any of his disciples did. They didn't, and she finally made her way back to her office. With a nod at Sisco, who stood guard in the doorway, she locked the door behind her.

Drew stirred in his sleep.

"Shh," she soothed, and checked the drinks fridge for something to scull and something to give Drew. Since he'd possibly be dehydrated, she chose an energy drink.

"Hey."

Startled, her head popped up, and the door slid out of her hand and slammed shut. "Hey."

He lifted his head. "Where am I?"

"My office. The Murphy bed. The one you eyed off that day you were here." She sat on the side and handed over the bottle. "Drink this, it'll help."

Drew leant on his elbow and drank greedily. Once

half the contents had been consumed, he capped the bottle and burped. "Ah, that was good." He rolled onto his back and bunched a couple of pillows under his head. "Why am I on the Murphy bed in your office?"

"Because you were stabbed in the neck with a syringe and my doctor gave you something to counteract it. You need to rest."

He'd watched her while she'd talked, and it unnerved her a little.

"I was what?" His hand went to his neck. "What?" Drew sat up and the blood rush spun him out. He grabbed his eyes. "Bloody hell."

"Easy, lie back down." Remi gently pushed him back and adjusted the pillows behind him. "We don't think you scored much, and Doc says you should be okay." She pulled the blanket up to his chest. "Just rest."

"Rest? How the fuck can I rest when I've been injected a third fucking time?" Drew spat. "How much was injected?"

"Don't know. The syringe was half full."

"So, half a syringe could be in my body?" Drew waved his hands in frustration. "Fucking fantastic."

"Calm down. You're not out of it and seem to be thinking clearly, so it can't have been that much." Remi took a mouthful of drink. "Besides, the vial barely looked like anything had come out of it."

"Vial? What vial? How do you have a vial and a syringe?" Drew slowly sat up and stared at her. "How do you know these things?"

"Ah…" Remi glanced away.

"Remi!"

"Well…" She dragged the word out and avoided his gaze.

"Remi!" Drew grabbed her arm, making her head swivel at the action.

She gazed intently at his hand and her tone lowered to menacing level. "Detective."

"For fuck's sake, call me Drew, especially since I'm calling you Remi. What happened?"

The fiery tingle meandered up her arm making her warm all over.

"Remi." His tone was softer. "What happened?"

She found her softer voice. "You don't seem all that doped up, detective. You should be able to remember." Her eyes finally found his. "You were coming here to search the lane behind the club."

Drew leaned back and breathed, his gaze wandering around the room. "I vaguely remember looking in the bins. I thought I might find something."

"What! Even after today when your people went through everything?" She was enjoying his manly hand on her arm and wondered if it would like to explore other parts of her body.

He sighed, rubbed his eyes and rested his elbow on his bent knee. "Yeah, I wanted to have a look for myself to see if I could find something." Flashes sped past behind his eyes like an old-time movie reel. He saw a black figure, arm raised, he dashed away but the man threw something at him, blinding him. Then pain in his neck and struggling. He turned to Remi. "I was attacked in the alley. What happened? I don't remember after the pain in my neck."

"Ah…" Remi considered how much to tell him.

"Remi!"

"Ah…you were attacked."

"I know that much. I just said so."

She blushed; his hand still held her arm making her want to do very dirty things with him. Dirty, sexual things. "Yeah, you were attacked, and I burst out the back door and did some karate moves on him and knocked him to the ground."

Drew saw flashes of that happening. "You came to me, but he came up behind you." He waited for the next image. His face crumpled up in thought. He saw the image. His face relaxed and he turned to Remi, mouth open. "You shot him."

She watched him, saying nothing, watching the emotion and conflict flit over his face.

"What happened to him? What did you do with him?" He pulled her close. "What did you do, Remi? Where is he?"

Her chin lifted and her gaze became steely. "I did what I had to do. I protected you and myself."

"Okay." Drew shifted towards her. "But what did you do? You shot him. Do you have a gun?" A thought occurred to him. "Did you use my gun? Where's my gun?" He looked around the room.

"It's on my desk for now. I could put it in the safe if you want."

"You shot him with my gun? How many bullets?" Drew moved over to the desk, pulled the gun from its holster, and clicked out the cartridge. "Three bullets. Fuck, Remi. You fired three bullets into him. How the hell am I going to explain that to my boss?" He shoved the cartridge back in and holstered it. "How the fuck am I going to explain three bullets and a dead body?" Slapping the holstered gun on the desk, he paced behind it, running his hands through his hair one moment, crossing his arms the next. He repeated the motions a few moments more.

"Do you have to?" Remi had no idea about the laws for detectives with guns. "What if you didn't have your gun on you? What if you'd left it at home? You'd be dead, possibly." She stood up in a rush and faced him from the front of her desk. "You had it on you. I know how to use guns. Do you even need to say your gun was fired three times and not by you?"

He stopped and stared, incredulous at what she was proposing. "My gun was used by a non-cop. That's not allowed."

"Even in dire circumstances?" Remi asked.

"Even in dire circumstances." Drew waved his left hand in frustration, while his right nestled on his hip. "And what about the body? How the hell am I going to explain this? Do we even know who this guy is?"

"Well…" Remi started slowly. "I took a photo, and we have a fingerprint app in our tablets so you could run it through a system." She watched his brows furrow and they reminded her of Rex. God, she wanted to fuck him. Drew *and* Rex. "But that won't be a good idea."

"And why's that?" He watched her pink tongue slide over her full pink lips and hardened.

Her head made small bouncy motions. "Because the body's not here anymore."

Drew's left hand landed on his hip. "What's that now? There's no body?" He cocked his head. "I don't think I heard you correctly."

Suddenly nervous, Remi shifted on her feet. "I took care of you and him and it."

Drew exploded, his arms flying from his waist into the air. "What the fuck does that mean? Fucking hell, Remi. What did you do?" He slammed his hands on the desk. "What the fuck did you do?" He stormed around to her side, grabbing her by the arms. "You killed him. Where's the body? What did you do to it? You've tampered with evidence and I'm going to take the blame for it."

His brown eyes reminded her of Rex's and she stirred between her legs. "Calm the fuck down. I shot the dude who tried to kill you and I've disposed of the body. Tell your boss you went out to the desert to shoot at targets but only fired three times. That's if you even need to tell him. Why do you even need to make a report? You're off the case for the rest of the week. Do you need rehab? I know a place."

"No, I don't fucking need rehab." He pushed her away. "What the fuck is wrong with you? Of course, I have to report this."

"Bullshit! Stop being a dick." Her temper bubbled below the surface, sick of his stupid shit. "No one except us needs to know and you're a cop. You can hide this from everyone else."

"How the fuck am I supposed to hide it?" he yelled in her face. "*I'm a fucking cop.*"

She stepped back and slapped him, and his hand

flew to his face in shock. "Snap out of it! You're being a dick. You were stabbed with a syringe full of dope that could've killed you. I saved you *and* me. You don't need to know what's happened to the body, so you have nothing to tell. I helped you, detective." She stepped forward, and her tone darkened. "I saved your life."

His eyes narrowed. "Am I supposed to be fucking grateful?"

She scoffed. "Yes, bitch, you are. You'd be dead now if it wasn't for me."

He stepped closer. "Bitch? Who the fuck you calling bitch?"

Her boot toes knocked into his. Her nose was barely centimetres from his. "You!"

Drew's breathing was laboured, heavy, his heart beat like a drum in his chest, and his penis was already waving hello at her. "Fuck you, Remi Steele."

"Fuck you, Drew Reilly."

He grabbed her face and planted his lips on hers, his tongue invading her mouth.

Her hands wrapped around him, her mouth accepting him into it.

The passion burst forth and clothes came off. Hands groped and grabbed, and they tumbled naked onto the bed.

Drew plunged into her, making her gasp and buck up.

She clawed him, cried out, and made her body receptive.

He pulsed into her with every grunting thrust.

The climax came quickly, and they collapsed, their breath coming in heaving gulps.

"Fucking hell," Remi gasped, her glazed eyes directed

at the ceiling. "Fucking hell."

"Ah… I was not expecting that." Drew ran a hand through his dark black curls, down the side of his face and onto his chest, where it lay. "Not expecting that."

"Is that how you resolve all of your cases?" Remi rolled towards him. "By fucking them. Or is it just me?"

His head turned toward her, and he saw how glowy she was in the half-lit room. His body followed so they were facing each other. "It's just you."

Her fingers found their way into the close shaved beard. "I didn't think cops were allowed beards. I thought you had to be clean shaven."

"We do. But this isn't a beard. It's a five o'clock shadow." Drew's joke was light, but the mood was not. "I don't like what you've done, Remi."

Her eyes fired up. "I saved your life, Drew."

The blood in his veins surged a little with the anger that was rising within him. "You did—and thank you. But you could have done that by knocking the guy out, so I could call the cops and have him arrested." His fingers slid up her arm along her shoulder to her face. "Instead, you've made it so I have to say nothing and a man is dead and I'm three bullets down. And where exactly is the body?" His hand rubbed back and forth across her face, his thumbs across her lips.

She knew a control action when it was being applied, and Drew was on the edge of controlling her. The thought titillated her. "Somewhere you'll never find it." Remi moved his hand to her breast and applied the same motions he'd just done to her face. "Besides, detective, you've been compromised. Stabbed with a syringe once, bitten twice, and drugged thrice, you could have died all three times."

"But I didn't." His erection was finding its way to its sanctuary and his mouth longed to envelope her delectable breast. He swallowed hard.

Remi saw the reaction and moved her hand to his penis, stroking it into submission. "Detective." She moved so her lips brushed his. "After what you've been doing in this club, you might not want your bosses to know what happened tonight. Or last night." Her tongue lashed out, tasting his. "Or the night before. Or do they already know about those?"

His tongue met hers for a languid kiss, and his penis wanted to do the same to the sanctum between her legs. "They know something happened. But not all the details." He rolled her over, his legs between her thighs, his hand moving over her breast, his mouth moving over hers.

They locked themselves into a passionate embrace, became one, and thrust their way to a happy ending.

Drew collapsed onto Remi; his breathing laboured. "Fucking hell. I'd sworn off sex and now for some reason, I've been fucking everyone."

"Everyone?" Remi's brows rose and her fingers trailed up and down his sides. "Have you been using condoms?"

His head tilted and he looked into her eyes. "I… don't know."

"Well, you're not now," she told him. "And considering your behaviour this week I probably should have swathed you in them."

"My behaviour?" His curiosity piqued. "What behaviour?

When behaviour? Do you mean the blonde and the brunette? I don't even know if we used condoms. I certainly didn't see them at the blonde's house, or any on the floor, but I'm assuming we did." He glanced around the office as he thought. "I certainly hope we fucking did. Fuck!" Drew slid out of Remi and sat up. "I don't know if we did, and I don't fucking know if we even had sex at all, and as for the brunette, well I ended up in my bed and there's no evidence that she'd even been in my house let alone me or we having sex—"

"Take a breath." Remi sat up beside him. "Jesus. Are you hyperventilating? Look…" She noticed his red, wild-eyed face. "The only thing you could do is to contact them and find out. Did you get their numbers?"

His gaze moved to her. "What? Um… I know where the blonde lives because I woke up there, but I have no idea about the brunette, or what we even did. Hang on…" Something she'd said earlier slid through his mind. "What do you mean, about not wanting my bosses to know what I've been doing in this club tonight and last night? What did you mean by that?"

"Just that…" Remi kept it casual. "Look what's happened now, tonight. Do you want your bosses knowing about it? Will you have to explain this?" She waved her hand between the two of them. "Explain how we've ended up in bed together. Why you were in my back lane searching for any kind of evidence when you've been removed from the case? And that's not a euphemism by the way. Will you explain how you were surprised from behind and jabbed in the neck with a syringe full of a party drug that could have killed you if he'd got the whole lot in? How would you explain all of that, detective? Do tell me." She rolled off the bed and picked up her knickers, holding them up in front of her. "Tell me how you're going to tell your bosses how you managed to get into these." She stepped into them and pulled them up. "Tell me, how are you going to tell him? What are you going to write in your report?"

Drew shook his head and rested it in his hands. "I don't know. I don't fucking know; I just know that what happened in the alley needs to be reported."

"How?" Remi fastened her bra and pulled her top over her head. When he didn't reply, she pulled on her skirt and sat beside him. "A lot of shit has gone down here, Drew. You getting doped, fucking strangers, blanking out, and now getting stabbed by some deranged disciple of Teeth's. So, tell me, does your boss really need to know what happened tonight?"

Another thought slid through his mind, a reminder of what she'd said earlier. "What did you mean by last night?"

Remi's blood ran cold. "What about last night?"

"Do I need him to know what happened last night?" Another memory came flooding back. A memory of him being led through the red curtains. "Fucking hell!" He spun off the bed to face her.

She stared at the sizable appendage flapping with the movement and the abundance of fur. "Whoa," she moaned. "I do love a good body of fur."

"I went through the curtains last night?" He waved a finger at her. "She led me through them and asked if I'd ever been. I didn't say anything, but we ended up in a hallway where she pushed me against the wall and bit me. It becomes fuzzy after that." He glanced away, trying to remember. "But I definitely know it was a hallway. We walked through the curtains into a hallway and after she bit me…" His voice trailed off, his eyes narrowed in thought, and he tried recalling the memories from the night before.

Remi carefully got off the bed, not wanting to disturb him. She didn't want him finding out but she could also argue he had a right to know. So, she watched him, and debated what to tell him.

"She led me down the hall to a door and knocked before opening it." His shoulders tensed then released. "I don't remember after that." He sighed deep and guttural. "I don't remember *anything* after that. Not even how I got home."

Remi battled her inner thoughts. *Do I tell him? He has a right to know. If he was drugged, which he was, he should know what happened. But what if he freaks? Then he freaks. He has a right to—*

"Rem?"

She breathed deeply. "Mmm?"

"Something you want to tell me?"

"Yeah. Put your pants on." She waved at his clothes. "And your shirt. All that glorious body hair is distracting. So's the size of your dick."

He blushed furiously and quickly pulled his clothes on.

"Look, detective." Remi paced the small room, pacing her words with her steps. "Do you really want to know what happened last night?"

"Yes. Yes, I do." Drew pushed his feet into his shoes.

"I fucking need to know. What if I did something stupid? Or illegal? I need to know in case I can fix it."

Deflating, Remi stopped, but didn't look at him. "Look…we…ah…don't film in any of those rooms as they're off limits, like the toilets, but we do have footage of you going in, and coming out of the room, and probably walking out of the club. And we have outside cameras, so we could possibly see what happened outside."

"What's the big fucking secret about those rooms?" He walked up behind her and spun her around. "You've always blocked me when it came to those rooms, wouldn't let me in, wouldn't let me see. You would only tell me about the musicians in a room full of cops. Why did I need to get them in the room?"

"There were only three besides you," Remi reminded him.

"Yeah, yeah, and the case was sensitive." Drew's brows slid down. "You said something about those rooms." He clicked his fingers, trying to remember. "That the people who go through those curtains book the rooms for the fun they can have in them. That they're each for different things." His fingers stopped; his eyes widened. "Oh, my God." Staring hard at Remi, he said. "Are they sex rooms?"

Remi rubbed her lips together. She didn't want to tell him due to the privacy contracts she had. But…he did have a right to know—

"Remi!"

She jumped, her hand flying to her chest. "Jesus fucking Christ. What?"

"Are they sex rooms?" He stepped closer. "Do people

have sex in them?"

Unable to speak, she nodded.

His heart beat faster and his stomach churned. "Are they all the same?"

A head shake.

"Different levels of sex room?"

A nod.

He stepped right in front of her. "And room three?"

Pained, she looked into his eyes. "Full blown."

His lips parted; his brows flickered in disbelief. "What do you mean?"

"Three levels," she managed. "Third's highest. I can't tell you. I have my privacy contracts. You'll have to—"

"Orgy?"

She felt herself diminishing in stature and felt very small in front of him in that moment. "Yes."

"Fucking hell!" burst out of him. He stumbled back, his hands covering his mouth. It was a few moments before he spoke. "You're telling me, that last night I went into a room where an orgy was happening."

She nodded and pursed her lips.

"Are you fucking kidding me?" he yelled. "You have fucking orgies and I participated in one." Unable to fully comprehend everything in that moment, he took a few steps one way and then a few back, and then swayed from foot to foot on the spot. "I fucking what?" One hand went to his forehead, one to his hip, and he thought about the implications. "Did I participate…?"

"More than likely." Remi's voice was soft and low. "There are no cameras in the rooms, so we have no way of knowing unless you contact the brunette. But…"

He swiftly turned on her, making her jump back in surprise. "But what?"

"But we have footage of the hallway, so we know you went in and came out rather rumpled."

He loomed over her, grabbing her by the arms. "Do you have any other footage of me?"

She shook him off. "I told you. We probably have you leaving the club and maybe outside."

He grabbed her arms again, his brows low in anger. "And you definitely don't have footage of me in that room? I need to know what happened. How many people, whether they wore condoms, men, women, how many. Tell me." He shook her, gripping her arms in anger.

"Stop it!" Remi demanded, placing both hands on his chest and pushing him back. "I can't tell you because I don't know." She took a breath and swiped a strand of hair out of her eyes. "We don't monitor who goes in and out, although we can see on the monitor, but there is a bowl of condoms, and, if I recall, they were all used up last night, and we restocked in the clean-up." She adjusted her top. "I know you're pissed, I see it, but don't direct that at me. You hooked up with both women, you allowed them to bite you and whatever happened next is on you, not me. Don't get angry at me; get angry at your God damn self." She watched the inner battle of emotion playing like a show reel on his face and softened. "Drew, I'm sorry. But what you did is on you. You went willingly beyond the curtain. What happened next, you went with it. I can't…" She glanced around the room and shrugged. "I can't help you with this. I can't do anything. You have to come to terms with what happened."

Drew slowly came to the realisation that he'd participated in the one thing he'd never wanted to do again. That the last two nights had landed him back in exactly the same place he'd been so desperate to leave. Addicted to drugs and sex. "I have a sex and porn addiction," blurted out of him. He sighed and rested his hands on his hips, deciding to just tell her. "It started when I was in my late teens and kept on for ten years before I finally got out of it. All I did was fuck. Fuck any woman who wanted me, one, two, three at a time. Until I was fucking groups of women and when they brought other men into it, I revolted and backed out." His head shook in disgust. "I don't do men. I'm not fucking gay. But I'd fuck any woman who wanted me, and by that point, I realised it had become a crutch for the real problem that went back years before." He rubbed his eyes and sank onto the bed. "It was just a cover-up for the pain. So, I got help. I finally went and saw a therapist who helped me work through the issue and made me realise why I was using sex and porn as an escape. Once I had my breakthrough, I vowed to never have sex again, or until I met a woman I really wanted to be intimate with." He shyly glanced at her as she sat beside him. "But now I find out I'm back in my old ways just when I found someone I might be interested in."

A small smile touched her lips, and she gave his hand a gentle squeeze. "I'm sorry. I know about addictions. I'm in the entertainment industry; that's why I help those who want out. And…some even had a sex addiction. How many years has it been since you gave it up?"

"Fifteen." He nodded slightly. "Since I turned thirty."

A small huffy sound came from him. "Fifteen fucking years and I haven't fucked anyone until this week."

She shrugged. "It's a good record. But it's also not to say you'll fall back into your old ways. You know what happened and you can stop it." She gently bumped her shoulder into his. "You're an adult and you had a good run. But a couple of nights of sex won't return you to the dark side."

His lips slid into a small smile. "No. I guess not. But a hell of a lot of shit has happened this week, and I really don't know how to explain it to my boss."

"You were drugged," Remi said. "Plain and simple."

"And participated in a fucking orgy," Drew quipped and squeezed Remi's hand. "But that also means not telling him about the shooting. I'm a cop, it's my duty by law. I'm *bound* by law."

"Get over it." Remi pulled her hand from his. "Teeth is out in the club, or at least he was before. After the attack he doesn't know his disciple is dead. He probably thinks *you* are, though. And if the guy's family pays a visit to the cops, which I doubt they will, then you can play dumb because you will technically *and* truthfully not know who he was or what he looked like." She noted his frown. "You need to get over it, Drew. After what's happened to you the last three nights, you need to let this one go. It's not on you. It's on me and my people. It's been dealt with. So, forget about it."

"But it will come back to me. *Especially* if footage of me in that fucking hallway comes to light." He pushed up from the bed and paced the room. "Imagine if my bosses find out what I've done."

Remi's brows slowly slid up. "They won't say anything."

"How can you know that?" Drew stopped and faced her. "You got a Magic 8 ball?"

Without looking at him, she said, "Because they have *their* secrets too…"

"Well, everyone's got secrets." Drew saw her expression and finally caught on. "Fucking hell," came out slowly. "In here?"

She slowly nodded. "So, you see what *they* don't know…"

Drew shook his head. "Fucking hell. Don't that beat all. Is that why you wanted them in the room that night?" He slumped onto the bed. "So, what do I do now?"

"How long are you off work?"

"A few days, until next week probably."

"Why don't you get away up the coast? A friend of mine has a spiritual wellness style retreat. You can go, relax, detox, think shit through. It's on the beach so you can swim, surf, whatever. Just relax."

"I don't know if I could relax, but it sounds nice." His thoughts wandered. "Could I get in?"

"I'll call. You can set off first thing tomorrow, being Friday. You'll get three full days of rest and relaxation."

"Teeth thinks I'm dead," he said. "What would happen if I walked out of here, walked past him, if he's still here, and went home?"

"He might try again," Remi replied. "You could go tonight. Go home, pack a bag, hell, you wouldn't even need to do that. My friend has spa wear for the guests, but you probably shouldn't drive, as you have been drugged for three days. I could get two of my men to drive you up, they can come back tomorrow."

"In my car?" Drew was starting to like the idea of getting away.

"One can drive you up in yours, while one follows to bring him back."

"I'll need to stop at my house, grab my personal effects, laptop, papers, in case something happens while I'm away. And I have the info all over my office because I was working on it today."

"That's fine. My men know to have go-bags on them at all times. They're prepared. But it would be dangerous to walk past Teeth. He could have someone follow you and do more damage."

"Probably. So how do I get out of here without being seen?"

She smiled brightly. "You're in the right spot. I need your car keys." She called two of her guards in and handed over Drew's keys. "Grab your go-bags from your cars, and drive Drew to his house to collect some belongings, and then up to Byron's wellness retreat. If you need to stay the night, it's on me. Meet us at the celeb secret getaway door in five minutes."

They nodded and went on their way, and Remi turned to Drew. "Get ready detective, it's a go." With a jaunty brow, she left the office and made sure the door to the club was locked and the door to the secret hallway unlocked. She told her staff member on the curtain to not let anyone in for ten minutes and waved at the staff at the back door to prepare them for exit. Back at the office, she guided Drew to the door.

He stopped her with a soft hand to her elbow. "Um, before I go, I just want to say…how the fuck did this just happen?" He motioned back to the office. "Everything. Tonight."

Remi shrugged. "Attraction, circumstance, it happens. You were drugged. Maybe I took advantage of you."

A smile touched his lips. "And maybe I took advantage of my situation to fuck you."

She grinned. "Twice?"

His smile widened. "And now I have to thank you again for sending me away to gather myself and my thoughts."

"Byron will give you a full medical check-up. It will be kept private and only you will know the results. You should be fine. And don't worry, I doubt you'll get addicted to porn again just because you've had sex three nights in a row. But feel free to talk to him about that too. You'll be fine, Drew. And I'll see you when you get back."

There was a knock on the door, and she opened it to see her guard in Drew's car, headlights off. "Right, now get in the back and stay down until they get you home, and don't take long once you're there. The less time the better." She opened the back door to his car and pushed him in. "Have a good break and try not to get yourself killed again."

"Ha-ha," he grumbled and held his hand up in thanks. "Thanks again for this."

"You're welcome, now fuck off." She slammed the car door and watched them drive off, with the second guard following. Closing and bolting the door, Remi went back to her office to wait. And plan.

*****

When they arrived at Drew's house, one guard waited at the dark front door while the other followed Drew inside. He'd closed the roller shutters before leaving, so found no forced entry at any door or window. It was a two-storey townhouse and everything looked untouched.

He hurried into the office, and after taking a couple of dozen photos, pulled all of the papers off the white boards and wiped them down. He shoved the papers into his laptop case, along with his computer and other tech gadgets, then hurried upstairs to pack an overnight bag and a suit for Monday morning. He dug in his bedside drawer for a few things and came across a small gold frame. He stared sadly at the photo before placing it in the bottom of the bag. With a quick glance around, he knew it wouldn't matter if he lost any of it in a fire, except for his leather jacket, which he grabbed before going downstairs into the lounge room. His collections could be re-collected and the knick-knacks and wall art were generic and in abundance. With a final look, he gave a nod to the guard, who turned off the light and opened the door. Drew set the alarm, locked the door, and they silently moved into the night.

*****

Once her guard confirmed they were on the road, Remi entered her club and looked straight at The Golden

Ring. Teeth was holding court, his disciples either at his feet hanging on to every word, or dancing like a frenzied wild child on the floor. With renewed anger, Remi plastered a conspiratorial smile on her face and slowly walked past the ring, her head turning to gaze at the man she was really hating in that moment. She caught his eye, held his gaze as she walked past and shook her head slightly. When she saw his expression change, she turned away and kept walking; knowing he'd received her point loud and clear.

Chapter 10

After a relaxing weekend at the retreat, Drew arrived at work bright and early Monday morning and knocked on his boss's door first thing. "Boss, are the test results on those teeth in yet?"

Waylon looked up from what he was reading. "I have it here. Close the door."

Drew closed it and sat down. "Well, is it in the teeth?"

"It is. A neat little injector system. Tiny little syringes in the canines. When you bite into a person's neck, they spring down and inject the drug. Hey presto, you get high from a kinky love bite." He handed the report over and leaned back in his chair. "You look better. Feel better?"

Drew glanced up. "Yeah, I do. Spent a couple of days up the coast at a friend's wellness retreat on the beach. Went swimming, surfing. I feel good."

"Good. But as much as I want you back to work, you were still compromised. So, you'll work with Burrows and Wong on this one."

"But sir—"

Waylon waved a hand. "No arguments. You were

drugged twice. You won't work this alone. And unless you have an idea of who's selling or giving out these teeth, and they're in the club, I don't want you going anywhere near it unless you've got Burrows or Wong with you. Got me!"

Flame-faced, Drew glanced back at the report. "Not even if it's for personal reasons?"

"And what personal reasons would you have for going to the club? Oh…" It dawned on Waylon. "Remi Steele. The owner. You and her a thing?"

"Um, no," Drew muttered and flipped the page. "But once this is over…" He noticed a couple of names on the paper and memorised them.

"Not the best move to make, especially with everything happening right now." Waylon finished off his morning coffee and noticed the squad slowly filter through the doors. "Leave it until after, but even then, do you think the person dealing out these teeth are in her club? Is it a staff member? Remi herself?"

"No." The word came sharply out of Drew's mouth, and his brown eyes flared at his boss. "I think it's one of her patrons, but I can't seem to find anything on him."

"And what makes you think it's him?"

"He goes by the name Dr Teeth and has a gold top plate that goes from incisor to incisor. Makes him look like freaking Dracula," Drew mocked. "Yet he dresses like a homeless bum. We think Merriam Webster was with him the night she collapsed. We have him on film pointing to her and one of the disciples threw her bag beside her before they all took off."

"Disciples?" Waylon leaned on his desk; his interest

piqued. "Why do you call them that?"

"Remi." Drew caught himself and flashed his boss a glance. "Ms Steele says that every time he books out The Golden Ring in the club, he always has twelve people with him. So, thirteen in total. They seem to hang on his every word, sit at his feet, and that he has creepy God-like vibes, or thinks he's the second coming of Jesus or something. I've seen him. That's definitely the vibe he gives off. But I just can't prove he's done anything. Especially *in* the club, where everyone who works there just thought the teeth were a new kind of kink or something. None of us knew they had drugs in them. Let alone, that's how the guests were getting high."

"Interesting." Waylon nodded and thought it through. "You have no proof it's him, but he wears a gold version of the teeth. Have you done a search of him?"

"A search how?" Drew shrugged. "We have no fingerprints, DNA, car licence, address. How are we going to do a search, because clearly, Dr Teeth isn't his real name?"

"Fair point," Waylon conceded. "Can you get fingerprints?"

Drew shook his head and remembered Remi hadn't said anything. "I asked Remi, ah, Ms Steele, to keep a lookout in case he drank or ate, but so far, nothing."

"He doesn't touch anything?" Waylon frowned and tapped a pen on the desk. "We're out of luck at every level. Okay, keep in contact with Ms Steele and if any of these Dr Teeth disciples touch anything, we can run a check and maybe *they* will lead us to *him*. That's all, detective."

"Boss." Drew hurried to his desk and scanned the report, tapping in each name on the DNA tests into the system. Out of the five, only one was in the system as a petty thief, once charged. Next, he scoured Google and social media, coming up with a few names that matched, but only two had photos. Neither looked familiar. Sighing, he sat back in his seat and stared up at the ceiling, blowing out exasperated breaths.

"Still high, Reilly?" Burrows asked over his desktop.

"No, Burrows, I'm not." Drew gave him a scowling glare. "I'm trying to figure out who's handing out the teeth we collected for evidence and I'm hitting dead ends."

"Huh, probably not looking in the right area," Burrows scoffed. "I could do a better job than that, come on."

"Better job at picking your nose, maybe," Wong joked, going through the files on his desk. "Do we have the test results from those teeth in yet?"

Drew thought quickly and closed the file. "No, got a few others to catch up on, though." He slid the file into his drawer out of view of the others.

"That why you come in early, or are you sucking up to the boss?" Burrows griped and lazily swung around in his chair. "The least you could do on this case is find a suspect."

"Oh, is that all." Wong crumpled a piece of paper and threw it at him. "You have some pretty lofty expectations, there."

Burrows threw the paper at Drew. "The least he could've done was get fingerprints."

Drew grabbed his phone and hurried into the hallway.

Burrows scowled. "What'd I say?" Wong threw the

paper back at him and he threw it into the bin.

Drew dialled the club and ducked into an empty office, shutting the door behind him.

"Cavern Club, Remi Steele."

"Remi, Drew, has Teeth left his fingerprints at all? Touched anything, drunk anything. I need some evidence to get this fucker."

"Hello to you too, detective," she said dryly. "No, nothing. We're keeping an eye out and he's touched nothing, drank nothing. The only thing we thought of was searching for DNA residue, skin follicles, hair, and such, anything he might leave behind. He did have his hands on the top of the couch last week and we took some samples." She paused. "But I guess you guys would need to take those samples yourselves. For a court case and whatnot."

"Yeah, we would, otherwise it won't stand up in court." Drew slowly paced, biting his lip in thought. "Is he in tonight?"

"Let me check." Remi found the client list on her desk and scanned it for that night. "Not tonight." She flipped a page. "But he's in tomorrow night."

"Great. Do you mind if we come in and collect evidence?"

"No, as long as you're not intrusive on other patrons."

"We'll have a small team and close off the ring."

"We can do that once he leaves. Do I call you when he does?"

"Not sure. I'll speak to my boss first and get back to you."

"Okay. How was your holiday?"

A grin lit up Drew's face. "Very relaxing. Thank you for suggesting it and getting your friend to agree to it."

"I own shares in it, so he'd better've let you in. Good to know you're okay. Anything else?"

"Ah, yeah. About the other night."

"Which night?"

"You know full well which night. Thursday night."

"What about it?" She held her breath.

"Well, a number of things. I was stabbed, you used my gun. There's a dead body, and we fucked not once but twice in your office."

Remi glanced at the upright Murphy bed and blushed. "And both times were incredibly hot."

A raging blush raced across Drew's face. "Um, I'm talking about the man in the alley and what happened with that."

"What about it?"

"The DNA results are in on the teeth we collected. We have one DNA match in the system. Petty small stuff, no one I recognise from being there and he's not Teeth. I searched Google and social media, and didn't really come up with much, so that might be a bust, but I never got to see the guy from Thursday night. I have no idea what he looks like so he could be it. Do you have photos? Did you take any?"

Remi replayed Thursday night in her head. She had taken photos, but was sending them to him a good idea? "How would you explain that photo to your boss?"

Drew thought on the question. "I guess I couldn't, but at least if I saw him then I could say whether his DNA is on our list."

"I don't want to text it. How do you want to see it?"

"I could come around after work, to the club. Technically I'm supposed to have a colleague with me, so that could be a bugger."

"I could come to your place," blurted out of Remi's mouth before she could collect a thought together. "If you…"

Drew's lips slowly rose into a smile. "You could. I could cook."

"You cook?" she asked dubiously.

"I cook," he said. "I make a mean steak and chips."

"With gravy?" She was hopeful and her mouth was salivating.

"With gravy. What time? I'll be home about six-thirty. I'll get it on then."

"I can come about then too, and we can get it on together." Remi left the line hanging.

"You are a very naughty girl, Remi Steele."

"I'm no girl as you full well know, detective. But I am *very* naughty when I want to be."

A little giggle came out of him and he blushed. "You definitely aren't, Remi Steele."

"I'll see you tonight. Text me your address and try and look hot when I get there."

He heard the dial tone and giggled some more.

"Why the hell are you giggling, you girly man?" Burrows mocked from the open doorway.

Drew spun around. "That's absolutely none of your business." He rushed past Burrows who called out, "Boss wanted to know where you'd rushed off to."

Drew headed for his office and knocked on the door.

He was waved in and closed the door behind him. "I just made some calls; one was to Remi Steele. She said Teeth is due tomorrow night and sometimes he puts his hands on the back of the couch. And he has long hair, so maybe we could get our tech guys down there, and once he leaves, collect epithelials or hair samples. Do we wait till she calls, or go in by the back door and wait until he leaves?"

Waylon nodded. "Good thinking. If that's the only way to get some DNA then we'll do it." He picked up his phone. "I'll call the CSI team and see if they can spare a couple of people to wait there until he leaves. It will be quicker than waiting for them to come. Pick Burrows or Wong to take with you." He waved Drew out of the room and barked a few orders down the line.

Drew hurried to his desk.

"In trouble?" Burrows grinned.

"Nope. Got praised for my good thinking instead." Drew saw the sour expression and turned to Wong. "Richard, you need to come to the club tomorrow night. A suspect will be there and we need to collect DNA."

"Not *the* suspect?" Wong asked.

"Not at this stage. We're to wait until he leaves and then the CSIs move in and collect any evidence he left behind."

"Cool. What time?" Richard checked his schedule.

"Well, he normally stays till late. We could go in at ten."

"Reilly," Waylon barked from the door to his office. "CSIs will meet you there at ten. I told them to go in the back door so this Teeth person doesn't see them."

"Thanks, boss," Drew called and turned to Wong. "Ten. Back alley where we were last week. Tomorrow night."

"Great, I'll be there."

*****

Drew arrived home early with two fresh steaks, two bags of thick cut beer battered frozen chips, and two packets of microwave gravy. He already had the ingredients in his freezer, but wasn't going to wait on the steak to defrost. He put the steak and chips into the fridge and hurried upstairs for a quick shower.

Fifteen minutes later, in a casual black t-shirt and old faded blue jeans, he was back in the kitchen preparing the food, and had just slid the chips into the oven and the marinated steaks onto the grill when the doorbell rang.

Wiping his hands, he checked the surveillance system to make sure it was Remi, before opening the door. "Hey. Steaks are on, come in, come in." He waved her in and checked outside before locking the door.

"I don't think anyone followed me," she said. "And I didn't see anyone sitting in cars when I pulled up." She handed over a bottle of wine and a six pack of light beer. "If you don't drink, you'll obviously have something else, but I brought them just in case and I'll have a beer." She followed him into the kitchen.

"That's fine." He took them from her and placed them in the fridge. "I do have the rare low alcoholic beer, but I generally don't drink. So, I do mean rare."

"Smells good." She breathed in deeply, and salivated. The sounds from the sizzling steaks sang in her ears and her stomach grumbled. "Damn, I'm hungry. I didn't eat lunch because I was waiting for this." Leaning over the grill, she waved the scent towards her. "Aw, yum."

Drew gave her a sly grin. "If it's one thing I know how to cook, it's a good steak." He checked the undersides and flipped them over. "Another ten minutes or so. And we have chips and gravy." He opened the oven door and turned the pan around. "I hope you like my speciality."

"Well, I certainly did the other night." She glanced around the kitchen; aware he was watching her. "Can I get one of those beers?"

"Ah, sure. Help yourself." Drew busied himself with getting things ready.

Remi opened the fridge and peered inside. "Interesting. A wide variety and selection. Rather healthy, Detective Reilly." She pulled a beer from the carton and closed the door. "A neat and tidy fridge, a neat and tidy living, dining and kitchen. I take it the bedroom's the same."

The living, dining and kitchen were all open plan on one side of the townhouse, the office, toilet and laundry took up the other half of the downstairs. Two bedrooms and a bathroom were upstairs.

She wandered over to the art on the wall. Old rock stars from the '60s and '70s, paintings from an artist she'd vaguely heard of. A surfboard stood in the corner near the window, a TV and music system took up the wall space. The sectional couch was black velvet. The dining space held a table and four chairs, with a painting of Africa looming over it. "Neat. Clean. Fresh," she said.

Drew turned off the oven and grill. "It is. I like it." He prepared the gravy and put it in the microwave. "Ready to eat? Everything can finish off and we can get stuck in." He laid out the table with place mats and cutlery.

"Quite the little homemaker," Remi joked. "You'll make someone a damn good wife."

"Cute," he said and straightened the floral arrangement in the centre of the table. "But I have no interest in being anyone's wife. Or husband."

Remi's brows flew up in surprise. "What! But you're a catch. You're hot as fuck, can cook, know how to lay a table, *and* a woman. Why don't you want a partner?"

He paused at the oven, mitt in hand. "I have my reasons." He set the microwave to seventy seconds and plated up the steak and chips. When the micro beeped, he removed the gravy sachets and poured half of each over the chips. He added a sprinkle of salt to both and carried the plates to the dining table and a stunned Remi. "Sit. Dig in." He sat and whipped a napkin across his legs.

She fell into the chair and stared from him to her plate. "You have no interest in getting married? What about shacking up? What about a relationship? Wait…?" She paused. "You said you hadn't had sex in fifteen years. Does that mean you haven't had a relationship? Oh, my God." Her hand went to her chest in shock. "Was I your first in fifteen, no, wait, you had the blonde, the brunette, and how many others before me." Her brows knotted in puzzlement. "You hadn't had sex in fifteen years until this week and then you had a whole lot of it. Does that mean you haven't had a relationship at all?" She stared at him unable to comprehend the fact a man like him hadn't fucked or dated or—

"I've dated." He sipped his cola. "But refrained from sex. Why are you so surprised? Not everyone has an active sex life. Or dating life, or relationship."

"Yeah, but look at you." She waved a hand over all of him. "*Look* at you. How do women resist you? How do you resist women?" She leaned forward. "*Have* women resisted you because I sure as hell couldn't."

He shook his head and cut a piece of steak. "It's none of your business, Remi. Eat your steak and tell me what you think." Shoving a piece into his mouth, he chewed and watched her frown, puzzled by his choices, until she finally picked up her cutlery and placed a decent sized piece of steak in her mouth.

She chewed three times and her eyes rolled back in her head. "Fuuuuck."

He grinned. "Knew you'd love it. Now eat up and no talking. You have a steak to finish."

Remi devoured the steak, and rolled the chips around in the gravy until they were thoroughly covered and devoured those too. Wiping up the leftover gravy with the garlic bread Drew had forgotten in the oven and belatedly rushed to the table, she placed the last morsel in her mouth, chewed, licked her fingers and swallowed. "That was just as thoroughly enjoyable as you are."

The blush raced over him. "Glad to be of service."

"And will you be in service tonight?"

His eyes widened. "Remi Steele, you are fresh."

"Kids haven't said fresh in decades," she argued.

"But I do and I say you're fresh." He carried the plates to the sink.

"And I asked if you were in service." Remi placed her bottle next to the plates. "Or is that not where this night is going? Which is disappointing if it's not, but understandable if it is."

He turned around, leaned against the sink, and crossed his arms. "Just because I've chosen to be like a priest and have no sex for fifteen years, doesn't mean that choice was never going to change. But I'm not saying it will happen. It's not what I invited you for. I invited you over for dinner and so we could compare photos. I managed to take pictures of the people in the file. Obviously, I couldn't bring the files home, but we can still compare." He rushed out of the kitchen into his office.

"Right." Remi wandered into the living room and pulled out the photo she'd taken of the Teeth disciple.

"Here are the photos." Drew handed them over and exchanged it for the one in Remi's hand. "Oh, wait—that's him."

"Him who?" Remi's gaze moved from the photo to Drew.

"Here." Drew took the photos back and sorted through until he came across the petty thief and held them up side by side. "That's him, right? Looks like he graduated from petty theft to attempted murder."

Remi studied both photos. "Looks like him but…"

She bit her lip and looked at Drew. "I can't give you his DNA samples for you to run. It would throw up too many red flags and then what would you tell your boss?"

That made him stop. "Shit! Hadn't thought of that, and there's no body. Fuck!" He ran a hand through his hair and moved around the room, muttering to himself. "No body, no DNA test, but his on file, dropped his teeth outside the club, tried to kill me." He stopped and sighed. "Yeah, I have no clue. I can't even try and look for the guy because if I do, we'll find out he's missing."

"And if he is…he could have taken off of God knows where…" Remi supplied. "Who knows where he's disappeared to? You may have to *try* and find him."

"Yeah." His head nodded in agreement. "Yeah. And we can *try* and look for him or not at all because he's in the system as a petty thief and of no real importance to this case."

"Not that your boss knows of. Can we fuck now?"

His head tilted. "Remi! That's not what you're here for."

"Could be." She lifted her top over her head and tugged at his t-shirt. The photos floated to the floor and their flaming attraction burnt the house down.

Chapter 11

At ten p.m. Tuesday night, Remi let Drew, Richard, and a team of four CSIs through the back door off the alley. Drew had been uncomfortable standing there waiting for Remi to open the door, as flashbacks of Thursday night pounded through his head.

The door to the club was closed, and everyone waited in the office, watching the monitors for signs of Teeth touching anything.

"He's stroking the back of the couch," one CSI said and pointed to the monitor. "We'll definitely get something off that."

"And he never eats or drinks, or touches a glass or bottle?" Richard asked, somewhat enthralled by being in *The Cavern Club* with Remi Steele. He'd had her posters on his wall twenty years ago, and had gone to several concerts.

"No." Remi shook her head. "He's never drunk a thing, never eaten a thing. I think he fills up before he comes, or after he leaves."

"Then why come here at all?" Richard questioned. "Does he even get up and dance?"

"Nope," Remi told them. "He clearly has other reasons for being here."

"Drugs. If he's the one handing out those teeth," Drew said and sipped the coffee Remi had passed around. She'd also laid out a buffet of food.

"So, he's using my club as a drug den, basically. Great." Remi's voice dripped sarcasm. "That's all I need. Some punk arse piece of shit who's in dire need of a wash using my club as a place to hand out experimental drugs."

"May not even be experimental at this point. He's already made them," Drew said. "He's either handing them out before he gets here, or it's not him at all."

"But I really want it to be," Remi murmured as she watched the screens. "I really want it to be him. I'm thinking of banning him because I've had enough."

"You can't do that until we find out who he is," Drew told her. "If we can't get decent DNA tonight, we'll have to come back, which means letting *him* come back."

She groaned. "Then get something on him because I'm sick of him being in the club. He stinks to high heaven and quite frankly, it's getting beyond a joke. No one else gets to book out the ring because he always does."

"How much does it cost to book it out?" Richard asked.

"A thousand per person, which is why him booking it out for thirteen people each night clearly shows he has money."

"A thousand for one person?" Richard whistled. "That's a lot."

"Everything's included. Food and drink, unless it's an expensive bottle of wine or champagne, that's extra. If you want something extra special, or brought in, you pay for that too."

"He's forked out thirteen thousand for every night he's been here, and not eaten or drunk anything? Neither have his disciples?" Drew shook his head. "That's a lot of money. So, the guy's rich or he's earning from those teeth. There is definitely something going on here and we need to find out. He could be into something bigger than drugs."

"To afford thirteen grand a night, yeah, I'd say so," Richard agreed.

Finally, at midnight, Teeth stood in the middle of the ring, arms straight out to the sides, head tilted back. His lips moved and the disciples swayed around him.

"What the fuck is he doing?" one CSI asked, as they all stood riveted around the monitor.

"What he always does," Remi replied. "When he first gets here, when he's ready to leave. It's like he's praying or something."

"Thinks he's Jesus." Richard sniggered. "Do the same people come every time?"

"Always different people. That's why it'll probably be hard to track him or them down..." Remi leaned forward. "He's leaving and they always follow." She spoke into her walkie-talkie. "Let me know when Teeth and his people actually get into a car and leave."

"Sure thing, boss."

They watched the four guards in the club casually make their way over to the ring, and once Teeth and his group walked out the door, they stood around it.

"Teeth just stole a cab from someone and took off. His goons are stumbling around looking for their way home," came over the walkie.

"Great, don't let them back in," Remi told him and turned to the others. "All yours, boys."

They collected their gear and made their way into the club and over to the ring, getting to work on finding hair and skin samples.

Drew, Remi and Richard stood by waiting, aware that many other patrons were watching them. Aware that many others weren't and going about their partying.

After an hour, they packed up their kits, having found multiple samples of skin and hair and not just from Teeth.

"We're ready to go." The lead investigator removed his mask and gloves. "I'd say we've got everything we need, it'll take a while to go through it all and get a good match, though. *If* we get a match."

"Okay, thanks Bob," Drew said. "Do what you can with Teeth's DNA and get that to us. We need to find out who this guy is."

"Will do. Okay boys, let's go. Ms Steele." He nodded at Remi. "Thank you kindly for your hospitality this evening."

Remi nodded in return. "You're welcome." She watched the investigator in the ring bump into the table and knock over the small vase of flowers.

"Bugger," he cried out and reached for it. "I'm so sorry, Ms Steele."

"Don't worry about it. We need to steam clean and

fumigate the place anyway."

"Ah, boss." He held up his hand. "We have a situation."

Bob Kenner leaned over the couch and looked at the object in his fellow CSI's hand. "Well, whaddya know." He picked it up and turned to Remi and Drew. "Someone's been watching."

"What is it?" Remi asked, frowning at the gut instinct in her stomach.

"A fucking recording device," Drew said and waved to a CSI for a glove." He took the camera and aimed it at Remi. "He's recording us."

Anger flared in her and she leaned towards the camera. "Teeth, you fucking cunt. You're done in my club. You hear that. Fucking done."

Drew turned it to his face. "Teeth, you are fucking dead." He dropped the camera to the ground and stomped on it, hearing the crack underfoot.

*****

Comfortable in his home, Teeth had watched it all on his phone, and seeing Remi and the detective made his blood boil. She was ruining all of his plans and *that* he wasn't going to tolerate.

"And I see the detective isn't dead. So that idiot clearly didn't do the job and he didn't even report in, so I have no idea where he is." He turned off his phone and sighed. Remi Steele was proving to be a very big problem. A problem he was going to have to do something about.

Chapter 12

Sunday morning, Drew called Remi. "Hey. I've finally caught you, where are you?"

"At home. Just got back."

"Where have you been? I've been trying to contact you about the DNA results. Sisco said you'd taken off for a few days after banning Teeth from the club."

"Yep." Remi pulled her lingerie out of her bag and placed it in the drawers of her massive walk-in closet. "After that bastard set us up with that fucking camera, I decided I needed a break. That bastard's no longer welcome, neither is his drug money, neither are his teeth, or his disciples, so I took off up the coast to my friend's retreat. Just turned my phone on today."

"Feeling better? You were *more* than pissed about Teeth leaving a camera in the flower vase."

"I was until we started talking about him." She hung up her tops and folded her pants. "God knows how long that's been in there, but since he books the thing out most nights, I have no idea what he expected to see. Or hear."

"Yeah, neither do I. But we've had our tech guys go

over it and had the lab run the DNA tests. I thought you could come over again and we could talk about it."

"Talk, as in with our mouths about the case, or talk as in fuck, in which case, I'm up for that as I'm sure Drew junior is," she teased.

"Drew junior? Jesus Christ! You haven't named my penis?"

"Why not?" Remi argued. "He was very inquisitive and needy."

"Fucking hell!" Drew pushed up from his place on his couch and paced around. "I just rang to see if you wanted dinner at my place again, so we could talk about the case."

Remi paused her unpacking. "How about you come to my place for a change? I'm out later to grab some fresh food; I could grab a chicken or two and roast her up."

"Yum, sounds good. What time?"

Remi gave her watch a cursory look. "About five. Being a Sunday, you might want to bring your suit for tomorrow just in case you and junior end up spending the night. There are parking spaces across the road."

"Bring my suit, huh?" Drew murmured and pulled the lace curtain at the front window aside so he could look out at the street. He didn't see anything suspicious. "You're expecting me to stay the night?"

"Of course. Just as I stayed the other night." She paused. "I do have a spare room in case nothing happens. But I expect it to."

"And what you expect and what you'll get could be two completely different things, Remi Steele." He let the curtain fall and turned his back, walking slowly through the living room. "You really shouldn't go through life expecting things."

"I don't. But I do expect sex with you. So, get those delectable buns of steel to my place about five. I'll text you the address. See you then, detective." She hung up and sent the text, then finished unpacking. The last four days away had helped her re-centre herself, so had banning Teeth from the club. The staff knew he wasn't welcome, his face was on a no entry list, and the teeth inserts weren't allowed either. Anyone seen with them, wearing them, selling or buying them, were also banned. The problem had gotten away from her and it was time to take back control. She was refreshed and ready to get to it.

At midday, she hit the shops for fresh food and had the chicken and veggies in the oven, and a saucepan of gravy ready to go at four. Checking the time, she had a quick shower, put on lacy underwear and a skimpy see-through silk slip dress and applied her favourite perfume that drove men wild. *Like Rex,* she thought. *Shit! I wonder what's happened to him.* She hadn't received texts for weeks, had assumed he was busy with the band, or fucking a lot of groupies. A frown crossed her face. *But he said he loved me and wanted me and no one else.* Thinking back to all of the words he'd said, she wondered if she remembered correctly. A stab of jealousy got her smack bang in the middle of her chest. *It's not like we were a couple,* she argued with herself. *We're both free to see other people, just like I'm seeing Drew, he's probably seen a lot of women. He's hardly a priest.*

Even priests don't stick by those celibacy vows, her brain argued.

True. She breathed deeply. *We're both adults, we love each other as hot people who want to fuck each other, and do. But we don't want a committed relationship. So, we fuck for fun. That's it. Just for fun. Nothing more, nothing less. So, I hope he's enjoying all the hot young pussy he's getting, and my pussy is enjoying Drew junior while he's interested.*

The intercom buzzed and she checked the security camera. Drew was waiting. "I'm in the penthouse, come on up." She pressed the button to release the front door, and then hurried into the bedroom for another spray of perfume, pulling down her knickers to add a spray to her pelvis so that hair smelt nice, and made it back to the door as he knocked. Flinging it open, she managed a "hey" before grabbing his arm and pulling him in. She slammed and locked the door behind him. "The chicken's been in an hour or so. It should be ready soon." She turned to see him staring wide-eyed at her and slid her hands down her dress. "You like?"

A guttural sound came from his open mouth. "Do you always wear nighties when you have guests for dinner?"

A giggle left her and she sidled up to him. "It's not a nightie, it's a slip dress, and I could slip out of it if you like. *Do* you like?"

Another groan. "Fucking love it, but I thought I came here to talk about the case."

"I thought you came here to fuck me," Remi replied.

"Ah, fuck, Remi." He closed his eyes and turned away. "I, uh, brought a pack of my favourite cola. I wasn't sure if you drink it or not, but thought I'd supply my own." He didn't offer her the six-pack, just stood with his back to her and stared out the floor-to-ceiling French doors overlooking the ocean. "What a fucking view."

"It certainly is," she murmured and patted his voluptuous behind before taking the six-pack from him. "I'll just pop these in the fridge and you help yourself, just like I did at your place." She padded over to the kitchen.

"That's a very loaded comment," Drew told her, finally moving from his spot. He kept on moving over to the French doors. "This is quite a fucking view."

"It is." She made her way to his side. "Very calming when you're having a bad day."

"Had a few of those lately," he joked. "I know the feeling."

"Between you being drugged three times, and me dealing with a Muppet wannabe selling drugs in my club, *and* a hot detective riding me in bed *and* at work over missing musicians, yeah, I've had a few days, a few weeks even." She cast a side-eye his way. "I mean *really*, it's so *hard* being ridden by a hot detective covered in fur. So, so hard."

The raging blush sped over his face. "Maybe we should move this conversation to the reason I'm here."

"Which is to fuck me." Remi nodded her approval.

He couldn't stop himself from grinning. "Remi," he warned. "I'm trying to be serious."

"And I'm trying to be fucked. But I do have a roast in the oven and I don't want that to go to waste while we're doing the tango *and* the fandango in bed. So, okay." She clapped her hands. "Let's get on with this and then we can eat. Or I'll eat the chicken and you can eat me. Chop, chop."

He shook his head in embarrassment, but his grin was ear to ear. "You just don't stop."

"Nope."

"Fucking hell. Okay." He breathed in and out to calm himself. "The DNA from the couch has come back, obviously male, but it's not in any of our systems, so he's not been in trouble before."

"Which means?"

"Which means we're no closer to finding out who he is or where he lives."

"Fucking hell." Remi ran a hand through her hair in frustration. "What do we do about that? We have DNA, but it can't tell us who he is because he has no priors."

"Right now..." Drew gave a nod of his head. "Nowhere. But we did get DNA from the others. Or some of the others, rather. We have samples from some of the people that were with him and two of those are in the system."

"So, they can tell us who Teeth is?" Excitement rose in her gut.

Another nod. "Well...yes and no."

"What do you mean by that?" she asked. "Can they tell us or not?"

"Can you stop interrupting me and let me fucking finish?" he said, exasperated. "Just shut up and listen." He watched her brows rise and her arms cross under her delectable breasts that made his heart thunder and his dick harden. His voice rose. "We have DNA from four others. Two of them turned up in our system, so they had priors. While you were"— he waved a hand at her— "sunning yourself up the coast, we hauled them in and interrogated them about Teeth. They swore up and down they didn't have anything to do with drugs and didn't know he did either. They both came across him after friends of theirs raved about him and the good times they had, and how he threw parties."

"Except Merriam Webster," Remi murmured, her brow creasing. "I suppose you could say she died from having fun and living her life."

Drew's mood sobered. "Yeah. I guess you could. But these two guys said they didn't go to any of the parties, so had no idea where they were and no idea where he lived."

"So how did they get on the list?" Remi asked.

"What list?"

"The list of people he paid for every night? Different people every night."

"He didn't pay for them." Drew shoved his hands into his old blue jean's pockets. "Apparently you text your name to a number and if you're chosen you send a thousand dollars to a bank account and then meet him at a bus stop. He gave them handfuls of drugs and teeth. And then took them to the club where they partied for the night. He was lorded as some bigwig celebrity to party with."

"Okay…hang on. They texted their name, so you have a number, and now you have two witnesses to say he gave them drugs and teeth. But why did they think he was some celebrity? Entry to the club is reasonable, you can see celebrities most nights, you sure as hell don't need to pay some dick you don't know a thousand bucks just to get into the club and sit in the ring. Jesus!" Remi threw her hands up in frustration. "How many people are paying this guy and how much more is he making. No drug dealer gives away their drugs unless they want to get them hooked on it. I've seen that way too many times in the industry I'm in. But he's gotta be making money somewhere."

"I'm sure he is. But to answer your questions, the number is disconnected, and no longer in use, and we can't trace it. We have two witnesses who want to co-operate, so they don't get into trouble. As for them thinking he's a celebrity, that's just the schtick going around. A rumour he or someone else probably started to make it bigger than it is. The disciples spread the word about it; more and more people become interested."

"So, where's he having his raves, or parties, or whatever we're calling it, because he has to be doing something somewhere?"

"We're looking into that too, and we're still tracking down manufacturers and other drug dealers that might have made the teeth, or the drugs that went into them. After all, I still have a death to solve."

"Oh, I think we know what happened there," Remi told him. "She was with Teeth; we have the footage of her entering with him and the others that night. We have her collapsing, him pointing, another minion throwing her bag at her and then taking off. Why else would they run?" Remi was interrupted by the oven bell going off.

She kept talking while checking the chicken. "Only guilty people run. You know that, you're a cop." She poked the chicken, saw clear juices run out and put it back in the oven and turned it off. "How many times have guilty people run from you?" She lit the stove for the pot of gravy and got it going.

"Yeah, a lot," he said and parked himself on the island bench stool to watch. "But we need proof that he gave her teeth, or any other drug. Her collapse happened while he was in the club, she was with him, and he and the others ran. It just proves she was there with him. Nothing else."

"She had bite marks on her neck. Did her tox screen say drugs?" Remi stirred the gravy. She wanted it nice and thick.

"She did. And *it* did. But she didn't have any teeth in her bag and none in her mouth—"

"Which meant someone else bit her, obviously," Remi interrupted. "And it still doesn't mean Teeth didn't give it to her beforehand." She sighed. "Was it technically an overdose? Or…what do you call it if she didn't inject herself?"

"Her stomach had no drugs in it, and the only injection point was the two on her neck. So no, she didn't ingest drugs of her own volition unless she knew drugs were in those teeth." He shook his head slowly; the whole case pained him. "She technically didn't overdose, but her body didn't accept the drug well and it wreaked havoc instead. Making her heart stop and her breathing laboured. It's a little complicated when a person doesn't ingest or inject their drugs. That means there's a perp out there who did it."

"How much drug is in those teeth? I've seen them, they're way too small for a large dose and don't look like they'd harm anyone."

"But they do. The stuff is potent and clearly lethal." Drew watched her turn off the gravy and pull the trays from the oven. "I had a couple of clean packs from the blonde." He paused and grew flame red, more so when Remi raised a brow. "I took them from her bedside cupboard. She had a lot. They were tested and the dose was five times the potency of the drug."

"Is it common? The drug, I mean." Remi expertly cut the birds and loaded the plates full of chicken and vegetables. "I wonder if it's the same as the syringe."

"The drug is common, just very potent." He cocked his head. "You mean the syringe I was stabbed with? Did you tell me what that was?"

"No, I don't think so." She poured gravy over the food. "Doc said it was a party drug and gave you something to counter act it. We don't know if it was full and you got half a dose, or barely got any at all. You seemed quite okay after your nap. Maybe you didn't cop a lot of it at all." She carried their plates to the table and sat on the long side. Drew sat at the end.

"I had a drug test at the retreat." Drew inhaled the succulent scents wafting up at him. "Minor traces of a party drug named Elmolucent. Elmo for short."

"That sounds like what Doc said. Certainly not something heard of coming through the music industry, but another reference to a bloody Muppet." She ate a piece of gravy covered chicken. "Mmm." She put her finger up, and when she'd swallowed, said, "I could contact Doug and see if he's heard of it and whether or not some of those he looks after had it in their system, or knows of some dude called Dr Teeth. Would that help?"

"Yeah, yeah, it would, but only as long as we could use it as evidence if needed. This fucking chicken is fantastic." He loaded another forkful into his mouth.

"*My* speciality," Remi told him. "And I'm not exactly sure Doug, or the privacy act would let you have it as evidence. But we won't know until we find out."

"And when do we find out?"

She checked the time. "We can call after dinner."

They took their time enjoying the food, the sunset, and their drinks. Making small talk, though mostly about the food, the sunset, and the view, and once the leftover food was put in the fridge, and the dishes in the dishwasher, they sat back at the table while Remi called Doug."

"*Holiday Meditation Centre.* We're currently not in as it's a Sunday and we don't work on Sunday because, you know, some of us want time off from doing this thankless job—"

"Ah, hello, Doug Western. Sorry about that. How can I help you?"

"Doug, it's Remi." Her eyebrows slid down from their surprised position. "I see Rachael's having some issues still."

"Ah, yeah. Sorry about that Remi. She's getting a bit sick of being here and wants out, so she's doing all manner of things to convince me to let her go. Like being rude to those on the phone."

"Well, it's probably not a bad thing. It must get very boring out there," Remi sympathised.

"It can do, some days. So, why are you calling us on a Sunday? Another musician? Another dead body?"

"Neither. I'm here with Detective Drew Reilly, you spoke to him weeks ago when the families of the musicians had put out missing person's reports, and you're also on speaker phone because we have some questions."

"Oh, right. Hello again, detective. Fire away."

"Yeah, hi. My first question pertains to the drugs the musicians were on. We're wondering if it's a new party drug called Elmolucent. We've seen a rise of it here—"

"And the dude I shot may have had it in his system," Remi cut in.

"Ah, yes, he did. I did an autopsy, tox screen, etc. Used his parts for the things I needed them for. But I definitely remember him having it in his system. And yes, detective, I've also seen it in a few of the patients that have come through here, but I won't mention names."

"I don't need names, I just need to know how long have you seen it, and in how many?" Drew asked.

Doug made small noises while he thought. "It's mainly the last year and at least a third, I think, of the patrons that have come here."

"Jesus," Remi murmured. "Is that considered a lot?"

"Not really, in the overall grand scheme. There are a lot of drugs out there and we've dealt with quite a few here."

"Okay, so we've established that this drug has been around about a year and you've dealt with it," Drew said. "Have any of the people there mentioned a dealer or party goer or—"

"Dickhead who thinks he's Jesus and stinking to high heaven," Remi cut in.

Drew shook his head and continued. "Or all of that, by the name of Dr Teeth who gives out plastic vampire teeth for party goers?"

"Huh, now that you mention it. I get the feeling the drugs are in the teeth," Doug said.

"And you'd be right." Drew nodded. "Heard of it or him?"

"I do remember one participant who boasted about biting groupies and having his penis bitten in return. He mentioned a set of teeth you pop over your own top teeth."

"That's it," Remi said. "There are small syringes in the canines that push down and dispense the drug."

"That *is* a new one," Doug replied. "I haven't heard the name, but did hear about the teeth about six months ago. A rocker from a band. They were touring Australia when it happened, but can't give you a name, of course, and again, haven't heard of Dr Teeth."

"Okay, thanks Doug, at least that's something to go on. He's been around for six months or more and the teeth would've been around just as long." Remi looked at Drew. "Anything else, detective?"

"No, no, that's all. Thanks for the information."

"You're welcome. Glad I could help. Remi, until next time."

"Bye Doug, and I hope you find another Rachael."

"So do I, unless I can convince her to stay."

"I somehow doubt it. Bye." She ended the call and turned to Drew. "I think we need a drink and an hour in front of that glorious view to unwind." She grabbed two sodas and poured them into wine glasses with ice, and they sat on the two-seater couch by the French doors to take in the remaining sun rays glistening off the dark night sky, and the scent of ocean waves rolling by.

"Well, that was something."

"It was, but it doesn't tell us anything more." Drew watched Remi wrap his arm around her shoulders and snuggle into his side. He was instantly aroused. Fuck!

"It tells us, Teeth had probably been around longer than first thought as have those fake teeth of his." She hooked her right leg over his and rubbed it up and down.

Drew bit back a moan. "More than likely. At least six months to a year. The drug was already around, so not completely new, and obviously the teeth have been manufactured long before now." He watched her right hand slide up his leg, over his crotch, and under his shorts. "Remi," he groaned, and closed his eyes as her hand roamed his chest.

"Drew," she groaned back. "We have the information; you've told me about the DNA tests and interrogations. So *now* can we stop and talk about other things?" She stroked the mess of hair on his sternum. It was darker than the rest of his chest hair, thicker, and softer, and she always got groans from him when she did.

"And what…other things…fuck." His eyes opened and closed against the onslaught. "Do you want to… talk…?" His voice lilted at the end and his head dropped back. "Fuck, Remi."

"Yes, Drew." She placed their glasses on the side table and planted her lips on his neck and her hands disappeared under his shirt. "I want you to fuck me and I want to fuck you." She kissed his neck, leaving a blazing trail up to his lips. "It's only fair after what happened at your place." Straddling him, her hands pushed the shirt over his head and trapped his arms in it. "Fuck me, Drew. You know you want to." She hauled him off the couch and led him to the bedroom. "And don't worry. I've got the handcuffs." She saw his eyes widen. "Standard issue. Of course."

They tumbled onto the bed and Drew managed to free his arms, encasing Remi within them as they kissed.

Her arms clawed at his back, her tongue delved into his mouth and her legs wrapped themselves around him.

"Fuck, Remi," he rasped, his hand sliding over the barely-there silk slip dress. He pulled the straps down, along with those of her lacy bra, and sucked on her delicious pink nipples.

She gasped and arched her back, giving him all access to her body. She pulled down the other straps, giving him both, and struggled to get both items off while he was on top. His hand pushed the fabric down because his mouth didn't want to let go of the delectable feast it was sucking on. His hands caught her knickers on the way down and soon she was free of all restraints and spreading her body across the bed for him to enjoy.

"Get your fucking pants off," she panted. "And get that dick of yours inside me."

He obeyed her command, his jeans and shorts falling beside the bed as he made his way inside, bringing almost instantaneous pleasure to her.

She cried out, having been so ready, and didn't stop while he pleasured himself, taking his time to speed up and slow down. Thrust then slide.

"God, fucking come already," she yelled, digging her nails into his round buttocks and riding him until he was spent.

They collapsed in a panting, sweaty mess of arms and legs and other body parts.

"Fucking hell, Drew. I've waited all day for that."

"Worth it?"

"Fuck yes." Remi tried swallowing, but she was too dry. "I'm going to grab our drinks. Get off."

"I already did." He grinned.

"You bastard." She swatted him away and hurried into the living room to collect their drinks. "Nope, not cold enough, need a new one." She quickly grabbed two cans from the fridge and hurried back to the bedroom. Drew was resting back on a pile of pillows. "Here, scull this."

They drank for a few moments and then lay back and rested.

Remi buried her face in Drew's chest hair, delighting in the mix of coarse and soft.

Drew's arms were around her, his chin resting on her head. Her hair smelled gently of apples, sweet and delectable.

"Are you staying?" Remi murmured into his fur. "I see you brought a bag."

"Figured I should bring that suit you mentioned in case I don't get back to my place in the morning. What time do you set your alarm for?"

"Ten."

He pulled his head back to look at her. "You don't get up till ten?"

She frowned, thinking it was a joke. "I run a club, why would I get up before that?"

"Huh, yeah, I guess. But I need to get up at six. So, if you don't mind me setting my alarm and waking up."

"No. I'll just let you out and come back to bed. Problem solved."

"Huh, yeah. Problem solved."

"Good. Now that we have that out of the way." Remi rolled towards her bedside table and dug in her drawer. After a bit of searching, she found what she wanted, and placing the key on the cupboard rolled back towards Drew, climbing on top of him. She held up the handcuffs. "Standard issue, like I said. Ready to get down and dirty?"

Before she could blink, he grabbed the cuffs, rolled her onto her back so he was on top, and cuffed her right hand and his left one, to the bed head rail.

With wide eyes, she looked at their hands and jiggled the cuffs. "Fucking hell! Where'd you learn that? You cuffed us both in seconds."

"Just a little trick." Drew shifted his legs between hers.

"What? They teach that at the academy, do they?" she teased, and gasped as his thumb rubbed her nipple. "That's so not fair, Reilly."

"Who said anything about fair," he muttered against the flesh of her breast bone. "Life isn't fair, Steele, not when it comes to love and war."

A small gasp came from her. Her head pushed back; her body arched. "Who said anything about war," she panted. "If you keep going, it just might be." She yanked on the cuffs but his lips took control. "That's not fair," she mumbled around them. "I'm right-handed."

"So am I." His right arm hitched her closer to him, holding her against his chest.

A banging sound mumbled through the walls.

"Ah, what's that?" She arched.

"I didn't hear anything." Drew pushed inside. "Just ignore it."

The sound came again. Louder.

"I think someone's banging on the door." Remi tried to clear her fuzzy brain.

"Leave it," Drew said against her lips. "They'll go away."

The sound came again. Louder, longer.

"Fucking hell," Remi yelled as she climaxed and shuddered to a stop. "It has to be a neighbour. Very few people can get into the building and up to the penthouse. Maybe something's wrong. Maybe there's a fire, or something."

More banging.

She growled. "They're clearly not leaving. Where's the key?"

"On the bedside cupboard where you put it." Drew groaned and roll off her. "Just leave it. They'll go away."

"Clearly not." She unlocked herself, slipped into the silk robe hanging on the headboard, and padded to the door, looking at the monitor before opening it. "Rex? What are you doing here? I thought you were on tour?"

He eyed her hungrily and leaned against the door

frame. "I was. But I missed my girl and came back to see her." He tugged at the tie around the robe. "Looks like you're ready for bed, and I'm just in time to join you."

She playfully slapped his hand away, her gaze roamed over his extra furry exterior. "You've grown your hair and beard. You know I like fur, but bedtime is otherwise occupied," she said saucily.

"Remi, who is it? Do I need my badge and gun?" Drew came around the corner into the entrance hall wearing just his jeans. He saw the man in the doorway and frowned. Memories flooded back, creating realisations. "Rex…?" Angry, and surprised, he crossed his arms. "What are you doing here? Do you know Remi? Jesus, what's it been? Not long enough, apparently."

Rex straightened, his shoulders back, brows deeply furrowing. "Drew? What the fuck are you doing here? How the fuck do you know… Oh…" His eyes widened, remembering back to the night he'd seen Drew at the club when the girl had collapsed. "What the fuck is he doing here?" he demanded of Remi.

Surprised, Remi had been glancing back and forth between them. "Know each other, I take it? Small world."

"Know each other?" Drew spat. "This fucking arsehole killed my girlfriend."

Remi's brows rose in shock, and she froze.

"I didn't fucking kill her," Rex bellowed, fists clenched at his sides. "You're the one who couldn't stand the fact she wanted me instead of you."

Drew took a menacing step toward him. "She didn't want you; she wanted the drugs you gave her, and you killed her."

"I didn't fucking kill her," Rex snapped and turned to a stunned Remi. "If he's the one you want now, then I won't be." Slamming the door behind him, he stormed off in fury down the hallway. "How…fucking…dare…he…she," he growled.

Remi, still stunned, turned to an angry Drew. "What's this about killing your girlfriend?"

Drew deflated and sighed. "It's a long story that goes back many, many years."

"We'd better get some coffee on then." Remi started for the kitchen, but Drew grasped her hand.

"No." He shook his head sadly. "I'm not talking about it. I vowed to never talk about it, so I won't. Not now, not ever. It was a long time ago, Remi, and nothing to do with now. But…" He pulled her toward him and held both of her arms. "I take it you know Rex, and I have deduced that you've slept with him."

Her cheeks flushed hot. "I've known him for four years, and only slept with him before he headed off on tour with his band. So, it was fairly new."

"Just like this," Drew said, kissing her and smoothing the hair off her face. "And now I'm right back to where I was before. Where *we* were before. A long, long time ago. But this time, I'm fighting."

She gazed into his soft brown eyes, seeing a whole range of emotions sweep through them. "Tell me."

He shook his head. "No. Not tonight. Maybe not ever. But just know this, Remi Steele. I'm falling for you, and so I'm going to fight for you."

*****

In the back alley behind the club, a figure dressed from head to toe in black set down a duffel bag and pulled out a bottle of petrol. He twisted off the lid, stuffed a rag into it, and set it aside. He did the same another nineteen times before zipping up the bag and taking a lighter from his pocket. He picked up the first bottle, lit the rag, and threw it at the back window. It smashed through with a tinkle of glass.

He rushed through the other bottles, throwing Molotov cocktail after Molotov cocktail through all of the windows, hoping to finish before the police were called. Once he was done with the windows, he opened the bins and threw burning rags into them and stood back to watch.

The man Remi and the police knew as Dr Teeth looked unrecognisable in a black balaclava and clothing.

"I'm getting my revenge on you, Remi Steele. So, you can burn, bitch, burn."

PART THREE

BURN

Chapter 13

Remi was having a delicious orgasm, her fifth for the night, when her phone rang.

"Don't answer it," Drew groaned against her neck. "Voicemail."

They settled, gasping for air, then Remi heard Rex's voice.

"Rem, it's Rex, you're fucking club's on fire and you need to get down here now. The fireys are trying to put it out. Get down here *now.*"

Stunned, Remi lifted her head. "Did he say…?"

"Yep." Drew rolled off her. "We'd better get down there."

They quickly dressed and took Drew's car to the club where Remi saw the fire service dealing with the fire, people milling around and pointing, and Rex standing by the road.

Drew stopped at the yellow police tape and flashed his badge, and the officer lifted it so he could drive under. They alighted to see other officers taking statements and Rex scowling at the sight of Drew.

"Rem," he yelled, and waved her over.

She ran to him. Fire radiated out of the alley, the building pulsating towards them in intense waves of volcanic heat. "What the fuck! Did you see it? How did you know? What the fuck!"

The sight of her hard-earned club going up in flames brought fear and despair to her heart. Her hands grasped her head, tears welled in her eyes, and her body was bending, leaning over, ready to collapse in shock. "What the fuck!" Her voice came out in a scared cry. "My fucking club!"

"Oh, Rem." Rex slid his arms around her. "I'm so sorry. I'm so sorry."

A hiccoughing sob came from her. "I have to, uh, call Sisco. He'll have to call the staff. Everyone's out of a job." Her face screwed up and she cried harder. "No one will come. I'm out of business."

Rex held her, soothing her while she cried, but his gaze followed Drew as he spoke to officers, the fire marshal, and other people on the outside of the police tape. He'd said his piece earlier; this wasn't the time to get back into it.

Drew finally made it over to them, warily eyeing Rex. It had been over twenty-five years since he'd seen him, and tonight had come as a very big surprise, but not one he was going to let get the better of him. "Remi," he said gently, reaching for her arm. "Remi, I have some news."

She pulled out of Rex's arms and turned to him. "What? Do they know who did it? I bet it was fucking Teeth and I'm going to smash his down his fucking throat the next time I see him." She ran both hands over her face to wipe the tears away. "What's happening?"

"Does the footage from the cameras in the alley only go to the monitoring system in the office? Is that the only place it's recorded and stored?" Drew asked.

She looked at him, confused. "What? Ah, no. It also goes to an offsite…oh…the footage will show who did it. Ah, okay. No, it's stored offsite for twenty-four hours then transferred into our own security backup. Yeah." She nodded enthusiastically. "We've still got it."

"Great," Drew said. "In the meantime, the other officers are seeing if the neighbouring businesses also have cameras pointing at the alley, or along the street to see if we can catch anyone coming or going, and they'll work through the night checking those. Hopefully, we'll be able to see someone."

"Great, but it won't save my club, though." Enthusiasm gone, she stared at her club. It was the one thing that kept her passion for music alive. Without it, she was back to being nothing, just as she had been when she'd quit music. All of the record execs had told her she was washed-up and over. The kids didn't want her songs anymore. They wanted Bieber, the Jonas brothers, and Taylor Swift. *'I was Taylor fucking Swift before Taylor Swift was Taylor fucking Swift,'* she'd muttered on her way out the door of the office belonging to the head of *CGB,* her record company for her entire career. But they'd taken what they wanted out of her and dumped her when they believed the well had run dry.

She'd already used all of her hard-earned money and turned it into the club she'd always wanted to perform at, and because she had so many famous musical acquaintances, she got them to perform at *The Cavern*

Club, making it the number one place to be. And now, it lay in smouldering ruins.

"Rem." Drew pulled her back to reality. "The fire chief says it looks as if the fire stayed on the alley side of the building and didn't have a chance to spread far. But the place might reek of smoke. There will need to be an investigation, and you'll have to deal with the insurance company, but, fingers crossed, it won't be as bad as it looks." He cupped her face. "It should be okay, Rem, it should be okay."

She gazed into his eyes and her brows dipped down in confusion. "Did you say the alley side is on fire?"

Drew nodded. "Yes. They don't think it had the chance to spread." He watched her pull her phone from her bag and dial a number. "Who are you calling?"

Remi placed the phone to her ear. "Sisco, Remi. Did you lock up last night?"

"Ah, Remi, do you have any idea what time it is?"

"Did you lock up last night, Sisco. Yes, or no?"

Sensing the urgency in her voice, he sat up straighter. "I did. I do that God damn fucking check list every God damn fucking night when I'm in charge, and I watch you every night you are."

"Did you shut the fireproof doors on the alley side? *All* sides?"

"Yes. *All* sides. It's the second thing we do after locking the back door."

She collapsed into Drew's arms and leaned heavily against him. "Thank God."

Rex sent a glare full of daggers at Drew, who sent them right back and tightened his arms around Remi.

"What the fuck's going on, Remi?" Sisco demanded. "What's wrong? What's happened?"

"The fucking club is on fire, that's what, and I fucking bet that arsehole Dr Teeth did it. They're going to search the surrounding cameras and we need to get the footage from the offsite storage centre."

"What the fuck!" Sisco collapsed back against his pillows in bed next to his toy boy lover who started kissing his shoulder. He was shooed away. "What do I do?"

"Get that footage, send it to Drew, ah, Detective Reilly." She rubbed her forehead and felt the opening pangs of a raging migraine coming on. "Once you've done that, send a mass email to everyone that the club has been burnt down and they'll be off work until the damage has been assessed and they can come back. Until I speak to the chief and can go in and have a look around, I won't know what needs to be done. But it'll definitely need a refurb, so make sure you have the numbers of the companies who did the last fit-out. We'll need to air out, pull out, and…" She sighed from the pit of her gut. "And work our guts out to get it back on track as quickly as possible. And then we'll have a grand re-opening. Hopefully, in a week or two."

"Okay, I'm on it. I'll call when it's done. Let me know if you need anything else."

"Will do. And you might need to be here tomorrow for the walk through. If we're allowed in."

"Let me know and I'll get to work."

"Okay, bye." Remi hung up and stared at her decrepit building. "Sisco will get the footage and send it to you. He says he shut the fire doors, so I hope the fire didn't spread."

"What do you *mean* fire doors?" Drew's arms fell away when she stood and faced him.

"When I gutted and made the club, I made everything fireproof. We have fire doors and corridors around the building. All up to code. We shut everything every night, so if there's a fire outside, it can't get into the club. And if there's one inside, it can't get outside."

"And if there's a fire while you have patrons? What then?" Drew asked.

"We evacuate and shut them down." A guttural sigh left her. "Do I need to talk to the fire chief tonight?"

"You probably should, yeah. Let him know what you just told me. If they've been trying to get through those doors and failing, they'll now know why. I'll take you over and introduce you."

She nodded and turned to Rex. "Thank you for calling. I'm glad someone did." She hugged him tightly. "You go home and get some sleep. It's already been a long night."

Reluctantly, and with a deep scowl at Drew, he kissed her cheek and let her go. "You're welcome. I'll drop by tomorrow." He nodded at the club. "Let me know if you need help and I'll push up my sleeves and get stuck in."

"Ha! You don't wear anything with sleeves *to* push up, but thanks for the offer. I'll see you tomorrow. Bye, Rex." She turned to Drew who slipped an arm around her and led her to the fire chief.

Rex stood rooted to the spot, his anger boiling with the same intensity as the fire. He'd been passing by when he'd seen the flames and called it in, then alerted the passers-by to clear the area before calling Remi. The fire brigade had arrived quickly, and Remi soon after. But seeing her with Drew, the way his arms were possessively around her, made his gut churn. *They obviously became involved after that night the girl collapsed. I saw him when I walked back into the club. Got quite a surprise at that. Hadn't seen him in over twenty-five years, but he still looked the same. Just older, and a fucking cop. Who'd have fucking thought it?* He was frowning so hard a migraine was developing and he rubbed his hand over his eyes. *Fucking Drew Reilly. Back in my life after twenty-five fucking years.* His scowl deepened and he finally walked away. *If he's the one Remi wants, then she's welcome to him. Why should I fight?*

Because I love her.

Fuck! He came to a stop beside his bike and glanced over his shoulder. They were still talking to the fire chief. *Why does my fucking brain keep arguing with me? Yeah, I fucking love her.*

Then fight for her.

Yeah, yeah. She's too incredible to give up. Yeah, I'm gonna fight for her, fuck Drew Reilly. He doesn't get the girl this time. He mounted his bike and rode off into the night.

Drew heard the roaring grunt of a Harley and turned to see Rex riding away. *What the fuck is that bastard in town for? How the fuck is he in this town? The one I'm in. The one Remi's in.* He blanked out from the conversation. Until today, he hadn't seen Rex since they were teenagers and he'd never wanted to see him again. *But here he was, on Remi's doorstep expecting what… sex? Remi's slept with him. Fuck!* He shuddered and came back to the conversation. *I can't let him have her, too. Not again. Not knowing what he's into. Although he didn't look like the drug addicted, rock wannabe he was the last time I saw him. But that was over twenty-five years ago. He's clearly cleaned up and got healthy. Unless he just hides it better.*

The fire chief thanked Remi and bade them good night before walking over to his squad.

"I'm ready to go home." Remi sagged against him, her arms sliding around his waist. "Take me home."

He hugged her and led her back to the car. After taking her home, he stayed the night.

*****

The next day they headed back to the club to survey the damage.

Drew had called into the office and his boss put Burrows on the surveillance footage and told him Wong would meet him there for more details.

"Fucking hell." Remi stood outside the police tape staring down the alley behind her club. "I really hope that's not as bad as it looks."

"The chief said it shouldn't be," Drew replied and saw Sisco hurrying towards them. "You're assistant's here."

Remi glanced at him and he grinned. "Ha-ha. You know full well he's not my assistant. I don't know how many more times we're going to do this joke." She turned her attention to her manager. "Hey. Get everything done last night?"

Sisco came to a stuttering stop in one of his expensive Armani suits and black leather loafers, staring in horror at the club. He absentmindedly smoothed the front of his blazer. "I did. Jesus Christ. What happened?"

"Teeth happened. That fucking little cunt," came out from between Remi's gritted teeth.

"We don't know that," Drew reminded her. "We need to check all the footage and see if we can get a clear image of his face to ID him."

"Oh, I know that," Remi spat. "I know that cunt gave out those teeth full of drugs. I know he killed Merriam Webster. I know he planted that fucking camera in the vase so he could see whatever the fuck he was watching for. I fucking know it was him."

"You don't." Drew put his hand up to stop her. "What we need is *proof* that he did all of those things so we can send him to jail."

"Jail." She snorted. "Yeah, coz real criminals get sent to jail." The scorn in her tone came through loud and clear. "He won't get jail time."

"You don't know that which is why we need cold hard proof," Drew said and noticed the fire chief getting out of his car. "The chief's here. You should be able to go through."

They greeted one another and the chief escorted them down the alley. The back door had been pried open and it was obvious the fire doors and walls were closed.

"How far did the fire spread?" Remi asked, poking her head into the back hallway. "We made everything as fireproof as possible, with doors that we shut every night."

"And that may have saved your club, Ms Steele," the chief told her. "What we're worried about is if it's spread *into* the outside walls, through the electricals, into the ceiling. We'll take our time checking those to be safe. But we need access to the rest of the club."

"Ah, yeah. You can unbolt the door manually from this side, or Sisco or I can run through the front and open it from the inside." Remi pointed to the handle that blended in so well to the design it was hard to see. "You pull it right and down."

The fire chief directed one of his men to open the door and after a bit of wrestling with it, it creaked open. The back hallway was fire and damage free.

"Oh, thank God." Remi breathed a sigh of relief. "I just hope the office is in intact as well as the mezzanine which backs against this wall."

"We'll check the club first and then call you in if it's safe. I already have men in the inside; we had to get in the front door last night."

She inwardly moaned, anger bubbling up in her gut. "Yeah, I saw that. The fire wall is all the way around."

"Umm…do you need to check every room in the club?" Sisco asked quietly. "We have a couple of floors… a lot of rooms." He eyeballed Remi who closed her eyes in despair.

"Fuck," she muttered. "I forgot about all the rooms. The kitchen is downstairs and we use gas."

"How many are there?" the chief asked. "We'll need to check everything including gas and electricity supply in case of damage."

"Ah…if we can get into the office, we can get you a copy of the blue print. We keep it on hand in case of fire, flood, gas leak." Remi heaved another sigh and waved a limp hand. "Just as well no one was around when it happened."

"Right. We'll check out the office and give you the all clear to come in." The chief nodded and motioned for his people to move in.

Remi and Sisco moved aside and exchanged a few low words.

"Everything all right?" Richard asked Drew.

"Probably not, considering," he replied. "There's a lot of work to be done, insurance, cleaning, and there's a lot of rooms in the club. I just hope it didn't get into the walls and between the floors or the electricals." He saw the chief wave them in and turned around. "Remi, they're ready for us."

She hurried inside, followed by Sisco and Drew, and headed for the office, finding it fairly smoke free, and no damage at all. She yanked open her desk drawer and pulled out the blue print, spreading it across the desk. "We have the kitchen, band rooms, bathrooms, and staff rooms in the basement." Her finger pointed it all out. "There are toilets, the stage, backstage, private rooms, the office, bar and dance floor on the ground floor, and the mezzanine and private booths above the dance floor. They back onto the wall, but there's a private staircase going up behind it so food can be taken up without staff traipsing across the floor."

"And we'll need to check all of it, especially the kitchen. Is there a utility room for air-conditioning, heating...?"

They looked at the prints and located it, and the chief directed his men to spread out. "We'll take most of the day, Ms Steele. We need to do a thorough job and check everything, every outlet, every wall, every floor, even the roof. We'll let Detective Reilly know when we're done."

"And I guess I'll have to get the front door boarded up because you wrecked my roller door. Same with the back door."

"Until you get them fixed, yes. You can leave now and we'll get to work."

Remi nodded, glanced at the closed Murphy bed and safe, and followed Drew and Richard out the door. She heaved a sigh. "I'm keeping my fingers crossed that the fire didn't go anywhere and we can re-open by next weekend. Sisco, organise for the insurance company to come out tomorrow, if possible. Organise a door man to board up the doors, and tell our guards they're pulling shifts this week by guarding the building. They'll still get paid, but I want at least four guards here in the alley, the celeb entrance, and the band entrance. Two can stay at the front door." She rubbed her forehead. The headache from last night was coming back. "I fucking hate this."

"I'll get on it. And be here with the insurer. Do you want me to stay today and lockup behind those hot fireys?"

She rolled her eyes and a small laugh came from her. "Trust you to notice their looks. But yeah, just…float."

"Sure thing." He gave a nod and moved off for his car which would be his office for the day.

"Float?" Richard asked as they walked down the alley.

"Float back and forth, keep an eye on everything, do everything," Remi told him. "I've got a massive migraine out of this and he's my manager, so he can handle this."

Richard nodded and pointed to his car. "I'm off back to the station. Drew, you coming?"

Drew glanced at Remi. "I'll be in later. I've sent the surveillance footage to you and Burrows. You'll probably crack the case before I get there."

Richard cracked a laugh. "Not with Burrows on the case. He'll take forever." He glanced between the two. "But sure. I'll let the boss know. Ms Steele."

"Detective," she said, not looking at him.

Drew watched him walk away then turned to Remi. "You want me to take you home?"

Her head bobbed, but pain followed. "Yes, please. Right now. I just need a dark room and peace and quiet."

*****

After seeing Remi to bed, Drew arrived at the station and saw his boss leaning over Burrows' shoulder. "Find something?" He left his blazer over his chair and walked around the desks. Surveillance footage of the alley showed a figure in black throwing burning bottles through the windows.

"I'm surprised she doesn't have smash proof glass or chicken wire in them." Burrows swung back and forth in his chair. "If she did, the bottles wouldn't've got in."

"Is that Remi's surveillance from the club?" Drew leaned in. "Can we get anything?"

"Too dark, probably not." Burrows swung around to face Drew. "You took your time getting here." He gave a slight head tilt at their boss.

"I took Remi home, since I took her to the club." A blush swept over Drew's face and he averted his eyes.

Burrows made a noise in his throat. "You took Remi home because you took her to the club," he mocked.

"Have you finished watching all of the footage, Burrows?" Waylon stopped leaning over the desk and smoothed his tie back in place.

"Ah, no sir. A couple more to go." Burrows snapped to attention and stopped swinging in his chair.

"Then get on with it." Waylon turned to Drew. "And how *is Ms* Steele?"

"Pissed," Drew said. "With a migraine. Her manager's dealing with the club for now."

Waylon nodded and murmured, "Good. Good. Dreadful thing, but that means you can get to work too, detective."

"Yes, sir." The blush deepened and Drew watched him head for his office.

"Sucked in!" Burrows hissed and slid the next disc into the computer.

Drew slapped him over the head and hurried around to his desk.

Chapter 14

During the week, Remi and Sisco met with the insurer.

Thankfully, the fire report had deemed the club safe and it could be assessed, but the payout would take up to a couple of months. Itching to get the club going, Remi told him she'd use her own money to fix the club in time for a two-week re-opening.

The alley and back hallway were flooded with water which had slowly spread through the walls and into the carpeting on that side of the building. Smoke had insidiously wafted through the interior via the back door and ventilation unit, so they brought in industrial fans to blow it back out. Sisco called in the carpenters, and carpet store. Remi decided she may as well do some more redecorating and ordered new curtains as well as new chairs, couches, and tables for the upstairs mezzanine. The ring would also get new seating as Teeth had left his DNA all over it.

Since all of this was going to take at least two weeks, Remi and Sisco organised social media, and a press release about the grand re-opening, with the first drink free for all, and the band, Skyway, would be performing.

Having been friends of hers for ten years, they had no problem saying yes to doing a concert for their good pal Remi. It also hadn't hurt that the guitarist *and* drummer had both had flings with her.

Exhausted after a long week, Remi and Sisco locked up after everyone on Friday night and went their separate ways.

Always on the lookout, Remi was the one to notice a car pull away from the side of the road once they'd left the alley. Noticed it, because it was still behind them when they were halfway home, and panicked because she knew in her gut it was Teeth or one of his associates. She told her driver to take her to Melanie's house instead and quickly called her. "Mel, I need help. I'm being followed and need to use your house as a getaway."

"Say what?" Melanie said.

"I need to use your house to run out the back alley. I'm being followed. We'll be there soon." She clicked off the call and said to her driver, "Once we get to Mel's house, I want you to wait until I'm inside and then drive off and call me. You'll need to make it look like you're heading for the main road, but double back and pick me up behind her house. A car's been tailing us, and if it stops or passes us then they definitely were.

"Playing a game of cat and mouse, are we?" her driver mused. "How long?"

"Ten minutes or so. It's a black sedan, dark windows. It pulled away from outside the club when we did."

The driver nodded. "I did notice that one and have been keeping an eye on it."

"Good. I wasn't imagining things. We're going to try

and outwit him. Here we are." She watched as they pulled up outside of Melanie's house. "Wait until I'm inside then call me and pull away. Be out back in ten minutes."

"Ma'am."

Remi alighted and hurried up the drive of her friend's house to be met with an open door and warm hug.

"What the hell is going on?" her friend hissed in her ear.

"Shut the door and I'll tell you." Remi moved inside and set her bag on the hall side table. Her phone rang. "Drive off, back alley in ten. Stay on the phone and let me know what's happening. I'll put you on speaker." She turned to Melanie and added, "We were being followed and I needed to lose him, so I'm going to pretend I'm here for dinner and you'll close the curtains in five minutes, and five minutes after that I'll slip out the back door and into the alley."

"What type of car is it?"

"Dark sedan." Remi shrugged. "Couldn't see much detail, but my driver noticed it."

"Four door sedan, dark blue or black, black windows, partial licence plate DRT," her driver said down the line.

"Dr Teeth?" Remi frowned. "Did you see anything else?" she asked him.

"No."

"Okay, eight minutes. Is he following you?"

"Not yet. I saw him by the road when I left. He stayed where he was, two houses down," he said.

"Okay, look Mel, we have to make a show about me being in the house. We need to go into the living room through to the kitchen because the lights are on and the curtains are open. He'll see I'm here."

"Okay, let's do this," Melanie said, and they walked through the living room and into the kitchen. "This is weird but not the first time we've done it. Remember back in high school?"

Laughter rolled out of Remi. "Oh, my God, that was hilarious."She glanced at her phone. Five minutes. "Time to shut the curtains." Setting her phone on the table, she turned to watch Melanie hurry to close them. "Are they see-through?"

"Of course not. What now?"

A check of the time. "In four minutes, I sneak out the back."

"Time for a drink then?" Melanie poured them both wines and they toasted their situation. "Ah, good times. Lunch this Sunday?"

"Don't know."

"You've been MIA recently," Melanie teased. "New man?"

Remi's brows rose and she took a gulp.

"Ooh, there is. Is he hot like Rex?"

"*Knows* Rex apparently and is very hairy just like him." She gave a quick rundown of the whole Rex Drew situation. "So, I'm not sure what's happening Sunday. I might have one of them over."

"Lucky you! How about both at the same time? Or, if you don't want one, send him my way." Melanie chuckled.

"I'm coming up the street now," her driver said.

"Shit." Remi slammed her glass on the bench and grabbed her bag. "I'll text you a pic of the hot detective.

But I gotta go tell him about this."

Without turning on a back light, Remi hugged her friend goodbye and raced across the back yard and through the back fence door and into her car just as it pulled up. The doors locked, and they drove away.

Once she was safely home, she called Drew. "Hey, can you come over for the night? I think I was followed by Teeth today."

"You were what? How do you know? Are you sure it was him?" Drew sprang to attention at his desk. "Describe the car."

"Ah, dark blue or black, four door sedan. Licence DRT. That's all I and my driver got."

"And did he follow you home?" Drew finished writing it down and clicked into the system for motor vehicles.

"No, my driver and I pulled a manoeuvre by going to my friend's house. My driver drove away and came back ten minutes later to pick me up in the back alley. The car was there when we left. But it followed us from the club. It pulled away from the club when we left."

"Okay. I'll do a search, but it's not much to go on and then I'll head to my place and grab a bag, then meet you at yours."

"Make sure you're not followed," Remi told him. "And check the CCTV to see if you can get him outside the club."

"We'll have to put in for that, but absolutely. I'll see you later." He ended the call and tapped in the partial licence, receiving 6300 hits in return. He added in navy black four door sedan and saw it narrowed down to 3600. "Jesus Christ," he mumbled and rubbed his face in frustration. "A fucking needle in a fucking haystack."

"What's that, Reilly? Not getting any tonight?" Burrows joked and shut down his computer. "Poor celibate you. Me, I'll be getting plenty." He pulled his coat from the back of his chair and slid it on.

"Good to know you fuck hookers on a Friday night, Burrows," Drew told him. "I'll just try and catch a drug dealer, a murderer, and an arsonist."

Burrows shrugged. "Whatever floats your boat, priest. I'm outta here."

Drew watched him saunter away then saved the search. Until he had more information to go on, there was nothing he could do. Sighing, he logged off, grabbed his jacket, and followed Burrows out the door.

After grabbing an overnight bag and a fresh suit from home, he made his way into Remi's penthouse an hour later.

"Were you followed?" She bolted the door and followed him into the living room. "Dark four door sedan with DRT on the plate."

He set his bags down. "Do you think the DRT stand for Dr Teeth? Did you get the numbers?"

"Well, no. Neither of us did. What about the CCTV?" She helped him out of his jacket and flung it over the back of the couch. "You look worn out."

"I *am* worn out." He slid his arms around her waist and pulled her close. "I'll check the CCTV next week; see if we can get anything to work with, but in the meantime. I need a beer."

Surprised, she leaned back to look into his eyes. "What? You actually *want* to drink now?"

"Yep." He sighed. "This case, this week, this month has just got to me."

"Rex?" She slid out of his arms.

"Fuck that bastard! Don't even mention his name to me." To prove his point, he pulled her back into his arms and kissed her with a passion that surprised them both.

*****

After a passionate weekend, Drew was back at his desk Monday morning scrolling through the CCTV footage. A dark four door sedan did indeed follow Remi's car, but he couldn't make out the driver or licence plate. He groaned and threw his head back, slumping in his chair. "Why can't we get this bastard?"

"We can't get a lot of them, sadly," Richard said, hitting a few keys on his computer. "It sucks when we can't."

"Especially for the victims." Drew moved from slumping in his chair to slumping on his desk. "Merriam Webster died from an overdose, probably from the teeth Teeth handed out. But we can't connect him to any of it. He's not in the system; we don't know his real name. We don't even have a fucking photo of…him…" Drew's head shot up and he quickly called Remi. "Did you ever get a photo of Teeth? I know the surveillance footage doesn't show him, but did you grab—"

"Nope. But you might want to check out social media because there are a lot of pissy little so-called influencers who come through here and they're always taking selfies. You might find something in that."

"Excellent ideas. I'll get on to that. Any hashtags in particular?"

"Just the club's, or the groups that played, hit those tags. They should help."

"Fantastic. Thanks, Rem." He hung up on her and pulled up *The Cavern Club's* social media pages. He scrolled back to the week before Merriam Webster died and carefully wrote down all of the hashtags the club used. He then right clicked and brought up each tag as a new page.

"Reilly, it's not time to browse social media. Do that on your personal time," Waylon said in passing.

"Remi suggested checking the social pages in case Teeth turned up in any photos and I'm checking the tags to see who else posted." Drew's eyes never left the screen.

Waylon mumbled something and back tracked. "Good idea. Found anything?"

"Just started. Richard gave me the idea; Remi cleared it up."

"Good for you Wong, help him out with this." Waylon gave a nod and walked off.

"Where do you want me to go?" Richard brought up Facebook and Twitter on his computer.

"*The Cavern Club*. Hit the hashtags. I'll take Instagram and TikTok, and they have a Pinterest page. Maybe it will be fastest."

"I'll do that." Richard pulled up a tab for Pinterest. "What about the website?"

"Try it, but I don't think they post photos except for bands."

After an hour of meticulous, mind-numbing scrolling,

Drew finally found something. "Here." He right clicked on the photo and made it larger. "Is that him in the background? Ah, fuck it! Let me just check her account." He clicked into the account of the young woman and found a selfie with Teeth clearly in the background. But his face was turned away so they only had a side shot. Drew right clicked it into a new tab and kept scrolling. "That's the only one she's got." He closed the tab and concentrated on the photo. "We have a few faces we could put through face rec but not his. Unless it does side views." He saved the page, made a note of it in the paperwork, and downloaded the image. He sat back, sighed, and rubbed his eyes. "I feel like I've been doing this all day."

"*The Cavern Club's* Facebook and Twitter is clean, but I followed the hashtags like you and found some of them post the same photos across their socials. *All* of their socials, because some of these people have ten accounts each. That's *a lot* of posting."

"Yeah, but they all think they're famous," Drew mocked. "Remi hates them, but knows they bring business in. Even though most of their clientele are forty-five and up."

"First name basis still, huh." Richard grinned. "Gone way past first base, too, I bet. Lucky man." He stretched out his back and noticed John wasn't in. "Wonder where Burrows is. He's not due for a day off."

"All right people, listen up, because we have a problem," Waylon barked as he walked into the room. He noticed two senior officers come in and nodded at them before continuing. "One of our own was found in the carpark of a club, Friday night. His wallet and phone were stolen, along with his keys. It was called in and his body's in the morgue. They only managed to identify him because he'd tattooed his badge number on his wrist as a means of identification. They also found two small marks on his neck, and a lethal dose of drug in his system."

And icy chill slid down Drew's spine and he glanced over his shoulder at Burrow's desk. "Fuck," he whispered.

"That's right, Reilly," Waylon called and Drew noticed all eyes on him. "Detective John Burrows was bitten with those fucking teeth and died of an overdose. Two officers checked his house this morning and found it trashed. We now have a real situation on our hands, people. Let's get to work."

It was all hands on deck, but Drew found a moment to call Remi.

"Fucking hell! He's moved on. But why'd he OD and not you? You had it three times."

"No idea. But it means I'll be busy for a while so stay safe and get yourself a body guard."

"Already organised. Two of my guards are on the job."

"Good. I'll see you when I see you. Stay safe."

"I will. Bye." Remi turned off her phone and shuddered. "Fucking hell. He can't help himself. Two dead that we know of and one's a cop. Thank God Drew's okay." Noticing the time on her wall clock, she grabbed her bag as the intercom buzzed. Remi saw her two body guards standing outside and buzzed them. "I'm on my way down." She left the safety of her apartment, checked the lift before entering, and made it down to the guards who drove her to the club. "Thanks boys. Home at five. But you can help out here."

The carpet was installed, the bar restocked, and the kitchen was filled with fresh food. They just needed the new furniture and *The Cavern Club* was good to go for its grand re-opening.

Chapter 15

Two weeks after the club was set on fire, it re-opened with a party to end all parties.

Skyway was playing on stage, patrons were taking photos and selfies to post to their socials, and there were no fake plastic teeth doing the rounds. And the best thing of all, there was no Dr Teeth and his twelve disciples sitting in the ring. With a lifetime ban, he would be arrested if he turned up.

Remi sighed and sank down on her stool by the bar. It had been a trying couple of weeks, and she was glad it was over. For now. She wasn't reliant on Drew to find Teeth, even though he and half the force were working on finding him and the person who'd bitten John Burrows. Drew had told her the coroner found that the drug was dirty. Cut with another substance. More than likely a knock-off or copycat of the teeth found in and around *The Cavern Club*. And Burrows, despite being in okay physical shape, had a bad reaction to it and collapsed, his heart seizing up and stopping.

Another sigh left her. Ever since that bastard Teeth had come on the scene it was one bad thing after another.

And she hoped he was done with her.

"Looks like everything is going well." Sisco stopped beside her and gazed around the club. "Everyone's back, they're having fun. The band is great and we're at peak capacity."

She nodded along with the music. "Great. What's good about tonight is it's just like the grand opening the first time. We built up a lot of excitement online."

"And it helps that we had a bit of a refurb as well. Spruced the place up a bit." He went behind the bar and poured himself a drink. "You know"— he sipped slowly— "I am yet to see either sexy Rexy, or the delectable detective."

Remi couldn't help but grin. "No idea where Rex is, but he said he'd drop in, and as for Drew, he's working the case but said he'd try and stop by."

"So…" Sisco leaned on the bar beside her. "Which one are you going to pick so I can have the other one?"

"Neither of them are gay," Remi told him. "Bedsides, don't you have a new flavour of the week?"

He pretended to yawn and made a show of patting his mouth. "Boring! More like flavour of the weekend. I'm a free agent. You know I love to roam around."

"Well keep your eyes off my men because I'm into both of them. But I'd sure as hell love to find out what's going on between them."

"Why haven't you?" Sisco sipped his drink and tapped his foot, gazing across the crowd. He saw Rex come through the door. "Oh, my, sexy Rexy just came in."

Remi's gaze moved over to the door and saw Rex notice her. He gave a nod and headed in her direction.

"No, they haven't, but it's clear they knew each other in their late teens or early twenties. And it's all about a girl." Remi slid off the stool. "Keep an eye on things for me. I need to talk to Rex." He found his way over and she grabbed his hand, leading him to her office. She shut the door behind them. "I haven't seen you since the club was on fire. Thank you again for calling it in."

Rex shrugged and shoved his hands into his pockets. "Just doing my duty as a responsible citizen." He hungrily eyed her. "How are you, Rem? You look a little tired."

"Ah…" She stood in front of him and pulled his hands out of his jeans and held them. "I am. I'm fucking exhausted. Between Teeth, knowing drugs were in my club, my club being set on fire, the refurb, being followed, it's a lot and I'm exhausted." She wanted to drown in his chocolate eyes she was so tired and found his hairy exterior clad in a black t-shirt and leather jacket incredibly sexy. She leaned into him. "I can't believe this shit has happened to me. Who the fuck wants to burn down a club? Let alone mine."

"Do you think it was that Teeth creep?" Rex was trying to control his penis, which was straining for release. His heart was thundering and the scent and touch of Remi was making his senses overload with electricity. But for all the physical reaction, and as much as he wanted to rip her clothes off and fuck her, she was seeing his arch enemy, Drew fucking Reilly.

"I certainly do." Remi slid her arms around his waist and rested her head on his shoulder. "That bastard brought those drugs into my club and we caught him.

He knows we're on to him which is why he moved on." She noticed his arms hadn't reciprocated. "Hug me. I need a hug."

Reluctantly, he put his arms around her, but held her lightly, putting no pressure on her body.

"Rex?" She gazed into his eyes. "You can't even hug me? You…" She shook her head. "You're barely responding to me."

He remained frozen, indifferent. "You're fucking another man."

She thought a moment. "Yeah. Just like I did before you. Just like I did after you. There was a hot guitarist in the orgy room."

His brows rose. "You what! You fucked a guitarist in the orgy room after I left? You brazen hussy. You couldn't even wait for me to come back."

"It wasn't just after you left. It was after your text about me missing your dick and your hair. I was sick of servicing myself, so I got him to."

"You couldn't even wait—"

"I bet you didn't!" she protested. "How many days did it take for you to fuck someone else?"

A guttural sound came from his throat as he thought.

"Ah-ha." She nodded. "Thought so. You couldn't even wait."

"A week," he finally said, turning beet red. "Okay, okay, I get it. Neither of us are tied to the other. We were free agents before, and clearly free agents during—"

"And you have no say in who I fuck, just as I have no say in who you fuck."

"But it's Drew fucking Reilly," he growled and turned

away. His hands went to his hips and he let out a deep sigh. "Fucking Drew Reilly," he repeated softly.

"Clearly you two have history you don't want to tell me and that's fine. It's your history not mine. But it just happened that I met him and find you both extremely attractive. In fact, you're a lot alike, physically. Both very hairy, sexy men who have big dicks and know how to manhandle and please a woman. Oh, my God…" Her eyes bugged out of her head and her jaw dropped at the thought she'd just had. "You're not brothers, are you? Is that the problem? You look so much alike."

"What! No, we're not fucking brothers." Rex shook his head and grinned. "Where do you get this shit?"

"Cousins?" Remi looked him up and down. "Same height, build, hair, probably weight."

"No, not fucking cousins, either."

"Well, if you were fucking brothers or cousins that would be a problem because you really shouldn't be doing that with a brother or cousin," Remi quipped.

"Fucking ha-ha!" Rex sniggered. "We're not related at all, but a lot of people thought we were as teenagers, we looked so much alike."

"Ah…as teenagers. So, you knew each other then." Remi tapped her finger to her chin in thought. "Thirteen, fifteen, eighteen?"

"None of your business." Rex pulled her in for a hug. "I'm glad you're okay, Remi. For a moment there, at your place that night, I thought I'd lost you."

Her brows furrowed. "Lost me? Rex, you don't have me. Not in that way. We're just a couple of single people who fucked a bit, and then went off and fucked other single people."

Rex pulled back, heart thundering. "I don't have you?"

"Well, no." She gazed into his eyes. "We're not a couple, you knew that. And we were friends for *four* years before that and are still friends now. We had fun. Didn't I just explain that?" She ran her fingers through his curly beard. "We're just a couple of hot people who fucked around and had fun. And then you fucked off with the band and fucked other people. Why? Did you think we were something more?" She saw doubt in his eyes and some kind of thought analysing going on. "Rex?"

"I'm not sure," he finally said. "I know that once I had you and then those other girls after you, that it wasn't the same. No one holds a candle to you, Remi Steele." Pulling her close, he kissed her. "I've been in love with you for so long and then I had you and I realised while I was away that no one else was you. No one came close. That it's you and only you. But then, I came back and found you fucking someone else, which, in all fairness," he conceded with a wave of a hand, "I had done too. But that wasn't the problem. The problem was who the fuck you were with. Fucking," he growled, "Drew fucking Reilly."

"Someone mention my name?"

Rex and Remi stared at Drew standing in the open doorway in stunned silence until Rex pulled away.

"Drew! You made it. Fantastic. Welcome to the grand re-opening of *The Cavern Club*. Drinks are on the house. Enjoy yourself. Have you found Teeth yet?" Remi saw the dark expression on his face. His eyes looked set for murder as they flared at Rex. "Drew?"

"What the fuck was going on?" he said, gripping the door handle, using it as an anchor for his anger. His gaze finally moved to Remi. "Remi?"

"Ah…" She tilted her head. "We were just talking about the club and how long we've known each other. Only four years to your twenty-five plus."

"We haven't known each other for twenty-five years. We haven't seen each other since then," Drew said through gritted teeth.

"And it didn't end well." Rex sighed. "I'm surprised we're in the same town after all these years. Drew, been a long time."

"Not long enough," Drew growled. "Remi, I thought you were done with this person. After he turned up on your doorstep and threw the tantrum he did, just like a child. I told you what I did for a reason."

Frowning, Remi studied Drew's face. "Rex called in the fire and then called me. I'm grateful for that. We've known each other for four years, Drew. I'm not just throwing that friendship away. He's brought a lot of bands to this club; it helps make them famous and the club the most wanted place to be. I'm not throwing away a friendship because he happens to be your ex-whatever." She glanced from him to Rex. "You two *really* look a lot alike. You sure you're not related?"

"Why the fuck would I want to be related to him? Look, Remi, if it's me you want then you don't get him. You don't get both of us. It's him or me," Drew declared. "Make a choice." He walked out and slammed the door behind him.

"He always was the dramatic type," Rex murmured.

"Oh, please," Remi scoffed. "*You're* the dramatic one with your leather and studs and grunty motorbike. Fucking hell." She ran her hands through her hair and let herself fall onto the couch. "I don't do well with demands. Never did."

"He's not wrong, though." Rex sighed and placed his hands on his hips. "Rem, he's right. It's him or me. You know I love you, and after being with you and then those other women, I know no one else compares to you and I want you. We could make a great power couple." He sat beside her. "Think about it. Remi Steele and Rex Titus, the power couple of the music industry. Remi and Rex. Ah, see, that got a smile out of you."

"Sounds great, but why can't you boys play nice? I want you both."

"You can't have both, Remi." He shook his head. "You just can't. Me or him. A hot band manager, or a boring old strait-laced dramatic detective."

"I'm a free agent, Rex." Her hand slid over his leg to his crotch and massaged him to an erection, which didn't take long. "I'll fuck who I want, when I want."

A guttural groan escaped him, and he slid down. "Fuck Remi. No fair."

She unzipped his jeans and pulled them down, along with his briefs. "Yes, Rex. Very fair," she said, before mounting him.

*****

Drew stormed out of the club and fumed around the block until he found himself at the back entrance. He took a breath, and pulled out a small flashlight from his jacket pocket, beginning a fresh search in case he found any evidence, especially any teeth or drugs. But after a sweep of the alley, he found nothing and put his torch away. He sighed and ran his left hand through his hair, and without thinking, punched the wall with his right.

"Fuck," he growled and waved his hand to lessen the pain. "Fucking hell. Fucking Remi in Rex's arms when I found her. What the fuck! After *everything* I told her, how I was falling in love with her and was going to fight for her. Yeah, right." Drew shook his head. "I'm really fighting for her. It's him or me. Fucking hell. What was I fucking thinking?" He shook his hand and flexed it. Nothing broken, that he could tell, but his heart was tearing into pieces. *Fucking Remi Steele. Why did I have to go and fall in love with you? Why did you have to know Rex? Why did I have to go and make a move and get you into bed, but fucking hell you're an incredible woman?*

The sigh left from deep within his gut, and full of heartbreak and tears, he allowed decades worth of pain out of its jail cell.

*****

"You know, Remi, you really shouldn't do that to a man when you're also fucking his enemy." Rex placed his left arm behind his head and stretched out on the couch. His right hand trailed up and down Remi's naked side, causing little shivers.

"You two need to fuck each other and get over it."

Remi buried herself in the forest of fur on his chest. "You're both so much alike physically; it's kinda creepy and scary. Maybe you're twins and just don't know."

"Ha-ha, funny little thing ain't ya." His fingers applied pressure to either side of her spine as they slid down. "But I'll say it again, Remi, he's not wrong. You can't have both of us. It's me or him."

"Why not?" She shivered as his fingers came back up. "As I told you before, just like you, I'm a free agent, I can see and fuck and talk to whoever I want. I don't need no man's permission," she reminded him.

"Yeah…" A long pause. "Including me." His fingers slid back down. "And if it were anyone but Drew—"

"Fucking Reilly. Yeah, yeah," she muttered. "So you said." Remi glanced at the clock and jumped up with a start. "Fuck! It's nearly eleven. The band's on again in a minute." She pulled on her clothes and picked up Rex's, ready to throw them at him, but the sight of his furry body spread out on her couch was incredibly tempting. "Ugh," she growled and flung his clothes at him. "Get dressed. We've got an hour to go."

"You closing at twelve?" Rex sat up and found his shorts.

"No, but I'm leaving at twelve. Sisco will run the place until two and lock up. When you're ready, come and party." She left him to dress and hastened into the club to see Skyway run out on stage for their second hour long set. They were playing their latest hit in seconds and encouraged the crowd to sing along.

Rex joined her and asked the bartender for a beer, pulling Remi to her feet to dance. With a beer in one hand, and Remi in the other, he was happy.

She laughed as he twirled and dipped her, and slapping him on his denim-clad voluptuous backside, walked off the see her patrons.

At twelve, Remi bid adieu to Sisco and collected her bag from the office. Rex met her on her way out and hugged and kissed her goodbye.

"You staying," she asked.

"For a bit longer, yeah. But if you want me to walk you out, I can do that."

"No. I've got my guards and my driver. I'll be fine."

"Okay." His thumb slid over her cheek and he sighed. "I love you, Remi. Think about what's been said tonight."

Her breathing became laboured and a feeling of suffocation came over her. "Whatever problem you two have, sort it out amongst yourselves, Rex. It's very clearly not about me."

"But that's just it, Remi Steele," he murmured and stepped closer. "It *is* about you."

She made a scoffing sound and swiped his hand away. "Sure, Rex, sure. I'll see you when I see you." She turned, waved to Sisco and her guards, and walked down the hallway to the alley door. A guard opened the door and she stepped out into the glow of the security lights they'd turned on for her exit. She turned right for her chauffeured car and a scream tore into the night behind her, then three gunshots, and her guards swarmed her and raced her to the back door of the car.

"Wait," she yelled. "Who was that?" Hiding behind the open car door they turned to see Drew standing over a prone figure in black talking into his phone. "Drew? What's going on? Who is that?" She shoved her guards aside and rushed over to him, staring down at the figure. "Is that Teeth?" She bent down to remove the balaclava.

"No." Drew grabbed her arm and pulled her back as he finished the call. "Don't touch anything," he warned them. "The police are on their way and we'll take the body in." He pulled a rubber glove from his jacket pocket and carefully pulled up the balaclava to reveal the face of a young red-haired woman. Not Teeth. He set the face covering back. "We'll need photos, evidence, especially that knife." He pointed to the long butchers' implement lying a few feet from the woman.

"Fucking hell," Remi murmured and covered her mouth in shock. Her gaze turned from the body to Drew. "Was she after me? Was she going to kill me? Did you see her? Why are you in my alley? Why was *she* in my alley? Why?"

"All very good questions and no doubt her intent was to harm you, if not kill you." Drew pulled her a few feet away. "But you're fine. I had my eye on her, and when I saw the knife, I took her down. You're fine."

"Fucking hell." Remi's body started to shake. "Fucking hell."

"It's okay." Drew pulled her close to stop the spasms. "You're okay. She's dead you're okay."

"You saved me," she murmured against his chest.

"Just repaying the favour," he replied, hearing sirens in the distance. "You saved me, I saved you, and now my colleagues are nearly here and I need to tell them what happened."

"What *did* happen?" She pulled out of his embrace. "Why are you in the alley? You stormed out hours ago."

"I, ah…" He hesitated a moment. "Went for a walk around the block to cool off and found myself back here. I thought I'd wait to see if anyone turned up, or anything suspicious happened, and by the way, those security lights"— he pointed up to them— "need to be on the entire night while the club is open. It will make it easier to see people coming and going on the CCTV."

She nodded in agreement. "Yeah, yeah. But why were you here for so long? And *where* were you?" She glanced around as the police turned up. "Were you sitting on a bin? What?"

"Hiding behind one, actually." Drew wasn't about to disclose what he'd been doing back there, but in the midst of his cryfest he'd seen a shadow approach and watched it. The closer it got, the more the outline appeared, and he's seen the glint of the knife and knew a person was up to no good. Things became a little complicated when the driver had come down the alley and the lights had been turned on, but he'd still managed to step out of the line of site of the perp.

Richard Wong walked up to them and saw the body. "Everyone okay?"

"Well, we are," Drew said. "Not so much her." He nodded at the figure.

"Her? You checked?" Richard asked.

"Lifted the balaclava. A red-haired woman, young, I'd say late teens, early twenties. She'll probably have teeth marks on the neck."

"And I take it the knife is hers?" Richard raised a brow. "How convenient to bring your own weapon."

"Very," Drew remarked dryly. "Can we get the interviews happening so Ms Steele can get home? She was the intended victim. And was on her way home when this happened."

"Yeah, sure." Richard waved several officers over and told them to interview the two guards and the driver. "I'll interview Ms Steele and you"— he pointed at Drew— "will need to write out your statement and hand over your gun."

They went about the protocols with Richard interviewing Remi who promised to send surveillance footage over that night. She rang Sisco, instead of going inside, and told him to get it sent over. When he found out what was happening, he bolted out the back door, but Remi brushed him away and told him to get back to work as he'd see it all on the footage. He went back inside, locking the doors behind him.

Remi thanked everyone and finally went home; knowing Drew or Rex wouldn't be following. *They both need to sort their shit out,* she thought as she slumped back in the car. *Whatever the fuck is going on, it's nothing to do with me. Even though it seems to include me. But either way, I'm hot for both and want both, but both clearly don't want each other.*

Chapter 16

It was three days before she saw Drew again. He showed up on her doorstep in jeans, boots, and a black t-shirt, casually leaning against the door frame.

She looked him up and down and instantly tingled. "Hey."

He did the same to her. "Hey."

"Here to apologise?"

His left brow rose. "Apologise for what?"

The spicy scent of his cologne wafted into her nostrils and made her sigh in contentment. "Your bad behaviour in my club the other night."

"*My* bad behaviour." He straightened and pointed to his chest. "*Mine?*"

"Yes." She nodded. "Demanding that I choose between the two of you when I've only known you a month or so and have only spent a few nights with each of you. Incredibly arrogant on your part. We're not even dating."

"Dating?" His brows lowered. "Whaddya mean, dating? Wait, what is going on? I just came here to let you what what's happening—"

"Oh, and not to see me?" she countered. "We aren't

dating, but you know that. We've fucked, a lot, and it's great. But so had Rex and I, and I'm not dating either one of you, so what was with the whole *it's him or me* garbage?"

"Ah…" He studied her, perplexed at the turn of conversation. "Of course, I came to see you," he said slowly. "I also came to tell you what's happening and to say I'm sorry for demanding anything of you." He shoved his hands into his pockets and saw her soften. "I was being a bit of a dick the other night. Rex and I have a long history and it's not about you. And you shouldn't be in the middle of it."

"Rex said I am. And it is. How is that? *Why* is that?" She didn't really expect an answer, as Rex couldn't even give her one. Right now, all she knew was she wanted Drew badly. She grabbed him by his t-shirt and pulled him inside, locking the door on the outside world. "Look, I don't fucking care what your beef with Rex is, but I ain't it," she told him, watching the expressions fly over his face. "I'm extremely attracted to both of you and I enjoy being with both of you. If you want to fuck that up, go right ahead. But I'm not staying in the middle of things. I'm way outside of it. If you're still interested and know you fucked up last night, then stay the night and show me that you're a secure, emotionally stable man who doesn't mind having casual fun with a woman who's also having casual fun with another man."

A slow grin slid across his lips. "I do want you, Remi Steele." He took her hands and pulled her into his arms. Her arms slid around his neck and his lips found their way onto hers. "I'm sorry I acted like an insecure dick.

We are grown adults in our forties, not children in our teens." Another kiss. "I apologise for being a dick and demanding anything of you. I know you are your own woman, and you'll see who you want to see whether we like it or not."

"Exactly." She pressed her breasts into his chest. "And I want to see you right now. How's the case? You said you came to update me."

He nodded. "Yeah. It's ah…going."

"That's rough." She smoothed her hands through his hair, which was slightly damp and curly, down the back of his head and around to his face where her fingers slid through his beard.

"Yeah, yeah, it is." He bowed his head so his forehead touched hers, resting a moment and closing his eyes. "We can't find Teeth, and we don't know who killed John. We only know he went into the club, came out later and collapsed. A couple of teens saw an opportunity and robbed him, then went and trashed his house."

"You found them?" she asked softly, stroking his face.

"Yeah, we have. They were on parole for another crime and confessed when we showed them the footage."

"Did Teeth have anything—?"

"No." He shook his head. "They said they came across him. They had nothing to do with Teeth."

"Bugger!"

"Yeah…bugger."

"You want to stay?"

Opening his eyes, he looked into hers and nodded.

*****

In the morning, Drew went back to his place to shower and change and headed to the station for another day of drudgery. They were no closer to catching Teeth or the killer, and he also had to deal with Rex which he didn't want to do. But for the sake of Remi's heart, he had to.

*****

That night at the club, Rex knocked on the office door and entered before she could say anything.

"I could have been naked," she complained, closing one file and opening another.

"That's what I was hoping for." He grinned and closed the door behind him.

"Bullshit!" she exclaimed. "You just wanted to see if I was fucking anyone other than you. Probably, specifically, Drew." She signed her name on multiple papers and closed the folder before looking up. He'd been silent after that comment, and was now standing uncertainly. "What's wrong? Was I wrong?"

His head shook slowly. "No…not really…no." He shifted from one foot to another until he just paced around the room, looking at certifications and photos on the walls, opened the fridge and pulled out a beer, cracked it open, noticed the Murphy bed was up, sculled back a few mouthfuls, looked at the awards on the wall behind the desk, kept moving until he came to the couch, where he slumped onto it and settled in.

"Have a nice walk?" she quipped and opened another folder. She read the file, signed her name, and closed it. "You know, Rex, there's clearly something wrong with you and you're moving around—"

"No there's not." He took a swig of beer.

"Yes, there clearly is," she went on, leaning back in her chair to watch him. "I don't think I've ever seen you so mopey. In fact, I don't think I've ever *seen you* mopey. Rough and gruff and sexy as hell, but not mopey."

That got a slight grin out of him. "Nah…you're probably right." He finished off the bottle, placed it on the side table and put his arm behind his head, using it for a pillow. "I don't know what's got into me."

"Bullshit! You were fine when you walked in, but the moment I mentioned Drew—"

"I don't wanna hear his name." Rex waved a hand in protest. "Nope. Don't wanna hear it."

"He came over last night."

"What!" Rex exploded off the couch, slammed his hands on her desk and leaned in close. "He did what?"

She arched a brow and tried not to laugh. "Well… that certainly got some heated action out of you. Yes. And he stayed the night, too."

"What the fuck, Remi?" Rex slammed the desk and started back and forth in front of it. "How could you do that? How could you let him come over and then let him stay?"

"He came all right," she murmured, remembering the orgasms they'd both enjoyed.

"Fucking hell, Remi. How could you?"

"Calm the fuck down, Rex. I fucked you the other night on the couch." She pointed to it. "And I fucked Drew last night in my bed, just like I did you months ago. Besides, he came over to update me on the case, *and* apologise for being a dick the other night. Are you going to apologise for being a dick now?"

"What? I…" He stopped; brows furrowed. "I'm… not."

"Bullshit!" she scoffed. "Of course you are, and I'll tell you what I told him. We're in our forties, act like it. Now…" She pulled another file towards her. "If you're not going to act your age, get out. Otherwise, what did you actually come in for?"

"Um…" He faltered, and took a moment. "Just wanted to see you. See how you were, are, if you're okay. I heard about the other night. Some woman tried to attack you?"

That stopped her. "That got around fast."

"Yeah, Sisco, I think. But I saw the cops when I left. You okay?" He shoved his hands into his pockets, nerves suddenly hitting him. Which was unusual, since Rex Titus had never been nervous in his entire life.

She sighed, watching his body language. "I'm fine. But what's your real reason for being here?"

"Jesus fucking Christ, Remi. Can't a guy just ask a friend if she's okay after being attacked?" blasted out of him. "Fucking hell. I'm not on trial for anything."

"Are you on drugs?" she demanded. "High on something, because you're swinging faster than a fucking pendulum. What is going on, Rex?" She pushed herself out of her seat and stalked around the desk. "Pull your fucking head out and get over yourself, and tell me what the fuck is wrong. Oh…" Her eyes widened. "You're jealous."

"What! Fuck no!" He viciously waved a hand and stormed around the room. "Why the fuck would I be jealous—"

"Because I'm fucking both of you."

He stopped, growled deep and guttural, grabbed her by the arms and pulled her to him. Their lips met with fiery passion and within moments they were naked and pulling down the Murphy bed to fuck like two crazy animals for a few short moments. Their cries were heard to those only in the office.

"Fuck you, Rex," she gasped. "You *are* jealous."

"*Of course I fucking am*, Remi. I want you to myself. I don't want to share you."

When they were done, Remi dressed and went into the club. Another Night, one of the top local bands was singing *Another Night, Another Club*, a slow rock ballad from their current album, *Segue*. They were going for a rockier sound with the new music and it seemed to be paying off. But that could also be down to Rex's management.

"Sound good? They've been working on this new sound for months." Rex stood beside her watching the band on stage.

"They do." She nodded in agreement. "You've got a good band there, Rex. Go and look after them, and I'll look after my patrons." She moved off and greeted acquaintances, old friends, and former record company execs she'd once worked with, before strolling along the mezzanine to meet more. When all had what they needed, she moved past Rex who was standing on the ring's steps watching the band, to make sure her private guests in their private rooms were also enjoying themselves. When she saw they were, she returned to the bar and sat on her stool beside it.

"Well, if it isn't Remi Steele."

Remi's head snapped to the right and she saw a slim man, no more than late twenties with short brown hair. "Yes?"

"I'm such a huge fan of yours, Ms Steele. You *and* your club." He reached for her hand to shake it and when she reciprocated, he clasped it between both of his. "It's such an honour to meet you. I have every cd, still, and had posters on my wall."

"That's nice," she said, getting a naggy little feeling. "A lot of fans did."

"Oh, I'm so much more than a fan. I'm an admirer." He drew her hand to his lips and kissed it. "I am so incredibly humbled and honoured to meet you."

She pulled her hand from his and frowned. Fans were normally respectful, but this was bordering on creepy. "That's nice." She noted the black turtleneck and pants, and paler than pale skin. "I hope you're enjoying yourself, and tell your friends about it. Word of mouth is important."

"Oh, very important," he agreed. "I'm in business myself, and it would not have succeeded without word of mouth. Can I get a photo?"

"A what? Oh…sure." She plastered a fake smile on her face as he stood beside her to take a photo of the two of them. His head was right beside hers and she detected the faint whiff of citrus. He took several before moving away.

"Thank you so much for that, Ms Steele, I'll definitely tell my friends about *The Cavern Club* in case they haven't already been."

"Great, you do that." She gave a slight nod of her

head as Rex interrupted.

"Rem, dance?" He held out his hand, gave the kid a side-eye, and escorted her to the dance floor, taking her into his arms. "Who the fuck was that twat?"

"Some creepy influencer, I think." Remi put her face close to Rex's so she could watch the man over Rex's shoulder. "He's still standing at the bar watching, and I got a creepy feeling when he was talking."

"Creepy how?" Rex slid his arms around her and sighed deeply, resting his head on her shoulder.

"Like he was a greasy little weirdo who was hitting on me." She watched him. "And that I knew him somehow."

"From where?"

"Don't know. But with everything else going on, I guess I need to be careful." She watched the guy order a drink, his back to her, but she sensed he was watching her in the reflection of the glass above it. Sisco was also at the bar sipping his drink. "Okay, I'm weirded out and need to get out of here." She stepped out of Rex's arms.

"Let's get out of here," he suggested. "My place?"

"You have the band; you need to be here. I don't. I'm gonna head out back." The music was giving her a headache on top of the gut clenches that her nerves were giving her. There was something about the guy that creeped her out. "I need to go home. Bye, Rex." She kissed him on the cheek and headed for the office, passing Sisco and flashing her eyes wide as a signal. She closed the hall door behind her and walked into the office. She was collecting her bag and putting her files away when Sisco walked in.

"I've locked the hall door. What's up?"

"I'm leaving because that guy at the bar is giving me the creeps, so make sure to lock up tonight after closing."

"Will do, boss. I'll get the boys."

"I'll call my driver." Remi called to let him know she was leaving and met her guards in the hallway. "It's an early night for me, boys. Let's go." They exited into the alley and into the car with no issues, and fifteen minutes later Remi was locked securely in her penthouse apartment, wondering why the creep in the club had hit a nerve.

Chapter 17

After an uneventful few days and nights, Remi got a call late Saturday night from Sisco.

"I gotta go, Remi. I don't feel good. My stomach's gurgling. I've had diarrhea twice."

"Don't want to know," she said. "Can you wait until I get in? I have to get my driver, my guards."

"I'm about to collapse and end up in the ER, Remi."

She heard gurgling sounds and then what sounded like vomiting. "Fucking hell," she muttered, and waited a few moments, hearing the toilet flush and the tap come on.

"Now I'm vomiting," he finally said. "I feel so sick, Remi. I can't close up."

She sighed and gave a little growl. "Okay. Hang on until I get there. Tell a couple of guards to meet me in the ally. I'll park there."

"Will do, ah, ugh."

She ended the call to save herself from the sounds he was making, and freshened up, changed clothes, and grabbed her handbag. It was ten on a Saturday night, her night now ruined. She left the penthouse, rode the elevator down to the basement car park and got into her Suzuki Grand Vitara. It was nowhere near her Lamborghini in style and comfort, which sat beside the Suzuki with a locked cover on it. But tonight was not the night for flash.

Within fifteen minutes she was parking in the alley, and her guards met her and escorted her in. She took one look at Sisco in the private bathroom and ordered him to the hospital. "You look like shit, you smell like shit, and you probably feel like shit."

He groaned, clutching his stomach as tightly as he was clutching the toilet bowl.

Her groan matched his and she turned to her guards. "Can you get him to the hospital? And if he vomits, or shits in your car, he'll pay for the cleaning when he's better."

"And if it doesn't come clean or just ends up stinking of said vomit and shit?" the guard asked.

"Then he'll pay for a new car," she replied and flinched at the sound of him vomiting. "Take a bucket and put him in the front seat."

The guards nodded grimly and each took one of Sisco's arms and hauled him to his feet. Remi handed them a bucket and they made it all the way to the car before he vomited again, all over the pavement out the back of the club in the staff carpark.

"Ugh. Get him out of here," Remi groaned and locked the back door. She took a breath and made her way back to the office where she left a big sign in red sharpie for the cleaning crew to clean the bathroom because of Sisco's vomit and shit. Both of which she underlined three times each. She taped it to the bathroom door and closed it against the smell that was making *her* want to vomit. "Ugh." She settled into her couch and waited out the next three hours with Netflix on the big screen TV.

She was awakened by the crew coming in to clean and a check of her watch said it was 2:30 Sunday morning. "Oh, God, time to lockup. Fuck. I fell asleep. Okay ladies, read the sign." She pointed to it. "And wear masks. He made a mess." They exchanged amused glances and pulled out masks.

Remi left them to it and walked into the club. Multiple crews were vacuuming and cleaning on all levels and in all rooms. Patrons were normally out by 2:20 but a few stragglers often had to be ushered out after that time.

"Check the toilets, the basement, the band rooms. Check all rooms. No one leaves until all staff are accounted for and everyone's fine," she said into her walkie-talkie so that all staff members heard. Remi knew it would be another hour before that happened so began her personal check of the dance floor and seating areas. Objects were often found, from escaped earrings, to broken necklaces, to house keys, to items of clothing. All and sunder were often found at the end of a night. People knew how to party and party hard they did. Not even realising they'd lost anything until a few days later when they called up to see if it had been found. Times were arranged for pickups, and many items found their way back to the owners, but some didn't and the lost and found box was filling up.

The dance floor held no secrets, but on her way

around the ground floor seating area she found a few costume beads, not doubt from a broken bracelet, and a used condom. "Jesus fucking Christ," she muttered, and then found a fake pink fingernail.

"Ms Steele, your office is done," a cleaner called, before she pushed the trolley down the hall.

Remi hurried to it and deposited the beads and nail into the lost and found box, chuckling at the assortment of items before grabbing a drink from the fridge. *I'd rather be at home in bed with Drew. Or Rex. Or both.* She smiled at the thought and sat behind her desk ready to go over the check list for the night. But what confronted her sent chills down her spine.

In the middle of her desk sat a pale translucent set of fake teeth.

"Fucking hell!" She shoved her chair back, thrust up, and raced to her bag where she grabbed her phone and dialled Drew's number.

"Please leave a message and I'll get back to you as soon as I can."

The beep sounded and Remi yelled, "Drew, Teeth was here at the club. He left a set of teeth on my desk. He must have done it after the cleaners because I came in after them so he must still be here…now…" A cold prickling creeped up the back of her neck and she slowly turned to the doorway to the hall. "Fuck!"

"Hello, Ms Steele." Dr Teeth stepped into the office and closed the door. "It's high time that we make acquaintances again."

Her hand fell to her side in shock. Her pounding heart and racing blood made her dizzy. And damn, she was scared. "How the fuck did you get in?" she whispered. Seeing he wore the same outfit he had every night in the club. Black turtleneck, jeans, long overcoat, fingerless gloves, old army boots, and a dirty top hat, and those God damn gold fucking vampire teeth. But she also picked up on something else. He didn't stink like he usually did, of moth balls, body odour, and garbage. But a faint whiff of spice.

"I came in the usual way, like everybody else. I just stayed a little longer, hidden away so no one would see me just so I could talk to you." He made small steps towards her, but she backed up until she was behind her desk.

"Get the fuck out. You're banned. For life. And I've called the police that you're here."

"Ah, yes. Detective Reilly." Teeth smirked. "Your lover. Is he as good in bed as I imagine?"

Her brows furrowed; her nostrils flared. The adrenaline kicked in. "Fuck off! Where do you get off asking that? Where the fuck do you get off killing people in my club? In any club. Where the fuck do you get off sending two of your goons to try and kill me? Because guess what, dickhead, *they're both dead.*" Without thinking, she threw her phone at him, and while he ducked, she ran around the other side of the desk and flung open the door. She grabbed the door to the club and turned the handle, but it wouldn't budge. What the fuck! They locked it from the other side." She banged her fists on it and kicked it, but a hand on her shoulder stopped her. With a quick glance over her shoulder, she scowled at Teeth. With both hands, she pushed him away and ran for the door to the alley, through it, and ran to the driver's side of her car to jump in, but it was locked and she didn't have the keys. "Fuck it!" she cried in frustration and saw Teeth in the doorway holding up her car keys.

"Looking for these?" he gloated, swinging them back and forth. "You'll need to do better than that Remi Steele."

Fire flared through her, bringing anger and hatred with it. With a loud screaming growl, she raced around the car and straight into him. She saw his eyes widen as she rammed into him, knocking them both to the ground. She landed a few punches to his face, scrambled for her keys, and climbed to her feet. Then she was off, racing back to the driver's side, unlocking the car, pulling open the door. But he was on her, clawing her, pulling her away. She spun away from it, into the wall, dropping the keys.

He came at her; she back kicked him in the gut, stumbled to her feet, yelled for help, grabbed her keys, and put the ignition key between her fingers, poking him in the eye. Her leg kicked out, and knocked his out from under him. She ran for the car. He grabbed a brick from the ground and threw it at her. It hit the car and set off the alarm.

With another growl and an adrenaline rush, she lunged at him and smashed her right foot into his gut. He rolled away, both arms wrapped around him and he managed to get to his feet.

They stood gasping for breath, nostrils flared. Two bulls ready to horn each other to death.

He ran at her, she ducked, but he grabbed her by the

arms and shoved her into the front fender of the car. She crumpled with a groan, but brought her boot heel down on his shin. He collapsed in front of her and she struggled to her feet, staggered around the front of the car, trying to get back in the club. He took her down from behind, both hands on her shoulders; he forced her face first into the ground and bit into her neck.

She screamed, "You fucking bastard," and clawed at his face, grabbing onto his hair as he pulled away, holding that hair as he stood and snatched up his hat. His phone beeped and he checked the time. A sly grin spread ear to ear. "It's time to say goodbye, Ms Steele."

She managed to look up at him to see short hair on his head and a wig in her hand, and him snatching up her car keys and climbing into her car. With a honk of the horn, he drove down the alley.

Remi struggled to get to her feet. Her head was woozy, her blood pulsating through her body. "Doc," she croaked, and managed to get through the doorway. "Doc. Where the fuck is everyone? Help," her voice louder but not a full yell. "Help. Doc." She stumbled down the hall into doc's office. "Help, anyone, help. Where is everyone?" Her head exploded in pain and her world went black.

*****

"Remi," Drew yelled over the cacophony of sound reverberating around him. "Remi. Where are you? Remi." Dread was beating his stomach into a bloody pulp. He'd heard her message at the same time the call had come in and knew Teeth was behind it. They'd mobilised and arrived to find the club blown to smithereens and blasting a fire as hot as a furnace. The explosion had also damaged surrounding buildings and the SES, and fire service was trying their best to deal with the mayhem.

"Remi," he yelled, cupping his hands around his mouth as a megaphone. "Remi, can you hear me?" The smoke overtook him, bending him into a coughing fit that watered his eyes and sinuses. "Fucking hell." He wiped his shirt sleeve across his eyes. A bottle of water was shoved in front of his face. "Thanks." He cracked it open, stood up to drink it and saw the person who'd handed it to him. Rex.

"Where is she? Was she in there? What the fuck's happened, Drew? Was it that bastard, Teeth? She doesn't work Saturday nights." A hand went through his hair and he stared forlornly at the burning debris.

Drew stared hard at him. "How did you get past the tape? Past the cops who're on crowd control. You need to get out of here."

"What?" Rex snapped, his attention back on Drew. "And let you find her and deal with all of this? You couldn't find a fucking needle in a fucking haystack, *cop.*"

Drew swung his right fist into Rex's face, and when he stumbled back, he pushed him to the ground. "Get the fuck out of here, Rex. You have no fucking clue what you're talking about."

Stunned, but not down for long, Rex touched his fingers to his mouth. Blood had been drawn and he wasn't about to let Drew get away with it. He climbed to his feet. "Remi's not even in there. She has Saturday's off." He glanced at the fire. "But the staff would've been clearing up."

"Which is why we're bringing bodies out in bags." Drew's clenched teeth made his jaw ache. "But I happen to know Remi was here because she called to say Teeth *was* here."

"What!" Rex's mouth opened in shock. "She…but she…" He glanced down the alley. "Her car's not there."

"What? What car? She has a driver. We found no cars in the alley."

"Not if she's called in last minute," Rex said. "If that happens, she drives herself and parks in the alley right outside the door. Are you saying there was no car there?"

They both stared down the alley and while there was a tonne of debris, it was clear there was no car.

"Richard," Drew yelled, looking around for his co-worker. "Richard?" After finding him, he waved him over. "Can you try and get the CCTV footage—"

"All ready on it. But we'd need Ms Steele or her manager to access the offsite servers. We're trying for the other street cameras as well."

"Remi drove herself to the club and called me about Teeth being here, but her car's not in the alley, so if she didn't leave then he might have drove off in it."

"What! Well, if she didn't leave then she's…" Richard looked towards the fire.

Drew spun on Rex. "Who does she fill in for? Sisco?"

Rex nodded. "If he had to leave or couldn't work."

"So, he's out there somewhere alive and we need to find him. Do you have his number?"

"No, just Remi's and the club's."

Drew pulled out his phone and dialled Remi's number. Nothing. Next, he called the club's number. Nothing. It didn't even go to another number. "Richard, can you track down Sisco's number?"

"Detective, phone call for you," a sergeant handed a phone to him. "Says he's the manager of the club and needs to speak to you."

Drew snatched the phone up. "Sisco? What the fuck happened? Is Remi in the club? Why aren't you in there? When did you leave? What the fuck is going on?"

"One thing at a time, detective. I'm on my death bed in the hospital, oh, I probably shouldn't have said that. I came down with food poisoning and called Remi to come in. That was about ten. She sent me off here and I've been here since. I saw what happened on my fellow patient's TV and knew I had to call you."

"Did she park her car in the alley?" Drew turned away from the fire and stuck his finger in his other ear to hear. "What type of car does she have?"

"She does. A silver Grand Vitara Suzuki. A few years old. Have you found it?"

"The car's gone. We don't know if she left or the car was stolen. We need to get the surveillance footage."

"Sorry, detective. There's not too much I can do from here on my own. But if one of your detectives can bring a laptop to me, I can login and send it to you."

"Okay, great. I'll send Wong and a couple of uniforms. Which hospital?" Once he finished, he gave the phone back to the sergeant and turned to Wong. "Get over to *Memorial Hospital*, third floor, ward thirteen, and take a laptop and a couple of uniforms. Sisco can log into the system that way and send the footage. We also need to get uniforms to Remi's apartment building to see if she went home. And if not, put out an APB on her car, a silver Grand Vitara Suzuki."

Richard nodded and took off, waving to a couple of uniformed officers on the way.

"So, if she's not at home and her car's been stolen, then she's in there." Rex breathed out and rushed a gasp of air back in. His heart palpitated and he started his breathing exercises to regulate his body that was freaking out at the situation.

"You need to get the fuck out and let us do our job," Drew told him and waved a uniform over.

"I need to do anything, hey—" Rex pulled his arm away from the cop's grasp. "Get your fucking hands off me."

"Get him out of here," Drew said. "And don't let him back." Now was not the time to deal with Rex Titus and his anger issues. He needed to find Remi. He saw the police chief and ran over. "Chief, when can I get in there? Remi's in there."

"Steele? The owner? Damn." He spoke into his communication device. "Be on the lookout for Remi Steele, the owner. She's in there. Where," he asked Drew. "Anywhere in particular?"

"No idea. Possibly her office towards the back of the club." Drew wiped the sweat from his brow and glanced at the alley, seeing a lone figure in black sneaking up from the other end. "Fucking Rex. Chief, I need to go in. Someone's sneaking in and he could get into trouble."

"No can do. The fire's still raging and the floor's blown to bits. From what we can gather, the kitchen blew the place to smithereens."

Drew shook his head to clear the brain fog. "The kitchen's in the basement at the back end of the club, as you know, the rest of it shouldn't have collapsed." He looked at the club and saw half the walls standing and nothing else. "That was done by something else. But either way, Rex just sneaked into the club and we need to get him out."

"Then my men will do that," the chief reprimanded. "It's not your job, detective; now let me get back to mine." He turned his back on Drew and walked away.

Undeterred, Drew kept an eye out for the perfect time to get down the alley. Inching his way closer to the tape, making sure no one was looking his way, when the chance came, he ducked under the tape and bolted down the alley and over the rubble, stopping where the door would have been. But there was nothing but a gaping hole.

"Fucking hell," he muttered, and took a deep breath, which was not a good idea. He choked on the ash and scent of fire and covered his mouth with his shirt tail before precariously picking his way through the doorway, keeping an eye out for crumbling walls and collapsing floors. Half of which was already gone.

"Rex," he yelled, choking on the smoke. "Rex! Where the fuck are you?" He made his way to where the office was, or used to be, and found Rex picking through the rubble yelling Remi's name. The walls were gone, as was half the floor.

"She here? You shouldn't be," he yelled. "Get the fuck out, Rex."

Rex's head popped up from behind a pile of rubble. "Not until I find Remi." He went back to moving blocks of rock and brick.

"That's not your job." Drew picked his way through, kicking aside bricks and plaster. His feet hit something that beeped and he stepped back, pushing aside the rubbish around it to find Remi's phone almost dead, but beeping an alarm.

"I found her bag." Rex stood up, showing her bag like a prize he'd won. He went through it. "Her car keys are gone. So's her phone."

"I've got the phone." Drew stood and waved it at Rex. "So, her bag's here, her phone's here. Her car and keys are not."

"But she could be so I need to keep looking." Rex zipped up her bag and flung it across his body. "I'm going to find her if it's the last thing I do."

"And it probably will be," Drew muttered. "Just be fucking careful." He made his way back to what was the hallway and saw the door to the club hanging off one hinge on what was left of the right-side wall. The bolt locked from the other side. There was a gaping hole in the floor, where the entire dance floor was blinking in the basement. The stage had collapsed on top of it and the mezzanine level had smashed down to the ground floor. The Golden Ring survived and sat where it always had. To the left, the bar was gone as were the private rooms along the hallway that now stood exposed. The rooms were gone, the hallway was gone, except for the doctor's office which was next to Remi's.

His gut churned. His brain thought about the situation. Why had Sisco not gone to see the doc for relief from his symptoms? Why had he demanded Remi come into work instead? If Teeth was there, what was he there for? What was he after? Was he there to do harm? To hurt Remi as two of his disciples had? They'd managed to ID the young woman. She had a petty crime background, with a few drug charges. Between her and the young man who'd tried to syringe him, what would Teeth have been up to?

She would've seen doc if he'd done anything, his brain told him. *She would've got to doc like she got me to him.* Holding his shirt to his mouth and wiping the sweat and tears from his smoke-filled eyes; he slowly eased along the remaining hallway, sticking to what little wall there was for support. He managed to get to the doorway, now devoid of a door, and most of its walls, and looked in. "Remi," he yelled. "Remi?" Half the floor was in the basement, but the desk and the patient table were blown against the leftover wall at the back. "Remi." Trying to find a way into the room, he stared down at the burning rubble hoping to see if she was there. "Remi," he called down. "Remi."

"Did you find her?" Rex asked from the doorway. "She's not in the office. And the toilet's gone, so not there either."

Drew threw a disgusted look at Rex. "No, but I have a feeling she came here."

"Why's that?" Rex inched up behind him and stared down at the mess.

"Because *Teeth* was here. If he did something to her,

she'd head to this office." Drew slowly moved towards the jammed-up desk and bed. "Remi? You here, Remi?" He picked and kicked at debris to get it out of his way, shoving it over the edge to fall below. "Remi?" He finally got to the bed and carefully pulled it away. "Remi?" He let it fall into the basement and lurched into a coughing fit.

"Here." Rex handed him a bandana. "I keep spares in my pocket."

"Then you should have given me one before," Drew chastised and wrapped it around his face.

"What are we, best friends or something," Rex mocked. "It's not like we know each other after all these years. We haven't seen each other in decades. Now move." He urged Drew out of the way and stepped past him, but the floor gave way and his foot flew out from under him.

Drew grabbed him and swung him back against the wall. "I fucking told you to be careful. Now fucking do what I say."

"You're not the boss of me, Drew," he spat.

"No, but someone definitely needs to be otherwise you'll get killed by your own damn stupidity," Drew threw back. "Now do as you're damn told." He gave Rex the evil eye and pressed back against the remaining wall. He shuffled along with Rex doing the same, until they were close enough to the desk to move it. They bent at the waist, planted their hands on the edge and shoved it. It only moved a few inches.

Drew glanced down and stuck his hand in the gap. "Move it again." They heaved and it moved a foot.

"I see a leg," he said and tried to look behind the desk. "Remi. Is that you? Remi."

Sick of waiting, Rex said, "Hold her," and shoved the desk away. The ground under it gave way and it toppled into the basement.

"Remi." Drew knelt over her, feeling for a pulse.

Rex bent down and smoothed her hair from her face. "Remi, baby. Wake up."

"What are you two doing in here? This whole place could collapse."

They looked at the doorway to see fireys hosing down the remaining interior.

"We've found the owner," Drew yelled and pointed to his badge on his belt. "We need to get her out."

"We'll get a back board. Just wait." The officer radioed through for help and within moments the rescue crew slowly made their way in, but when the floor gave way, they were cut off.

"Fuck." Rex huddled closer to Remi and the wall. "How are we getting out?"

"Go back," Drew yelled, waving them away. "Can you get a board over to us? Or come through the other office, the wall's half gone; we could pass her through or over."

It took another few minutes to figure out a plan, and then the rest of the wall dividing the offices came down. The back board was handed over and Drew and passed it to Rex. They carefully wrapped her neck in a collar, and after listening to instructions yelled by the paramedic, lifted Remi onto the stretcher and strapped her in.

"On three, we lift her and shuffle back to the wall. I'll

turn and we slide her over my shoulder," Drew told Rex.

"Being the big hero," Rex remarked.

"No, you jack arse," Drew said. "It's just something I've done as a cop. On three, one, two, three." They lifted Remi and slowly moved towards the wall. Drew ducked down, turned around while holding the back board, and slid it towards the paramedics who carefully pulled her through. Rex kept walking until he was behind Drew and was able to let go of Remi.

"May as well keep going," Drew told him and linked his hands together. "Over you go because we can't get out."

Rex looked at Drew's hand and nodded, put his foot in, grabbed the wall, and was hoisted over.

Drew grasped the wall to follow, but the remaining floor fell from under him and he fell with it. He screamed as his shoulder lurched out of its socket. He'd manage to grab a piece of rebar protruding from the floor and was dangling over the basement.

"Oh, for fuck's sake. You always did get yourself into trouble." Rex leaned over the edge. "Give me your hand." He was kneeling, holding onto the wall stud.

"Can't," Drew gasped. "Shoulder's out, can't move it."

"You always thought you were Superman. Why can't you fly?" Rex leaned down and grabbed Drew's good arm. "I can knock that shoulder back in."

"Yeah, you would." Drew gritted his teeth. "Argh, it fucking hurts. Just get Remi to the hospital. Everyone else can get me out."

"Fine by me," Rex said, but a tugging in his gut held him back. "For fuck's sake! Reilly, look, I'll grab your bad arm, it might pop back in if I pull it—"

The remaining floor fell, taking Drew and the rebar he was hanging onto with it.

"Drew," Rex yelled, seeing the fear in his old friend's eyes.

Drew landed awkwardly on the rubble, hitting his head. The last thing he saw was a fading image of Rex before the world went to black.

"Drew. Drew. You all right, man?" Rex yelled down. "Drew."

Seeing he was unmoving, Rex looked over his shoulder. Remi was being taken to hospital; Drew was unconscious. Remi was the woman he loved. Drew was the best friend he'd lost because of a woman.

"Except we're not friends now, but Remi would kill me if I didn't help him," he muttered. "I really hope you're okay, Remi, because if you die and I'm not there, I'll kick myself for the rest of my life for doing this. Drew." He carefully dropped down and climbed over the blocks of cement to Drew's side. "Drew." He slapped his face. "Drew. Wake the fuck up because I'm not going to carry you."

Drew coughed and grasped his shoulder, crying out in agony. "Fucking hell."

"Let's see if we can fix that, shall we." Rex handled Drew's arm and pulled it, pushing the shoulder back into its socket. "All done."

Drew yelled at the pain and lay panting before he opened his eyes. "Fuck you, Rex. What the fuck!"

"We did that as kids. Comes in handy, doesn't it?" Rex slapped his face. "Wake up. We've gotta get out of here."

"And how are we going to do that exactly?" Drew doubled over in a hacking cough, spitting out ashy saliva.

Rex noticed. "However we can. There's a band entrance down here and we're near it, so let's go." He grabbed Drew's left arm and hauled him to his feet. "We'll need to climb over a pile of junk, but we should be okay."

"We should just stay put and let the emergency services do the job." Drew grimaced at the pain in his body.

"Why would we do that now, when we didn't before," Rex argued, and pulled Drew over more rubble. "We're almost there." He kicked aside a chunk of wall and they stepped into the corridor with the secret band entrance right in front of them. "See, we're here." He leant Drew against the cinder block wall that remained intact, unbolted the door, yanked on the handle and pulled it back. It stuck halfway. "Ah fuck. Okay." He wiped the sweat from his eyes. "It must be warped but we should be able to get through." He pushed his head and torso through the opening and saw the stairway smothered in debris. "Fuck."

"Are we stuck? We should've just stayed where we were." Drew slid down to the ground, his energy was gone and the pain threshold was hitting a million.

"We're not stuck, for fuck's sake. You're being a drama queen like always. I'll go up and see if anyone's there, if not, I'll pull you out. Keep your face covered." Rex looked down at Drew and saw his red hooded eyes. "I'll be back in a minute." He pushed through the doorway and climbed through the rubble to the carpark, seeing fireys and cops. "Hey," he yelled, waving his arms. "Over here, help."

They noticed him and ran over. "Are you okay? Is it just you?"

"No, no, my friend, he's inside. We can't get the door open anymore and he's sick and busted his shoulder. We need to get him out."

"Get a ladder, get the Jaws of Life, get the oxygen," the fiery yelled.

Rex nodded and turned to go back down, but was stopped.

"We can't let you back down there. It's too dangerous," the fiery yelled.

Rex shook him off. "I'm not leaving him there," he yelled and stumbled back down to the door. The fireys quickly cleared a path and followed Rex who pushed through the door. "Drew. Drew." He slapped his face a couple of times. "We're getting out of here. Wake up."

Drew mumbled something and Rex saw the oxygen tank being passed through the doorway. He grabbed it and pulled it over Drew's head, whipping off the bandana.

The oxygen revived Drew a little, and by the time they got the door open, and him outside and into an ambulance, he was able to talk. But Rex promptly shushed him and climbed in after him.

*****

Richard Wong met them in emergency. "Way to go, Reilly. Not only do you save the owner but you get yourself wrecked as well."

Drew could only raise his brows as he was wheeled into a cubicle and the doctors went to work.

"How's Remi?" Rex asked Wong. "Is she here?"

"Being closely monitored. A few fractures, a concussion, the usual."

"How'd you know we'd be here?" Rex glanced around to see if he could find her.

"Her manager's upstairs. I was here when the word came in, so I stayed. She's in ICU, no one can see her."

Rex nodded and managed to look back at Drew before lurching into a spasmic coughing fit.

"You might need to check this one for inhalation," Wong called and waved over a doctor who pulled Rex into another cubicle.

"I'm fine." Rex waved him away, but coughed again. "Maybe not."

*****

The hours slowly slid by, and night turned into day and then afternoon before Rex and Drew were able to see Remi.

Drew had had full body x-rays. He had severe smoke inhalation, and his shoulder was in a sling. Rex only had a mild dose of inhalation, but both would be fine after fluids. They weren't allowed into ICU, so stayed outside looking in. Remi was unconscious and on a ventilator.

"I'm going to find that fucking bastard," Rex said and finally turned away. He paced with his hands on his hips, his body ready for a hot shower and a cold beer.

"We need to find him first." Drew manoeuvred his wheelchair around with one hand. "We also need to know if it was him, or whether this was a gas explosion from the kitchen, or something more."

Rex spun around. "What do you mean by that? Are you saying it was a bomb?"

Drew took a deep, slow breath. "The fire chief doesn't know. He's going by gas explosion, but until the investigation is done, he won't rule out anything else."

"And how long is that supposed to take?" Rex demanded. "How long is *any* of this supposed to take?"

"I don't know," Drew yelled, but his voice came out in a croak and he coughed up phlegm. "I don't fucking know. But what I *do* know is Remi's club is gone, her staff is dead, and she's in the ICU, and, with no fucking thanks to you, so am I. So just fuck off and go home, Rex. We'll deal with this."

"Like you've fucking dealt with this so far," Rex demanded. "If it weren't for me going in there, we wouldn't've found her."

"Ha! Some ego you've got there. I'm the one who knew to look in the doctor's office. Just get the fuck out and go home."

Fuming, Rex gritted his teeth, gave Drew his filthiest look, and stormed off. A hot shower and a cold beer would do better than Drew fucking Reilly.

Chapter 18

Two days later, Drew was released from the hospital, and two days after that, Remi was awakened and moved into her own room.

Sisco, Drew, and Rex converged on her at once.

"Oh, my God, Remi, I'm so sorry. I didn't know that was going to happen and I wish it was me instead of you," Sisco chatted incessantly.

"Remi, baby. I'm so glad you're okay." Rex held her hand to his mouth. "I love you so much. I don't know what I'd do if I lost you."

Remi raised an amused brow and watched Drew roll his eyes. "That's all very nice, Rexy, but Drew, did you get Teeth yet? He did this."

"No, Remi, we haven't." Drew placed his hands on the foot rail of the bed. "But we've seen the CCTV footage, and saw you and a man fighting in the alley. He jumped into your car and drove off, but the vision wasn't overly clean. Was it Teeth or not."

"*Of course* it fucking was. And he was wearing a fucking wig. I pulled it off and saw him with short hair…" Her mind blanked and she smelled citrus. It triggered a memory and she held up her hand for silence. After a few moments, she said, "That dirty little fucking arsehole. The dirty fucking arsehole. That's not how he looks at all. It's a fucking disguise. I pulled off his wig and he picked up his hat and put it back on." She sat up in the bed and her head pounded. "And earlier, when he was in the office, I got a faint whiff of citrus, not what he normally smelt of."

"Garbage." Rex nodded.

"So, why'd he smell so different?" Sisco asked, confused.

"Remember that guy, all in black, blonde brown hair, who came up to me at the bar weeks ago and said he was a fan and wanted a photo?" she asked him, not waiting for him to remember. "*That* was him. The scent, the manly, spicy aftershave. Short hair, tall, thin, that's the guy I saw when I caught a glimpse of him without the hair. That dirty fucking bastard. I bet it was a bomb." She paused, pulled her hand from Rex's grasp and rubbed her neck. "Fuck, the bastard bit me. We fought in the alley and he got me down and bit me. The doctor told me I'd been drugged, and being unconscious for so long slowed the blood flow down. I tried to get to doc, not even realising he wouldn't even be there, but my head exploded."

"That wasn't your head," Rex told her. "It was the club."

"Fucking hell!" She slumped back against the pillows and saw Drew place his phone on the roller table.

"From the beginning," he said. "I want every word you can remember."

She started from Sisco's phone call, recalled seeing

the plastic teeth on her desk, Teeth in her doorway, and calling Drew, to the fight, and why was the hallway door to the club locked. She turned to Sisco. "Since when do we lock it from the club side and who would've done that?"

"No idea." He shook his head. "We never have. It's always been from the office side."

"But someone did." She nodded as thoughts came. "Teeth could've, he was on my side. So, someone on that side would've had to…what? The cleaning crew, guard, staff? No one locks up except us and only after everyone checks out. We have protocols in place for a reason."

"Are you saying someone let him in and then locked you in together?" Drew asked. "Is that possible? Is it an inside job? Would he have someone on staff, on the inside?"

"Or it's possible one of the staff completely forgot that we don't lock the door from that side and did it anyway. Many people naturally lock doors when packing up for the night," Sisco said. "Look, Remi, I'm so sorry. It should've been me. I work Saturday nights just as you work Friday nights so we can both have an extra night off, so it should've been me."

"No, I don't think it should've been. I think it was meant for me." Remi's face was screwed up in thought. "If he's after me, and wants to destroy me and my club, why would he do it on a night I'm not there? It would have more impact if I was."

"Or," Rex interjected. "If you're not there, then he knows you'll suffer while watching it."

"He tried to burn it down knowing I wasn't there. He sent two goons after me knowing I was, so it had to be him," she argued. "And he clearly wanted the highest impact."

"But the highest impact would've been a full club," Drew argued. "And it was nearly empty. So, what are you saying? That you were the intended target, not Sisco? That Teeth waited until you were in the building, not Sisco. How did he know Sisco left and you…oh, yeah…?" He nodded. "He must have someone on the inside to know when you were and weren't in. What time did you arrive?"

"After ten," Remi and Sisco said together.

"And the club closes at two?" Drew scribbled some things in his notebook. "And the blast was when?"

"Ah…" Remi sighed. "Don't you have it on camera?"

Drew checked his notes. "2:40. He had at least four hours to set it up or get someone else to." He went on to ask what time the kitchen shut, and when the staff are normally done by.

"How many did we lose?" Remi asked quietly and watched all three glance at each other.

"About half," Sisco finally said. "Cleaning crew and guards, mainly."

"I remember being woken by the cleaning crew. I'd fallen asleep on the couch so I left them to it and did a round of the club. Found some beads, a used condom, and a fake nail. I went back to the office, the cleaners had gone, and put the things in the lost and found box." Remi scratched her head and thought back. "I didn't hear the door shut and I didn't shut the office door, but

I grabbed a drink and sat down at the desk. That's when I saw the teeth sitting there mocking me." She sighed and directed her attention to Drew. "That's when I grabbed my phone and called you. My back was to the door, but I got that prickly feeling on the back of my neck. He closed the door, but when I got out, the hall door was locked, the alley door wasn't." She frowned and shook her head. "Someone locked the club door so I couldn't run for help."

"Where were your guards to take you home?" Drew asked.

She shrugged a shoulder and winced. "No idea. I didn't try the door in the private hallway, I just bolted into the alley to get in my car and realised I didn't have the keys. But he did and was dangling them at me. I ran at him, knocked him down and punched him, grabbed the keys and ran, but he grabbed me and we fought. I still can't believe he's been wearing a wig."

"Not that it matters. We have skin epithelials and couldn't find him. But we have found your car and have gone over it with a fine-tooth comb. We finally have fingerprints and hair samples. We were also able to find trace amounts of a powdery substance on the wheel and keys, so he probably wore gloves while putting the bomb together, if he *did* put a bomb together. Tech also found trace on the floor, no doubt from his shoes, *and* he managed to lose some hair for us."

"How thoughtful and kind of him," Remi said sarcastically. "And?"

"And we still don't have him because he's not in the fucking system," Drew said. "This fucker is pissing me off and we can't actually find him."

Rex's brows rose. "Listen to the detective. Getting all sweary. He was straight and tight-laced once upon a time."

"Not now, Rex," Drew and Remi said at the same time, startling him.

"So, what's next?" Remi went on. "I guess I'm going to need guards."

"Twenty-four-seven protection," Drew insisted. "We need to keep you safe. You need to stay safe."

"All well and good for you to say that, you're not the one being targeted," she told him and turned to Sisco. "Insurance is up to date, it will take time to demolish and rebuild, and I don't want to lose my reputation, so I want site B up and running full bore while we catch this fucker because it could be a year or two or more before it's completed."

"Site B?" Drew and Rex asked.

Remi nodded wearily. "Yes. I have a second club that most people don't know belongs to me. It does exactly the same thing as Cavern. After the fire, it also got a refit."

"Certain *patrons* know it belongs to you, though," Sisco murmured. "Privacy for special clients."

A wry grin slid across her lips. "Yes, *certain* people know it's mine, they patronize both."

"Okay, so looks like you'll still have a club to run." Drew closed his notebook and picked up his phone. "Anything else?"

She shook her head. "I just want to get home to my own bed and see that fucker dead."

"Don't we all," Rex muttered, and kissed her cheek.

"I'll go and let you rest, and Sisco can organise the guards since he's clearly recovered from his ill-timed bout of food poisoning." He sent a pointed glare his way.

Sisco turned red and clasped Remi's hand. "I will, and I'll stay until they get here. Some of the boys will welcome work. They can do three shifts a day."

"And I'll get back to work solving this mystery." Drew switched his phone off and slid it into his pocket along with his notebook. "I'll be back tonight to see you."

Remi smiled wanly. "You don't need to do that. You need to rest too, by the look of you."

"He should. He was injured, and sexy Rexy saved him while they were searching for you," Sisco told her. "The delectable detective spent two days as a patient and then two days by your bedside."

"Sexy Rexy?" Drew turned his lips up in distaste.

"The delectable detective," Rex mocked. "Blech." He gave Remi another kiss. "You rest and I'll be back tonight." He left her bedside and walked out of the room.

Drew took up his vacated position by the bed and motioned for Sisco to step away. He moved to the doorway and blocked his ears. "I love you, Remi." Drew picked up her hand and held it to her lips. "I knew that before this and I'm even more sure after it. And I know Rex feels the same and I know you need to pick, but that can come in time. In the meantime, you rest up and I'll search for this prick and I'll see you tonight. Okay?" He leant in and kissed her cheek. "And Sisco…" He glanced over his shoulder to find him listening. "Don't leave her side."

Sisco saluted. "Yes, delectable detective, sir. I'll be

right here until you get back and her guards are in place."

"Good. I'll be back later." Drew strode past him and out the door, heading down the hall. Rex joined him in step. "What are you doing?" Drew asked.

"I'm helping you to track down this fucker."

"No, you're not. Remi needs to be safe. She doesn't need you interfering."

"Exactly how am I interfering?" Rex pulled him to a stop. "I'm helping track down this fucker whether you like it or not. And since you clearly don't want to work together, then I'll track down my sources and find out what they know and no"— he stopped Drew with a finger wave— "I won't be telling you. I'll be giving the information to your boss." He spun on his heel and strode down the hall, slamming open the exit door.

"Always was a fucking idiot," Drew muttered, and headed in the same direction.

*****

While Rex rang, tracked down, and spoke to people he knew, Drew kept on digging into the club disaster.

Preliminary reports showed there was indeed a bomb, with secondary explosions caused by the gas connected to the kitchen. But fingerprint and DNA tests still showed no sign of who Dr Teeth really was. And it was frustrating Drew to the point of murder.

"I just want to kill this bastard," he growled through gritted teeth. His head rested on his hands; his elbows rested on his desk. "I want this bastard dead for Remi, and if he killed John, then we'll get him for that."

"What if he didn't?" Richard clicked out of the web page he was viewing and stretched back against the back of his chair. He heard his spinal discs crack and release.

"What do you mean, what if he didn't?" Drew cocked his head enough to look at him.

"We don't know it was Teeth who did anything. John had teeth marks. We know the drug was inferior. It could be a copycat trying to get into Teeth's business. It could be someone completely different cutting into the market. If a woman wore the teeth and bit him, then where did she get them from? And besides…" He sighed and rubbed his tired eyes. "We checked the CCTV in and around the club he was found at. We never saw him being bitten, so don't know if it happened before, during, or as he was about to leave. But we did see those kids rob him after his collapse. We've rounded them up and they've been charged with theft and a whole bunch of other stuff."

"Yeah." Drew sighed and ran his fingers over is scalp, scratching the back of his head in thought. "We don't know that those teeth were from Teeth, and we know Teeth didn't rob him and his house, and that those kids deny knowing of a drug dealer called Dr Teeth. They just made the most of a stupid opportunity."

"As so many do," Richard said.

*****

On the other side of town, Rex was talking to an old

friend in the music industry about Dr Teeth and the local club scene.

"Yeah, I've seen those teeth, no idea where they come from," he said. "And no one's telling me. Just thought it was a kink, didn't know they were a drug thing."

"Yeah, they are." Rex was thoughtful. "This Teeth is also responsible for Remi Steele's club being blown to smithereens, so if you do meet Teeth, try not to go up against him because he might take it out on you."

"Will do. Sounds like a right piece of work," he said.

"He is. All right, my friend, take care." Rex grasped his shoulder in farewell and went about his business.

Chapter 19

After four days in the ICU, and two in a private room, Remi was on the verge of insanity. TV was boring her to death, her brain refused to turn off and thought of nothing but Teeth, and what happened to her club, and her butt was numb from being in bed all day.

Growling her displeasure, she threw back the covers and carefully slid out of bed. "If no one's coming to help me pee, I'll do it my damn self," she muttered and slowly made her way into the bathroom. After relieving herself and washing her hands, she looked in the mirror and screwed her face up when she noticed how deplorable her hair was. "Ugh when the hell can I have a shower? I need one." Frowning, she realised there was nothing stopping her, and using the shower chair to sit on, soaped herself up and washed her hair with the items Sisco had brought for her. Once done, she carefully dried herself and dressed in a light blue velour tracksuit and fluffy slippers he'd also brought from her house.

Feeling refreshed on every level, she pulled out her notebook from the bedside table, and began making notes of everything she'd just thought of. It was amazing what a good hot shower could do for the mind. She was interrupted by an orderly with a wheelchair.

"Ah, Ms Steele. We need to get you downstairs for some tests." He manoeuvred the chair beside the one she was sitting on and waited while she carefully stood and tucked her notebook back in the drawer before sitting in the chair.

"And what are these tests for?" She set her feet on the footrest and he pushed her through the door.

"We're having some scans to make sure you're doing fine," he said, pushing her along the corridor, fully aware her two guards were following. He noticed the nurses at the station and did a quick turn down a corridor on their left. "We need to go this way because the floor is being cleaned so we're taking a detour." He turned down a corridor on their right and stopped at the elevators. The door opened a moment later and they entered, going down to the basement.

"Why are we in the basement?" she asked, only briefly seeing the signs on the wall in front of her before he turned left.

"This is where the machines are. Don't you remember?" He rolled her down to the dark end and turned into an even darker room.

"Then why are the lights off?" She heard sounds behind her and turned to see her guards fall face first to the ground.

"So, no one can see you disappear." The orderly slapped a white cloth over her mouth and it was then that Remi realised what was going on. She saw two people behind him and realised that with her guards on the floor, the other two must have been waiting for him, and so that must mean… She looked into his face properly for the first time and realised who he actually was.

*****

An hour later, Drew got the call. "What do you mean she's missing?" he demanded so loudly the squad room turned to stare, and he thrust up from his desk. "How the hell can she be missing?" He listened to the rest of the call, ended it, and grabbed his coat from the back of the chair.

"Reilly? What is it?" Waylon called across the room.

"Fucking Teeth!" Drew growled. "Remi Steele's gone missing from the hospital; her two guards followed her to the basement for tests and were hit over the head. When they came to, she was gone."

"Right. Get over there, Wong, go with him. This bastard just keeps adding to his rap sheet."

Drew and Richard used their lights and sirens to get to the hospital, both of them impatiently running from the lift to Remi's room. "Where the hell is she?"

Sisco turned a whiter shade of pale. "Ah…we don't know."

Drew turned on the two guards. "From the beginning. What the fuck happened?"

They glanced at each other and then Sisco, who nodded.

"Fuck him, tell me," Drew demanded.

"Ah," the first guard started. "An orderly came for

Ms Steele to take her for some tests. He wheeled her out of here and we followed. Took the corridor left, then right, then down in the lift to the basement. We turned left and walked into the last room on the right, then we were hit over the head and blacked out."

The second guard picked up the story. "When we came to, Ms Steele was gone, so was the orderly, and we have no idea what the two that hit us looked like. They came from behind."

"And the orderly looked like what?" Drew asked. "Tall, skinny, short hair?"

The guards nodded. "Exactly that. Tall, skinny, short brown hair, and wire framed glasses."

"Sounds like that fucking bastard, Teeth." Drew slammed his way around the room, muttering about killing him if anything happened to Remi.

Remi!

He stood at the window, gasping. Remi. The woman he'd lost his heart to after so many years of not allowing himself to love or fall in love. And once again, his heart was breaking for the women he'd lost.

But she's not lost, his brain told him. *She's out there and you'll fucking well find her.*

"What's going on? Where's Remi?"

Drew knew the voice and knew shit was about to blow.

Silence followed for a few moments before he asked again. "Where's Remi? Drew?"

"She's missing," Richard told him. "Kidnapped by someone passing as an orderly."

There was another silence quickly followed by an explosion from Rex.

"How the fuck did you let that fucking happen?" he yelled, waving arms, and pointing fingers at the two guards. "You two fuckwits were supposed to be watching her, guarding her, fucking looking out for fucking Teeth. Was it Teeth? Was it that fucking arsehole, Teeth?" Rex grabbed one of the guards by his shirt. "Was it fucking Teeth who grabbed her, and why the fuck didn't you do anything to protect her?" With flared nostrils and spit flying from his mouth, he continued berating the guard while Richard and the other guard tried pulling him off. To no avail.

"Let him go," Drew finally told them and turned around. "He needs to vent."

Rex let go and turned to Drew. "And where the fuck were you, Mr Big Shot fucking detective? Why weren't you here?" He pushed Drew back and copped a fist to the face in retaliation. He stumbled back and his hand flew to his cheek. "Mr Big Shot detective still has it, I see."

"Listen here, you piece of shit." Drew advanced on him with a warning finger. "You weren't fucking here, either. So, I could accuse you and blame you too, but I'm not. So shut your fucking mouth with the insults because I'm not fucking interested. I'm here to find Remi and kill Teeth, and you'd better stay the fuck out of my way or I'll kill you, too."

They stood toe to toe, same height, same dark hair, same brown eyes, same flaring nostrils and heaving mouths.

"Are you two related?" Richard waved a finger between them, surprised at the resemblance up close.

"No!" they both yelled at him.

"But you are certainly both delectable," Sisco murmured,

incredibly aroused by the similarities and wishing he could be the meat in that very hirsute sandwich.

They both directed filthy looks his way, and Drew added, "We don't need shit like that now, we need to find Remi." He pointed at the guards. "You two, take me the exact way you went down to the basement. Richard, see about CCTV footage. Sisco, you stay here in case there's a phone call or another visitor. We'll be back shortly. Let's go." He charged out of the room, Rex on his tail. "And where are you going?"

"With you and the guards. I want to see for myself how they got her out."

Drew stopped him with a hand to the chest. "I don't need you interfering."

Rex slapped the hand away. "Fuck you, Drew. We haven't seen each other in over twenty-five years and now for some reason we've reunited over a woman who's gone and got herself kidnapped. There's no way I'm backing off and not interfering. I'll do my own damn search whether you like it or not."

"Do you want to see it or not?" one guard asked, prompting the two men to glare at him silently and nod. "Okay, this way." He led them down the corridor, took a left and walked down, took a right and stopped at the bank of elevators. "This is where we went down to the basement." He pressed the button and waited.

Drew had been taking photos with his phone and making note of where the cameras were while they'd been moving, hoping it would help him piece together how Remi had disappeared.

They stepped into the lift and went down to the

basement where Drew took a photo of the sign on the wall opposite them. They walked down the corridor into the last room. "Was it dark? Were the lights on?" Drew asked, taking a video of the room.

"It was dark, the doors were open, we walked in and bam, hit over the back of the head." One guard motioned to the spots they woke up. "It was still dark. We stumbled out, called Sisco, and the security of the hospital."

Drew studied the room. "No windows, no doors except the one they'd come in. A bed in the middle, shelves of supplies. Did you not know there was nothing here? No reason to be here?" he asked, walking around the room until he came back to the doors.

"No. We just followed," a guard said.

Drew moved the door to see how much room was behind it. "There's enough room for a person to fit behind."

Rex did the same with the other door. "Same here.'"

"That means that Teeth had two disciples, at least, helping him." Drew breathed deeply, trying to stop the raging anger building within him. "He had helpers, wore no disguise, except for the orderly outfit, and maybe the glasses." Something sweet drifted into his nostrils. "Do you smell that?" He breathed again, trying to identify the scent.

"Smells like it did before," one guard said. "Like a hospital room."

"Except it's not." Drew slowly moved around the room, trying to pinpoint where it was coming from. "Take a good look around. There's no sign on the door to say what it is, it looks like a storage room, or spare whatever room. A bed, shelves, it doesn't actually do much. There's no x-ray machine, scanner, nothing, they do nothing in this room." He saw upended items on the shelves and found a couple more on the floor. "This could've happened in a struggle. Maybe Remi threw things, tried to get away from him." He breathed again, but couldn't find the scent, so he went back to the door. "There it is again. I couldn't smell it over there, but it's here."

"We don't have fucking time for you to worry about what you're fucking smelling," Rex barked. "We need to find Remi." He watched Drew bend down, sniffing around, and pull a glove from his pocket. "What did you find?"

Drew bent down and pulled a white cloth from under the shelving unit by the door. "This." He held it up and carefully sniffed it.

"A rag?" Rex scoffed. "That's what you were sniffing? Fuck's sake, Drew. I'm outta here. Off to find the real criminals while you play house."

"It's drenched in chloroform," Drew told them. "He drugged her. Knocked her out."

Rex stopped, his heart did a tap step and ice slithered through his veins. "He what? She was what?" He turned around slowly, and saw Drew on the phone.

"We need CSIs down here now. Ms Steele was drugged before she was kidnapped and I want fingerprints, DNA, anything and everything on them. In the basement, east wing." He ended the call and dialled Richard. "I found a chloroformed rag in the room; the CSIs are on their way. You find anything?"

"Just the orderly doing exactly what the guards said. I've got the footage; I'm just waiting on the elevator and basement footage. I'll get back to the station once I've got it."

"Right. Are you in Remi's room?"

"No. The security room."

"Okay. I'll ring Remi's room and check with Sisco to see if anyone's rung." He called the room, but found out that no one had. He ended the call and sighed. "No one's called the room. We're still waiting on CCTV and the two of you"— he nodded at the guards— "will need to give statements to the officers when they get here. You can wait out in the hall." He followed them out, along with Rex, and stood holding the cloth. "She was in a wheelchair, would've heard you two be hit, turned around, seen the disciples, and realised it was Teeth."

"Do you think she fought? She would've." Rex stood by his side. "You've got your serious thinking face on. You're thinking about how it happened."

Drew huffed. "Of course I am, I'm a cop. She was still weak from the explosion and drug he bit her with, it might not have taken too much to sedate her." He turned to the guards. "Did you see a cloth in his hand at all? See him get it out and cover her mouth." When they shook their heads, he sighed again. "She would've heard you fall, would've turned around to see. Seen Teeth for who he was. Then what? She fought; he drugged her." He stood in the doorway imagining the sequence of events, and realised the bed was oddly placed in the room. "Was the bed in that position when you two walked in?"

They looked over his shoulder and one shook his head. "No, now that you ask. It was facing us, the feet at this end."

Drew noted it was now placed across the room, feet to the right, head to the left. "She fought, possibly got out of the chair, made it around the bed as a buffer between them. Threw stuff at him, them. But it wouldn't have been effective."

"Three against one," Rex murmured, looking around.

The team of investigators arrived and took the cloth, bagging it as they set up.

"Check the doors, behind the doors for hair, saliva, DNA, everything. They were standing behind it. Check the bed for fingerprints. It's been moved." His phone rang.

"Reilly, it's Richard. I'm watching the footage and they took her out the door to your left."

Drew frowned. "How do you know…oh…you're also watching the monitors?"

"Yep." Richard grinned. "It should be unlocked and leads out to the underground section of the carpark."

"Okay, if you've finished up there, can you come down here and take over. I'll follow the yellow brick road and see what I can find." He saw a group of officers walking down the corridor and waved them over. "The UNIs are here, gotta go." Ending the call, he said to them, "Can two of you take statements from the guards, and two of you stay here and guard the room. Two of you come with me." He walked to the door and pushed the metal lever down. The door opened without a sound.

"How convenient for them," Rex remarked dryly. "Unless they oiled the hinges."

"Probably." Drew walked through the doorway and pulled his gun out. Steadying it in front of his face aimed ahead. "Stay on your toes; we don't know what's down here." They walked the long stark corridor, empty of everything except for a faint medical odour. The light bulbs flickered as they made their way along and through the door that led to the carpark. They didn't have to search far to see an empty wheelchair against a nearby industrial bin and skid marks on the ground.

"Fuck!" Drew growled and got on the phone. "Richard, you in the basement yet? Good. Send a couple of CSIs out here; we have a secondary crime scene here as well. Photos, fingerprints, collection of evidence." He shoved his phone into his pocket and growled again, grabbing onto his hair and almost pulling it out by the roots.

"You'll go bald doing that," Rex murmured beside him. "Not that I care. Remi loves my hair, so if you're bald she won't give a shit about you anymore. I still have mine."

Drew turned his anger on Rex, both hands sliding around his neck and squeezing for a moment. Rex's eyes bulged in shock, but he quickly crossed his arms in front of him, grabbed Drew's thumbs, and bent them backward, yanking Drew's arms away from him so they were now crossed. He saw the officers move for them. "It's okay, we're old friends. He does that when he's angry." He released Drew and pushed him back. "Calm down. Getting angry at me won't help Remi."

The unsure officers looked at Drew for guidance.

He waved them away. "He's right. I'm fine."

Two CSIs came through the door and took charge, and Drew instructed one of the officers to stand guard and the other to follow him. The two of them, and Rex, made their way up the carpark lane that led directly to the exit. Drew took photos of everything and noticed the CCTV cameras. He called Richard. "It leads to the exit and the exit has CCTV. We should be able to find something."

"Already got it and checked it out. It's been emailed to the team back at HQ. It looks like a typical nondescript car."

"Can you get a licence plate?"

"I couldn't on the hospital system, but I'm sure the tech guys can. Not that it will help."

"Why wouldn't it help?" Drew demanded. "Any lead that leads to the capture of that fucking arsehole will help."

"Of course, I wasn't thinking," Richard placated. "I'm sure the tech guys will have a plate number and owner by the time you get back to the station."

"Yeah." Drew relaxed a little. "I'm sure they will." They made their way back to the basement door, along the corridor, and into the hospital where they checked on the crime scene before Drew and Rex left. Drew headed for Remi's room and Rex followed. "Why are you following me, Rex? Go home." They exited the elevators and walked down the corridor.

"Because I love her just as much as you do, and if we have better luck finding her together, then I'll damn well be by your side every second."

Drew's heart quivered and he came to a halt. He breathed and breathed again.

"I knew her before you did," Rex said quietly. "I've known her for four years and I've loved her from the moment I met her. But she's a free spirit when it comes to men. Wanting who she wants when she wants and nothing happened between us until a couple of months ago, just before you came along. If not *when* you came along. I won't let her go, Drew. And if I have to do round two with you and fight over another woman then I will. Because Remi Steele is more than worth it." He saw Drew's gaze dart to him.

Drew gritted his teeth. "We're not children, Rex. I'm not going to fight you for a woman who can make up her own mind. And *I* don't need your help finding her. I have the whole police force to back me up." He started off, but Rex grabbed his arm and he glared down at it.

"Maybe so, Drew, but I know more about Remi than you do. So, what helps you more? A police force who knows nothing about the victim, or someone who knows everything."

Drew shook himself free and stalked off to Remi's room to find a frantic Sisco.

"He's called. He's called for you, detective." He pointed at the phone lying on its side. "It's him."

Drew hurried to the phone. "Teeth, she'd better be all right. If you've hurt her—"

"Calm down, detective, she's just fine. Not that she will be for long, and the fact that you called me Teeth tells me you still don't know who I am. You are very behind the eight ball, detective. I just rang to see what you were up to and say hi. And that you and the band manager will never see Remi again."

"And if that happens, I will personally make sure you never see the rest of your life again," Drew threatened. "Let her go, or I will kill you."

Teeth laughed. "Not a chance, detective. Not a chance."

The dial tone sounded.

"Hello, hello." Drew slammed the phone into its cradle several times, breathing hard. He pointed at Sisco and Rex. "You two, come with me." He took them down to the police station, marched them into the office, pointed to his and Richard's chairs and said, "Sit. Talk. Everything you both know about Remi Steele. Now!"

"Even the private steamy parts," Rex teased, swinging side to side in the chair.

Drew grabbed the chair arms and glared into Rex's eyes. "Keep the private shit to yourself, and don't embarrass her. Everything public. Now!"

Multiple detectives came over to listen, including their superintendent.

Rex and Sisco gave them the rundown on Remi's business dealings, the club, her extracurricular activities, within reason, and her life in general.

"Have you told any of her friends, yet?" Rex asked. "She hangs out with a bunch of them on Sundays. Has a meal, a few drinks."

"Not lately, she hasn't," Drew said, pacing in front of them. "She warned them that they may not see her until this shit was sorted out."

"While all that was interesting, it doesn't get us any

closer to finding Ms Steele," Waylon said. "What we need to do is find who the hell this Dr Teeth is and where'd he take her."

"Have we found the car yet?" Drew yelled out. "Did you get a license?"

"We did. The car hasn't been reported stolen and we called the owner. They said the car had been borrowed for a few days."

That gave Drew food for thought and he stopped pacing. "Wait. So that means the person who took the car knows the owner."

"Don't know, but the owner said their keys were where they'd left them."

"So, the person who borrowed it has a set of their own?" Drew asked. "Kids, grandkids, houseboy, gardener, house sitter, who's in the owner's life?"

A detective did some digging on the computer. "Twenty-three-year-old son lives at home. He would have access to the keys. Or his own set."

"And he is currently where?" Waylon asked.

"He is…" the detective read something. "Don't know current whereabouts." He clicked on an email that came through. "Fingerprints from the hospital flagged him as one of the people in that room."

"And we get closer." Drew fist bumped the air. "Do they own property elsewhere? Does he have friends, family, anyone, someone with something?"

The detective dug some more. "A couple of priors for petty theft. There's an old report of a car being stolen, and then pulled because the owner found the son had taken it. Don't really have much else." Another dig. "And we have more fingerprints. Remi Steele, and a Madonna Chapworth, nineteen, from the inner city."

"Do we have her for anything?" Waylon asked.

"Again, petty theft," the detective said. "What is it with all of these people, they're all petty crims."

A light bulb went off over Drew's head. "Can you search petty crimes for a tall, skinny guy with blonde brown hair? We have Teeth's DNA from Remi's car. If we can pinpoint the stuff found in the car when he abandoned it, and reference all of that…I don't know, maybe it's a long shot."

"Everything is at the moment. Although weren't you unable to find him in the database?" Waylon wearily climbed to his feet. "Do what you can. Find what you can. Any lead is worth it." He headed for his office and a stiff drink.

Drew leaned against his desk and gave a half growl half sigh. "We need to do every fucking thing to find her and then I'll fucking kill him."

"If I know Remi, and I do," Sisco told him. "She's already beaten you to it."

Chapter 20

Remi came to, foggy, and with no idea of what in the hell had happened. She tried to move, but found her hands tied behind her back, and her feet tied together at the ankles. She was able to breathe through her nose, but her mouth was covered with something, so she breathed to clear the fog. As her eyes were also covered, she couldn't see, but tried to kick her senses into overdrive. Her hands reached only so far, her legs felt for the edge of the object she was lying on, her head sensed a pillow under it, and she guessed she was on her side on a bed. But where that bed was, was a different matter.

Remi rubbed her face against her shoulder and managed to move the blindfold until her eyes were uncovered. She was in a room in what looked to be a warehouse. High windows, metal walls, and tilted roof. Not seeing anyone, or hearing any noises, she moved her arms down into the crook of her knees, rolled onto her back and tucked her feet into the loop of her arms, and brought her arms around to her front.

Pulling off her blindfold and the tape over her mouth, she slowly looked around. She was on a cot bed against one wall of the room, and there was no one with her. She had to get herself untied and out of there ASAP.

She quickly untied her feet and then used her teeth to undo the rope around her wrists. There was nothing else in the room, no toilet, desk, chair, just the bed and her on it. Careful not to make a sound, she tiptoed to the door and listened. If there was anyone out there, she had no weapon in the room to defend herself, and her strength was not up to par. After being drugged and knocked out in an explosion, she knew she didn't have it in her to do all that was necessary, but she would try. She grasped the handle and slowly began to turn it.

*****

"Come on, come on," Drew growled, his patience worn thin. "There must be something, some connection we can get between this jerk and Teeth." He paced back and forth in the squad room. "Is he on social media? Yes. Have we found him on a photo of Teeth? No. Has the computer come up with petty crims matching his description? No. Do we have DNA and fingerprints? Yes? Can we use them? No."

"Fucking hell," Rex complained. "How the hell do you put up with this drudgery?"

"I don't see you helping or going out to talk to your sources," Drew told him. "If you don't like it, fuck off and let us do our job."

"If only," Rex snarled. "You're stuck with me, Reilly. Just like the old days. Always about a woman, besides…" He swung around in his chair, but Drew stopped him, glaring into his eyes, leaning over him. Rex breathed to calm his nerves. "I told you I loved her too, and I loved her first, so you're stuck with me while we find her."

Sisco took in every word from his spot at Drew's desk, delighting in all of the juicy details. He was definitely going to be telling Remi all about it. He sobered. When they found her and she got back, that was.

"Got something," a detective yelled and they all rushed over.

"The owner of the car has a distant cousin of her father, who owns a track of land out in the country about an hour from here. And CCTV footage traced the car all the way to the highway out of town heading in that direction."

"Great, let's go. Tell the local cops we're on our way." Drew grabbed his gun and checked the cartridge.

"You do realise it's an hour away, Reilly," Waylon said. "Take the chopper. You'll get there in half the time and I'll get onto the local cops to monitor the place until you arrive."

Drew grabbed his spare cartridge from his desk drawer and slid it into his jacket pocket, then slid into his jacket. "Who's coming with?"

"I am." Rex stood.

"No," Waylon said. "Detectives only. Wong, you go with him."

"You're not stopping me, cop." Rex pointed a threatening finger at him. "If I don't go with Drew, I'll find my own way there and do it by chopper as well." He glared at Waylon who glared back.

Drew shook his head and noticed every cop in the

room was on edge and ready to pounce. "Everyone, calm down. He may be a dick, but he's not that much of a dick that he'd go against a roomful of cops." He glanced back at Rex. "Don't be a dick. Sir, he's coming whether we like it or not. And believe me, I don't, but he can't be stopped when he's started. If Wong's coming and we find Remi, how are we getting home?"

"I'll have officers get out there to bring everyone back, and get a team of investigators out there too."

"And what about me?" Sisco waved a hand. "Can I stay until Remi gets back? If she even comes back, because you're all going out there, but you have no clue if she's even there, and if she's not, what a waste of time sending everyone."

Every cop in the room looked at each other before turning to their superintendent.

Waylon's head dropped in worn out exasperation. "I'd better put a call in to the town's department. He can send someone out to see if the car's there." He hurried to his office and made the call which didn't last long. "He's sending someone out there to take a look, in the meantime, everyone keep searching for clues about these people and put together a case. Once we have confirmation, it's a go. I'll tell them to get the chopper ready." He made another call.

*****

The door creaked slightly as Remi opened it a crack and peered through. She saw no one, heard no sounds, but knew Teeth or his disciples had to be somewhere. They wouldn't drive her all the way to wherever they were and then leave her. Knowing she had to take the chance, she slowly opened the door and leaned into the room. It was fairly open, a few rooms down the side to her right, but it was clearly a metal shed made for storing farm equipment. The light aroma of engine oil mixed with hay told her as much. No one was in view, and from her position she couldn't see a door at her end of the shed.

"Fuck," she muttered, realising she'd have to make her way to the other end. She scanned her options. To her immediate right, there were rooms that Teeth could be in. In front of her was a free lane of grease-stained floor she could bolt down, but if anyone was in any of the rooms, they'd see her. Three massive farm trucks were in the second lane, closer to the opposite wall. She could use them as cover and make her way to the door. The only problem then would be would it be open or unlocked. She couldn't even see it from where she was, but knew enough about sheds that they had doors as well.

Remi moved her left leg forward and heard the scuff of her slipper bottom. *Crap. Gotta take them off or they'll alert Teeth. Thank God I've got socks on.* She quickly removed her slippers and made a run for the truck on the other side of the shed, taking a quick look to see if anyone was behind it. They weren't, so she quickly tiptoed along and came to the end. The door was on the side of the shed, hidden by the machinery which is why she hadn't seen it. With a glance towards the rooms, she stepped over to the door and grasped the knob, but heard a click behind her. She froze.

"That's far enough, Ms Steele."

*****

Drew had paced for another twenty minutes until the call finally came through. The car they were after was definitely on the property, but the officers hadn't been able to get close enough for a visual on people.

"Okay people, it's a go. Reilly, Wong, get to the chopper. Baker, Taylor, prepare for a drive and get yourselves out there in your own cars to bring everyone back. We'll get squad cars and CSIs out there." He clapped his hands twice. "Here we go people. Go get our man."

Drew and Richard grabbed their stuff and headed for the lift, Rex following behind. The helipad was on the roof, and it wasn't something they normally got to do.

Drew climbed into the front, Richard and Rex into the back, and within a minute, they were flying west into the country.

*****

Remi sat dejectedly on the cot bed. Teeth had caught her, thrown an old chaff sack over her head, tied both of her hands to the wall, and then left her.

Fucking arsehole, she thought. *I should've just run out the door.*

But what if the door was locked?

Then I should've run to another door and fought my way out.

But you don't have the energy.

She sighed. *Why the fuck am I arguing with myself? Now I have to figure out* again *how to get out of here.* She leaned towards her hands and grasped the chaff sack, pulling it off. He'd taken her slippers and yanked off her socks, so she sat cross-legged to keep her feet warm. "Fucking arsehole," she muttered and looked at her hands in the dim light, flexing them, twisting them, trying to find a way out of the bonds around her. Her body heaved in exhaustion. The effects of the drug and explosion had taken most of her energy.

Resting, she realised she must've been right. Teeth and or his disciples were in the room next to hers. She could either try going out the door again, or just take matters into her own hands—if she could get them free—and attack first. But that would require a weapon, and except for the tools in the industrial tool boxes she'd seen, there didn't seem to be anything to use. So, what the hell was she going to attack with?

She tried to formulate a plan at the same time as figuring out how to get her hands free.

*****

The helicopter landed on the hospital's helipad as it was the only one in town, and they'd be able to refuel. The town's Sergeant met them there.

"Sergeant Vista." He shook their hands and noted Rex wasn't a cop. "He along for the ride?"

"Yeah, I fucking am," Rex declared. "Now let's go get Remi."

The sergeant looked at Drew who wearily nodded

and said, "Right. I'll take you in my car. We have teams around the property in plain clothes and vehicles. So far, no one's gone anywhere." He led the way to his car and they got on the road.

"Has anyone gone in or out?" Drew asked from the front seat. "Has anyone been seen, namely Remi or Teeth?"

"We haven't seen anyone outside, and no one's gone in since we first set up." Vista turned off the main road onto a smaller side road. "We haven't sent anyone in to look yet; we were waiting until dark to not be seen."

"We can't wait that long," Rex argued. "He could be doing God knows what to Remi. And if he isn't, what the hell is he waiting for?"

Drew's sigh was full of anger and hurt. "I agree. We can't wait until after dark. We need to get in and take them all down and get Remi out. Is the owner home? It's the father's cousin or something."

"He's not. Out of town for a few days, which is why it's probably being used." Vista turned off the side road onto an even smaller one. "We're getting close, but we'll have to park on this side of the property so we're not near the shed. It's not far, just don't want them to see us."

"We can't say we're bringing them something," Drew muttered, looking at the pasture land and wheat fields. "We have no excuse for being here and going into the shed."

"The warrant came through while we were waiting for you." Vista pulled to the side of the road and stopped the car. They could see the house in the distance. "We can search every building, vehicle, underground bunker the old geezer has."

"Are we assuming the two goons he had helping him are still with him?" Richard asked. "Those two and Teeth make three. The son of the car's owner won't necessarily know where to run and hide just because he's related to the property owner, and that means the other two most definitely won't."

"My men do, though," Vista said. "I made it a prerequisite for working out here. Know every person and the layout of their property, so we can help if there's a problem and we know where to find you. We'll use the wheat crops for cover. Stay down in case someone's in the house watching the road." He picked up his walkie-talkie. "We're coming in from the front. Everyone get ready because once we get there, we're going straight in. Converge on the shed and catch whoever flees. Okay, boys, let's go."

Rex was first out of the car and striding his way down the lane, not even bothering to hide behind the wheat.

Drew caught up to him and grabbed the back of his jacket. "Get down, you idiot. We don't want to be seen." He pulled Rex into a half crouch and kept walking.

"Is it really going to matter?" Rex snarked. "Either way, I'm going in and getting Remi."

"And getting yourself shot, no doubt," Drew said. "You always were a hothead."

"Not that you'd know." Rex kept pace with him. "You haven't seen me since you walked away twenty-five years ago."

"Gentlemen." The sergeant stopped them at the driveway. "We'll need to divide and conquer. You two go down the side of the driveway and we'll go down this side. Use the wheat as cover, don't be seen, we can take each side of the house when we come upon it. The old man always has a few car wrecks in the yard and piles of crap. Use them as cover."

Drew nodded and pushed Rex across the road into the wheat field to use as cover. He saw Wong and Vista do the same on their side, and they quickly made their way forward.

"Why does the whole *we haven't seen each other in twenty-five years* keep coming up?" Drew kept his eyes on the house for movement. "I'm sick of hearing it. We *used* to be friends. *Once.* When we were kids. That's it. We moved on. Got lives."

Rex rolled his eyes. "Because that's how long it's been. Twenty-five fucking years since you walked away like the gutless coward you were."

They came to the edge of the field and the yard of the property opened up before them.

Drew kept his seething in check, saw Vista indicate where they were going, and nodded. He saw a few junked cars they could manoeuvre around, drew his gun, and moved forward. Rex followed on his tail. "I didn't walk away like a coward. I walked away from a bad situation." Drew ducked behind a wreck and glanced over the house before moving to the next car.

"It wasn't a bad situation *until* you walked." Rex bent down beside him. "She loved you; you know."

The pang hit Drew's heart and he took a moment to breathe. "But *she* chose *you.*" He looked at the house and moved on, only briefly stopping behind a pile of old fruit crates before running for the side of the house and ducking down.

Rex followed. "Yeah," he whispered, knowing the gravity of keeping quiet. "She chose me because I gave her drugs. After you walked away, *she* chose the drugs."

Drew faltered and glared at him. "That's *your* fault. *You* introduced drugs into the group, *you* got her hooked and nearly hooked me. *She* chose *you.* I loved her, but *she* chose *you.* So, I chose myself and walked away." He moved on, running to the back of the house which was quiet.

They could see the shed just down the hill and a few bushes and trees to hide behind on the way. The sun was setting, so the yard was half dark, but he saw Vista and Richard on the other side run to a pile of crates.

He nodded and ran for the first tree he saw. The situation was what it was, there was no point rehashing something so old.

"I don't think she ever loved me the way she loved you," Rex murmured behind him. "She chose me because I had the drugs, but she loved you."

"Too late now." Drew ran for the next tree.

Rex ran after him. "And I have a feeling that life is repeating itself."

Drew rolled his eyes at him. "Gee, what gave you that fucking idea?"

Rex grinned. "Yeah. Twenty-five years on we're back in each other's lives fighting over a girl."

"Remi's no girl." Drew moved on, gun pointing skyward beside his ear. The trees were getting fewer and there were only bushes left.

"No, she definitely isn't," Rex said. "She's an incredible,

amazing, beautiful woman who has a mind of her own and doesn't do drugs."

"Unlike you." Drew raised a brow.

"Not since then," Rex replied. "Once it all happened, I went cold turkey. Haven't touched the stuff since."

"And I'm supposed to believe that, am I?" Drew dashed to the bushes, Rex right behind him.

"It's true. Emily's death knocked me on my arse and really destroyed me."

Drew's heart froze, his blood becoming ice in his veins. He hadn't heard or mentioned that name since the funeral.

Rex grabbed his arm. "Listen to me, Drew. I'm only to blame for the drugs. I'm not to blame for anything else. But you walked away when you could have stayed and fought. For her. For us. For all of us."

Drew shook him off. "I'm not responsible for you. I wasn't then, I sure as fuck aren't now. I was dumb enough to try drugs when you brought them to us, but smart enough to extricate myself when I saw where it was going. *You* got her hooked, *you* got her killed."

Rex's head shook violently. "I didn't kill her, the drugs did. Killed her and her baby."

Drew faltered. "What! What baby? My baby?" He grabbed Rex by his jacket lapels. "Your baby? You killed her baby?" Twenty-five years of pain and torment rained down on him. There had been gossip among the women at the reception after the funeral. Whispering gaggles full of lies and innuendo spreading like vile wildfire. He'd heard it, frowned, and scoffed at it. Emily would have told him if she were pregnant. Would've begged him to help her get clean and make a life together. He desperately stared into Rex's eyes. "She was pregnant?"

Rex gave a slight nod. "I didn't kill her, Drew. You'd left. She was heartbroken by you leaving and I knew then that she loved you and not me, and that she'd chosen me for the drugs. So, I tried to get her to quit. Tried to get her to cut down. But she wouldn't." He shook his head sadly and rubbed his eyes. "She wanted the drugs more than you or me and so she found someone who could give them to her."

"Who?" Drew demanded, shaking him. "Who? Is he dead? Did he kill her?" The information was pounding his head with the knowledge he'd refused to learn for so long. He'd lived and breathed by knowing Rex had done it. Emily had chosen Rex even though he loved her. She'd died because of Rex.

"He's dead. Died of an overdose after she did. We ah…" Rex took a deep breath. "Only a few people knew she was pregnant. I managed to find out how pregnant thinking it might have been mine or yours."

"Yours! You fucked her after I walked away?" Drew pushed him back. "She was *my* girlfriend."

"Not after she chose me," Rex said. "I'm sorry, Drew. She chose me and you left. We fucked a couple of times, but that was it. It felt weird and wrong because I knew she still loved you and was devastated when you left. But then she left me and overdosed months later. I figured it wasn't yours, doubted it was mine. Turns out, it was his."

"I heard whispers at the funeral," Drew whispered. "But I didn't believe it because if it were true, she could have come to me and told me." He slumped to the ground. "It wasn't mine and I lost the girl I loved."

"I'm sorry, Drew. I really am." Rex wiped a hand over his mouth. "I have always been so fucking sorry. Sorry for bringing the drugs into our friendship. Sorry for not listening to you. Sorry for getting Em hooked, sorry for not stopping it. I know it's all my fault. All my fault because I started it and didn't stop it, and I lost my best friend and his girlfriend within a matter of months." He swiped at the tears falling down his face. "I'm so fucking sorry for what I did. And I know Em would be sorry for what she did. But she's been gone twenty-five years. The day we last saw each other was her funeral when we were twenty. I completely deserved the beating you gave me that day. Fully deserved it. But that was twenty-five years ago. Two and a half decades ago. And now here we are again. Fighting over a girl we both love."

Drew finally looked up, decades of pain on his face and in his heart. "I stopped thinking about her to survive. I stayed angry at you because you were to blame. But I also knew she made a choice, and even though it broke me, heart, body and soul, I *still* loved her. Even now." He breathed slowly. "Even now a part of me loves her and hates you. But I didn't know about the other guy and only heard rumours of a baby. I had years of therapy to deal with it and I know none of it's on me. Only my choices. Em made hers, and you made yours, and I've loved her and hated you since. But you're right. We're here to find the woman we both love, and I do love her Rex. And I am *not* walking away from her this time." He shook his head and climbed to his feet. "This time, the girl is mine, regardless of how you feel, or what you want."

Rex stood up and nodded. "If that's the way it's going to be, fine. But first, let's go get that fucker and kill him, and then we'll let Remi decide." He strode with determination towards the shed, Drew following with his gun drawn.

Chapter 21

Remi couldn't be half-arsed waiting any longer. If anyone was coming to save her, more than likely Rex or Drew, or both, then she couldn't wait. She had to save herself. Without shoes, she couldn't go far, and without strength, she couldn't really fight, and what the fuck Teeth was waiting for she didn't know, but she no longer had the time to wait and wasn't about to hang around and find out.

One last yank on the rope around her wrists and she was free and getting to her feet. Careful to open the door quietly, instead of running, she looked over the tool boxes and saw they were all unlocked or open. There had to be something in them to use as a weapon. She tiptoed to the first one and opened the door, quietly rummaging for something to use.

"You don't give up, do you, Ms Steele? Why don't you just die already?"

Her head popped up over the top of the toolbox. "Why don't you, you dirty little fucker? Your drugs killed people, one of them a cop." She hurled a piece of machinery at him.

He ducked. "If I wanted you dead, you would be."

"Then why did you just ask why don't I die already, dickhead? It's a stupid contradiction. And bullshit!" She threw a wrench, but he swerved. "You expected me to die in the explosion, but I didn't, so you kidnapped me from the hospital instead. You clearly don't want me dead or I would be, and buried in some hole where no one can find me, or ground up in some meat grinder." Another tool went flying.

"You're right." He fired a shot at her, but she ducked. "You should be, but I'm waiting for something specific to happen."

Remi grabbed a heavy piece of car part and hurled it. "Fuck you; you're the one dying today?"

"And are you going to do the killing?" he mocked, advancing on her. "No one's coming to save you, bitch." He waved away the two disciples who'd come out of the room.

"Fuck you, cunt. I know full well who's coming to save me, but I'll be the one saving myself." Another heavy wrench went flying Teeth's way, and another bullet came flying back.

"That's two gun shots," Rex said, as they approached the shed. "I'm going in." He grabbed a pitchfork from a bale of hay as he passed.

"*We're* going in." Drew moved up next to him. "I'm the one with the gun and the badge, remember."

"How could I forget," Rex replied. "Oh, wait, you won't let me."

Drew saw Wong and Vista coming up fast from the other side and they reached the door as another shot rang out.

"Fuck you, you bastard," Remi yelled, throwing tools with both hands at Teeth as he advanced on her until he was a few feet away. The gun aimed at her face.

"Teeth, you fucking bastard I'm going to kill you," Rex yelled, running and aiming the pitchfork at him.

Teeth spun around in shock, watching the scene unfold.

Vista and Wong raced in behind them, their guns aimed at the disciples who immediately threw up their hands and fell to the floor in surrender.

"You're not getting out of here alive," Teeth screamed, firing the gun at Rex and Drew who ducked out of the way.

Remi crouched down behind the tool box so Drew could fire back, and her hands closed around the tool she'd seen moments earlier.

Drew saw her duck and fired; Teeth turned and stumbled on one of the tools she'd thrown, falling straight onto the weapon Remi held in both hands as she stood up before him.

She clenched the two pronged fork with a death grip, pushing it further into Teeth's neck. "I thought this was appropriate," she told him. "Two prongs to the neck. Two teeth marks to so many others."

His blood spurted and gurgled out of his neck and mouth, his eyes wide in pain and knowledge of death most imminent. His body leaning into it.

"Bite this, you bastard," she said and shoved it further in.

"Remi." Drew and Rex raced for her.

Drew holstered his gun as he approached. "Remi, you need to let go."

"Not until he's dead," she said, staring into Teeth's

eyes. "He needs to die for what he did."

"He certainly will now." Rex was on her other side, taking in the glassy expression and blood pouring from his neck. "Highly appropriate way to go, I suppose. You gave fake teeth to people to get high, and end up having two prongs shoved back in yours. Tit for tat and all that." He waved his hand in front of Teeth's face and saw no eye movement. He clicked his fingers in his ear. "I think he's dead."

"Not yet." Drew put his arm around Remi. "You need to let him go."

"Not until he's done," she said and watched the life go out of his eyes which rolled back into his head. His body finally surrendered to gravity and sank to its knees. Her hands went with the fork, only letting go when his body fell backwards.

"Fucking hell," Rex rasped, looking down at the body. "Fucking hell."

"Let's get you out of here." Drew pulled her aside as officers swarmed in.

Richard came towards them and Drew told him to take over. The CSIs came pouring in and wanted Remi's clothes. The two handcuffed disciples were taken away, and Drew and Rex led Remi outside where she changed in the back of the CSI van.

She was given two gowns, one she put on backwards to cover her rear, and was wrapped in a blanket. Standing at the door, she watched the scene unfold around her.

"Come on, we're getting you home." Rex wrapped his arms around her and carried her to one of the cop cars Drew had commandeered. They climbed in the back and sped off for the hospital.

"How long till we get home?" Remi noticed how dark it was on the lonely country lane. "I'm so freaking tired." Everything was a blur to her, happening in slow motion. "I'm cold; my feet are cold, my tracksuit's gone for evidence. I have no idea where my socks and slippers are."

"Give 'em 'ere." Rex lifted her legs and put them on his, rubbing them to warm them up.

Drew had his right arm around her and wouldn't let go.

Remi sat sideways facing Rex, knowing she was safe and Teeth was dead. And her feet and legs were being heated up by a very hot furry man. She turned her head to look at Drew. "Do we know why Teeth did what he did? Tried to burn down my club and then blew it up, then kidnapped me, and tried to kill you. He never told me, just that he was waiting for something to happen."

Drew sighed and rubbed his face in her hair. "We haven't found out yet, and may not now he's dead. Unless he left a manifesto or something."

Remi rolled her eyes. "Well, that was fucking anti-climactic then, wasn't it? What was the fucking point to any of it? The little fucker told me nothing, and now I'll never know why he targeted me and did what he did." She heaved a deep, guttural sigh, rested her head against Drew's shoulder, and closed her eyes against the nightmarish terrors she'd lived through.

They arrived at the hospital soon after and were met by a doctor and nurse with a wheelchair.

"What's going on?" Remi asked when Drew alighted.

"You're getting a check over before we go, and we'll

take the chopper back so it's quicker." Drew helped her from the car and into the wheelchair, and thanked the officer for the ride before wheeling her inside.

After a fifteen minute check, a spare change of clothes, and a pair of slippers, Remi was wheeled out to the helipad and lifted into the back.

Drew thanked the hospital staff and climbed in beside her.

Rex sat on the other side.

"Been a long time since I've been in a chopper." Remi tightened the blanket around her. "Not since my rock star days."

"You're still a rock star, Rem." Rex grasped her hand as they lifted off. "And don't you forget it."

She gave him a weary smile, and grasped Drew's hand, holding them both on her legs.

Rex and Drew exchanged glances and sat like that all the way back to the city.

A half hour later, they touched down on the police helipad and saw several officers waiting for them. They climbed down and helped Remi inside to a standing ovation.

Sisco ran over and enveloped her in a big bear hug, not wanting to let go.

"I can't wait to get home, have a hot shower, a hot meal, and go to bed for a week," she said, finally letting go.

"Can't do that yet, I'm afraid, Ms Steele." Waylon shook her hand. "We need a statement about everything that happened from the hospital."

Remi physically deflated. She was worn out and had little energy. "Then I'm going to need Pepsi Max and a chocolate bar, unless someone has pizza or burgers on them."

"Someone order twenty pizzas?"

They turned around and saw two pizza guys holding ten boxes a piece.

Remi grinned at the superintendent. "Perfect timing."

"Help yourself to whatever you want," Waylon told her. "You deserve it." He paid for them while Drew set her up at his desk.

In five minutes, she finished her third piece and washed it down with an ice cold Pepsi from the drink machine. "I need another three pieces and another Pepsi, and then I'll be ready to give that statement." Fifteen minutes later she started her statement, and was ready to go home thirty minutes after that.

"I'll take you." Drew stood up and stretched his back, hearing it crack.

"No. Sisco called my driver, he'll be waiting downstairs. You stay here and wrap up this case, and Rex"— she cut them both off with a warning finger— "you need to go home too. I don't want to see either of you for a few days because I need rest, and there's clearly still shit you two need to resolve. So, deal with it and I'll see you both in a few days. Sisco, let's go." She left them staring after her.

"I get the feeling it's going to be *her* picking one of *us,*" Drew muttered.

"Because she's an independent woman with a mind of her own. That's Remi Steele. And that's why we love her." Rex sighed. "Looks like I'm headed out too. But as for what she said, I think we've dealt with all we need to. There's nothing left. We *were* best friends, once. Em was *your* girlfriend. I fucked up by bringing drugs into the mix and we all paid for it. I'm sorry, Drew. I truly am."

Drew's lip quivered. "So am I. I always have been. But about not saving her. It was never about you. My hate is what's for you and I have nothing more to say except I will fight for Remi and I will win. It's time for you to leave, Rex." He turned and walked away.

Rex watched his retreating back, sorrow for the past washing over him.

*****

A week later, Remi called both of them to her apartment. She'd made up her mind about a few things, and had come to a decision about both men.

They both arrived at her door at the same time and she invited them in.

"So, who's it gonna be?" Rex demanded.

"Geez, you don't wait," Remi remarked dryly, closing the door. "I have something to say and I want you both to be quiet until I've finished." She led them to the living room and offered seats. When they refused, she sat on the chair opposite the couch and pulled a blanket over her legs. "Sit your arses on the couch." She watched as they obeyed. "Now, I have a proposal. I have no idea what went on between you two decades ago, but I've come to the conclusion that I want you both and want to know if you'd be happy to share?"

Their frowns were identical. "What?"

"You two really do look like you're related. Cousins, brothers. Maybe that's why I'm so attracted to you both and you're both so hot and horny you could have me a week on, a week off, or month on, month off. Depending on when you're actually in town, Rex. We could set up a schedule."

"Wait." Drew put up his hands to stop her. "Are you asking us to *share* you? To both sleep with you and have a relationship with you?"

She shrugged. "Sure, why not? I'm crazy about both of you. You look so much alike and it's my type. I don't want to give up either of you and I'll be exclusive to both of you. No more fucking musicians, just the two of you. Exclusively."

"Oh, aren't we lucky and so special," Rex said sarcastically.

"Yeah, you are, so if you can both grow up and get along, you wouldn't even see each other if I do a schedule. So, no fights will happen."

"Are you suggesting a threesome?" Rex asked.

"God no," she exploded. "My body can only handle one of you at a time. I couldn't handle two."

"No," Drew said. "You're suggesting an open relationship. Suggesting we share you. No. I don't want to share you, Remi. I want you for myself. Just you and me in a relationship."

Remi watched him fidget, watched Rex shift uneasily, and listened for the words she wanted to hear. But she only heard them from one man. "Rex?"

"What do you actually want, Rem?" he asked. "Because I want to keep having fun with you. Drew wants a relationship. I've known you for over four years. He's known you for over four weeks. I love you, Remi. I want to keep seeing you and fucking you and having fun with you. But I just got this feeling"— his clenched fist lightly pounded his chest— "in here, that something's wrong. Something's different. *You're* different. *The situation's* different."

"It is different, Rex." Her voice was quiet. "Very different. I've done a lot of thinking in the last couple of weeks, especially since the explosion, and I've come to the conclusion about what I want. Some bastard blew up my club, tried to kill me, and I had to figure out what I wanted so it could actually come to fruition. After everything that happened, and since Teeth is dead, my club is gone, my career's over, it's time to change how I do things."

"What do you want, Remi?" Drew asked. "Which one of us do you want, because I want you? I want *us.*" He waved a finger between her and himself. "*Not us.*" He waved a finger between all three of them.

Her smile was soft as she looked at Rex. "And you?"

"Ah, Rem," he growled. "I'm getting the feeling you've chosen."

"I want a relationship," she said. "After everything that's happened, I've realised it's time for me to have a relationship with a man. I want to play house. I want to know he's there when I get home, whether his or mine. Or I'm there when he gets home, whether his or mine. I want to know he's there, that I can rely on him, and not wait weeks if not months for him to come home."

"Ah, Rem," Rex gasped and lurched to his feet. "Ah, fuck. I fucking love you, but it's not me and I know it's not me and I am so fucking sorry."

Remi saw a stunned Drew out of the corner of her eye as she got up to embrace Rex. "I love you. The fire, the passion, the sex. You are an incredible man, Rex Titus."

"But not relationship material." He reddened and gasped back tears. "I'm so sorry."

"No, don't be. Sorry for what?" She wiped his tears away. "We're two adult human beings in our forties who were free to have fun with each other. That's now come to an end because neither of you wanted to share, but that's okay because I needed to know."

"Yeah," he said. "I know. I think I've known it from the start. Sex was all it was ever going to be. But that doesn't stop me loving you, Remi, and wanting you."

"And I'll always love you and the times we've had together." She kissed him. "Be happy Rex. Go and find the woman who has the same life as you, or can go with you so you're always together. She's the one for you, not me. And I hope you're happy."

"Maybe one day I will be, but I'm certainly not now." He pulled her into his arms for a tight hug. "And it's going to take me a long time to get over you."

"I know. I'm hard to forget or get over," she murmured into his curly beard. She ran her fingers through it. "I love you. Go and be happy."

"I'll try." He nodded. "But it's going to be hard to replace you." He let her go and walked for the door, only stopping when he'd opened it. "Bye, Remi. Be happy. Drew, you're a lucky fucker, take care of her or you'll have me to answer to." He walked out of the door. The click reverberated in the silence.

"What the fuck just happened?" Drew slowly rose to

his feet. "What just happened?"

"I chose," Remi said. "I chose you."

He stared at her, his brows furrowing, his head shaking slowly. "You what? What was all that about sharing and setting up a schedule of when we could have you?"

"I wanted to, believe me, that was definitely my first option," she said with a small laugh. "But my second was my choice. I knew which one of you I wanted, and I saw which one of you fought for me."

The light dawned on him. "And Rex didn't tell you, didn't fight for you."

"Nope." She shook her head. "Besides, I want a man who's actually here and not travelling. A man who actually wants a relationship and not just a good time. But just know this, Drew Reilly." She moved into his arms and kissed him. "If you decide you don't want a relationship, then he's my backup. So, you'd better man-up and be the man who actually wants me."

"Is that so?" He kissed her passionately. "Believe me, Remi Steele, you don't need a backup. I'm all the man you need."

"Is that so?" she remarked and kissed him passionately in return.

Epilogue

One year later, on the exact date of the explosion, *The Cavern Club* re-opened with a massive bang. It was such a bang; they were going to be open for twenty-four hours with twenty-four bands and artists playing an hour each for twenty-four hours straight.

Everyone Remi knew offered their time, talked it up on social media, and the re-opening was bigger the second time around.

Sisco was back as manager; the staff who'd survived the bombing had moved on or stayed. The private rooms were back, the basement kitchen was safety fitted, the band area separated from it. Fire doors and walls were everywhere, and the no drug policy was back in full force. The Golden Ring hadn't been replaced, but another private area was under the mezzanine.

Not replacing The Golden Ring was something Remi was absolute about. She didn't want memories of what Teeth had done spoiling her business, or her life. They hadn't found out his actual reason for everything he'd done to Remi. Surmised it was because she was trying to stop his drug business from succeeding in her club, so he'd tried to take her down for her interference.

His disciples had given up almost nothing. They were drug users, doing his bidding, but didn't know what his actual business was, or the reason behind it. The ones the police caught scored ten years in prison. Teeth, whose real name was Marcus Holmstead, was dead and buried, with no one showing up to his burial except for his lawyer. He'd had a will, and the lawyer proceeded to execute his wishes. That included closing down the business he had, which turned out to be a very lucrative drug business in the millions. As the money was made from illegal means, the government seized it and it disappeared.

Remi glanced around the club and thought about Rex. He'd called in his apology, unable to make it due to his latest band travelling overseas, but he'd be watching the livestream on the club's YouTube channel. He'd also met someone and was happy fucking her exclusively.

I can see why, Remi had thought when he texted her a photo. The twenty-three year old up-and-coming singer was fucking gorgeous. "Just as long as she's not using you to climb her way to the top," she told Rex.

"She's got a long way to climb to my top," he'd quipped in return.

Remi's gaze came to Drew, who was watching the band on stage, and she smiled at how lucky she was to have him beside her. Her pregnant hips and baby bump couldn't help but sway to the music, and her hands were protectively over it. The pregnancy had come as a complete surprise to both of them and she was about to drop any day. She'd made the decision to take time off once their daughter arrived, and Drew had as well, but he was looking into another job, so he wasn't in the line of gunfire all the time.

That was fine by Remi, she liked having him home. He'd moved into her apartment and rented out his townhouse for extra income. She'd also played house with designing the baby's room and buying a ridiculous amount of clothes and toys, reasoning it might be her only child, so it was being spoilt.

And now, her first baby had finally re-opened and it was all coming back together.

She swayed her hips into Drew's and he gently bumped back, his hands sliding around to her swollen belly, his hips swaying with hers. Her hands slid over his.

He grinned and nuzzled her neck, leaving a kiss on her shoulder. He felt his baby kick inside of her. A joy he'd never known had gripped his heart the day she'd announced her pregnancy, and he'd been in a panic ever since. Between trying to find a calmer, safer job, he'd been worried about her every day. The health of the baby, Remi's age, whether he would be a good father, a good partner.

They had discussed marriage, but figured that would come when ready, just like the baby would. And they had discussed names, but Remi was firm that she'd already picked one out, and she'd tell Drew once the baby was born.

A pain ripped through her stomach and fluid poured from between her legs. "Fuck!" she growled, gripping her stomach. "The baby's coming."

"What! You're not due. We're not due. She's not due." Drew panicked. "What do we do?"

"You're the cop, you tell me," she snapped.

Sisco came up behind them with a mop and bucket. "Either way, get the hell out of here. You'll disgust the clientele." He shoved her bag at her. "Go."

With a pained grin, Remi set off with a worried Drew, ready for the next grand opening of her life. The one that was going to make them a family of three.

About The Author

L.J. has been writing since 2006, when her first of many novels, ***The Road To Vegas,*** was born. In 2016 she created the ***Porn Star Brothers*** series about three sizzlingly hot Australian born Greek Island raised brothers who became the hottest porn stars in '70s America.

L.J. lives in Australia, loves '80s music, disaster movies, and collecting Jackie Collins books as Jackie is her inspiration and mentor.

L.J. Diva is the adult pen name for author Tiara King. You can find more about Tiara on her website; follow her on social media, or visit her publishing house, Royal Star Publishing.

Socials

tiaraking.com.au/ljdiva

royalstarpublishing.com.au

Sign up for *Tiara's* Newsletter…

Make sure you're always in the know and never miss free exclusives, the latest news, book updates, and so much more with newsletters from…

tiaraking.com.au

Have you read these?

The Porn Star Brothers Series

Porn Star Brothers
Forever
Love Never Dies
Stefan: The New Generation
DeLuca
Spiros & Jenny
And Always

The Illicit Things Series

Her
Him
Madam X

A Novel Investigation Series

Designs in Crime
A Killer Plot
Murder on the Set
A Novel Investigation (omnibus)

Or These?

NOVELS

Burning Desires
Anything for You
Falling for London
The Road to Vegas
Hollywood Dreams
The Billionaire's Dirty Little Secret

SHORT STORIES

The Body
The Perfect Plot
The Star of Your Own Crime Scene